the
WRONG KIND
of **MAN**

by LOLLI POWELL

Copyright © 2014 Laurel Heidtman
All rights reserved.
ISBN: 0692365338
ISBN-13: 978-0692365335

This book is protected under the copyright laws of the United States of America. Any reproduction or other unauthorized use of the material or artwork herein is prohibited.

This book is a work of fiction. Any resemblance to persons, places, or events is purely coincidental.

***

Cover from: Bill Wilkinson at format-your-book-4u.com.

DEDICATION

This book is dedicated to anyone who has ever loved the wrong kind of man. Hang in there, sunshine—and don't give up hope! The right kind does exist!

.

ACKNOWLEDGMENTS

A special thanks to Bernie, Tony, Cassie, Janet, Amberisa, and Angela for your time and input. It helped tremendously.

Chapter One

The pale gold of the early morning sun shining through the trees outside the window painted a ragtag pattern of light and shadow on the blue and white linoleum as Maggie entered the kitchen, a bounce in her step. It was spring, it was Saturday, and she felt fantastic for a change. She was also hungry, and she breathed deeply of the tantalizing aromas of freshly brewed coffee, sizzling bacon, and the homemade biscuits her grandmother was in the process of removing from the oven.

"Morning, Gran." She crossed the room and kissed her grandmother on the back of the neck. "Breakfast smells great! I'm so hungry, I could eat a horse."

"A horse might be what you need to eat." Dora Jacobs frowned at her granddaughter. "It might put some weight on those bones of yours."

"Gran, you worry too much." Maggie took a heavy white mug from a hook under a cabinet and filled it with coffee. "Didn't you ever hear that saying? A woman can never be too rich or too thin?"

"Rich, I won't argue with. Thin, I will." The petite woman put her hands on her hips and frowned. "It's time you stopped treating yourself so poorly and started living again. I hate seeing you tying yourself to the past the way you do. You're still young."

"Gran, please." Maggie held up a hand. "Not today. Okay? I'm in too good of a mood."

"Oh." Dora looked surprised, then smiled. "Good! I'm glad to hear it. Then you can do me a favor and get that tray down for me."

She gestured to the top of a cabinet before taking a plate and ladling a large spoonful of scrambled eggs and another of home fries onto it.

"We've got a couple of house guests," she said. "Your Uncle Lee came in last night after you were asleep, and he brought a friend with him. They'd had an accident and your grandfather had to do a little work on Mr. Brady. He's in the guest room, and I'd imagine he's ready for some breakfast by now."

Dora laid four strips of bacon and a couple of biscuits on the plate, then filled a mug with coffee, all the while keeping her back to her granddaughter as she worked. Maggie knew it was because she didn't want her expression read, but Maggie didn't need to see her grandmother's face to know what was there. Lee was home and that could only mean one thing. He was in some kind of trouble, and this time he had brought someone with him.

"What kind of an accident?" Maggie heard herself say and wondered why, with all there could be to say on the subject of her grandparents' eldest child, those were the only words she could bring herself to speak.

"Oh, a little trouble with their car," Dora said vaguely, busying herself with arranging the food on the tray. "Their jack slipped while they were changing a tire, and Mr. Brady hurt his arm. Your grandpa fixed him right up, though. With a little rest, he should be as good as new. Now run this on up to him before the eggs get cold."

Dora shoved the tray into Maggie's hands and turned back to the stove. Maggie knew the conversation was over regarding the stranger and Lee, at least for the time being. She resolved not to let the subject stay dropped.

It never changed, she thought, as she started down the hall to the stairs. Lee had always been the black sheep of the family, dropping out of sight for months, even years, with not a letter or phone call to his parents to let them know if he was alive or dead, then suddenly, with no advance warning, popping up at the most unexpected moments, usually in need of something. When she was younger, she had idolized him, mesmerized by his rakish good looks and charming ways, and, yes, she had to admit, by his reckless, irresponsible lifestyle.

But she had grown up, and with that maturity, she'd come to resent what he was doing to her grandparents, two people who were more like parents to her since they had raised her from the age of ten. He was their only living child, yet Mother's Day and Father's Day and all the special days of the year when people remembered those they loved, even if they were unable to at other times, came and went with not so much as a card from Lee. Every time she saw the hurt on her grandparents' faces, she idolized him less and less until, finally, she wasn't even sure she liked her uncle anymore.

As she'd grown older, she'd become aware of one other thing about Lee, something that might be considered even worse than his neglect of his family, depending on how a person rated such things. She had come to suspect that Lee was a criminal. Maybe not one who had ever been caught, although that might explain some of his absences, but crooked nonetheless. And she knew that her grandparents knew or at least suspected. She knew from the way they sidestepped her questions about her uncle, the vague answers about what Lee did for a living, the way conversations stopped when she entered a room on the few occasions when Lee did come home. It made her sick for them and sometimes even angry with them. But Lee was their son after all. She knew that no matter what, they loved him. In spite of herself, she did understand, not that it made her any less angry.

Another thing she'd always suspected was that most of her uncle's calls and visits usually indicated he was in some kind of hot water and needed money, shelter, or both. There was no reason to think that his latest arrival in the middle of the night was an exception. Only this time he'd brought someone with him. Maggie couldn't help but wonder if that meant even more trouble for all of them.

The door to the guest room was open a few inches. Through it, Maggie could see the figure of a man lying in the bed. She balanced the tray against her hip and gently pushed the door open. Apparently the stranger was still asleep, a fact for which she was grateful. She would have an opportunity to get a good look at him without his being aware of it, and she might even have a chance to search through anything he'd brought with him.

She crossed to the dresser to the left of the window, careful to walk lightly on the hardwood floor. She set the tray on the dresser and turned to look at the sleeping stranger. At that moment, the blue curtains stirred in a gentle breeze wafting in through the open window. A shaft of morning sunlight fell on the man's sleeping face, and Maggie forgot to breathe.

She had never in her life seen anyone so handsome. "Golden" was the only term she could think of to describe him, a golden creature lying there on her grandmother's crisp white sheets, the white chenille bedspread covering him from the waist down. His hair was sun-streaked brown and lay in unruly curls around his face, a frame for the finely chiseled features, the dark blond stubble, and the long golden lashes that hid his sleeping eyes. He was breathing deeply, and she watched for several seconds, marveling at the way his nostrils flared ever so slightly with each breath. Then, in spite of herself, her gaze drifted downward over his bare body.

It was as beautiful as his face, and like a connoisseur of fine art, she took her time admiring every inch. His skin was a golden tan, stretched taut over finely muscled arms and a broad chest, the skin glowing even darker against the stark white bandage that her grandfather had applied to his left shoulder. Over it all grew a mat of curly golden hair, thinner on his upper chest, thicker as it traveled across the curved planes of his developed pectorals, thinning again as it disappeared beneath her grandmother's bedspread.

Maggie's gaze lingered there at the edge of that lucky spread. She fought a surprising urge to reach over and pull it back, to see if the golden hair continued on down. She couldn't have said how long she looked and wondered, but finally her gaze began to drift back up, taking in the scenery one more time. She silently admired each swell and curve of muscle, each tight brown nipple, each tuft of hair, until finally her eyes reached his face, and she found herself staring into amused amber eyes. At that moment, she wished she were dead.

"Well. Hello," he said, slowly looking her up and down. "I must have died during the night and gone to heaven."

"Hardly." She turned to the dresser in an effort to hide her rapidly reddening face. What was wrong with her? She was behaving like some sex-mad teenager, ogling boys through a hole in the locker room wall. Worse yet, she'd been caught at it! She picked up the tray. "My grandmother asked me to bring you breakfast."

"Your grandmother?" he said, as she gingerly set the tray on the edge of the bed and stepped back, putting several feet between herself and the bed. "So you must be Lee's niece. Maggie, right? Let's see, what was the last name? Fields? Yeah, Magdalyn Fields, but you go by Maggie, right? Lee told me you were pretty. He wasn't exaggerating."

"How kind of my uncle." Maggie didn't bother to keep the sarcasm out of her voice. "I'm at a disadvantage. I don't know your name."

"Brady. Seth Brady, and I'm very pleased to meet you." He emphasized the "very," his eyes twinkling.

"Mr. Brady, what are you and my uncle doing here?"

She had not intended to be so blunt, but his manner and those eyes disconcerted her. If her grandmother had been in the room, she would likely have keeled over from the shock of her granddaughter's rudeness.

"My arm," he said, the twinkle gone from his eyes. "It wasn't planned, but it couldn't be helped. We were nearby when it happened, and since your grandfather's a doctor, Lee brought me here."

"My grandfather is retired." Maggie could hear her voice quiver with the suppressed anger she was feeling. "And retirements are supposed to be peaceful. My uncle's presence has never brought peace to this house, and somehow, Mr. Brady, I doubt that yours will either."

He stared at her, apparently surprised at her outburst.

"Well," he said. "I see you've got the temper to go with that gorgeous red hair. I just don't understand why you're so upset."

"I'm upset because I love my grandparents." Maggie turned away, busying herself with straightening the blue and white doily on the dresser top. It distracted her to look at him, and that bothered her. She did not want that kind of distraction, not from the kind of man she knew he was.

"Maggie." His voice was gentle. "I give you my word that Lee and I won't cause you or Dr. and Mrs. Jacobs any problems. As soon as your grandfather says I'm able to travel, we'll be out of your hair. I promise."

She turned and looked at him. The cocky flirtatiousness was gone from his eyes. He had made her a promise, a promise that he would leave this house as soon as he could. Looking at him, she could almost believe he meant it. The sooner, the better, she thought to herself. She knew beyond a shadow of a doubt that this man was trouble.

Seth Brady shifted his weight in the bed and leaned forward, trying to move into a sitting position. He groaned as he involuntarily moved his shoulder in the attempt and slumped back onto the pillows, his face white. He closed his eyes for a moment. When he opened them, Maggie could see that he was hurting.

"I think I'll pass on that breakfast, if you don't mind," he said. "I don't think I'm up to it just yet.

"You need to eat." She looked at his arm lying useless on the bed, then at the tray sitting beside it.

"I suppose I could feed you." She felt her face growing hot, as if she'd just suggested she get naked under the spread with him rather than just offer to help him eat. "If it hurts too much to sit up."

He smiled weakly. "I would love to take you up on that offer," he said, a hint of the earlier flirtatiousness in his voice. "But I think, for now, I'll settle for a little more sleep. Tell your grandmother I'm sorry and that I do appreciate all the trouble she went to. I just don't think I can tolerate food yet."

He closed his eyes. Within seconds, his breathing had slowed, and Maggie realized he was asleep. Maybe she had been too hard on him, she thought. She was angry with her uncle and had taken it out on him. She mentally chided herself for not thinking before she spoke, a character flaw she had tried all her life to overcome—with little success. Maybe Seth Brady was right. Maybe she was just a hotheaded redhead. Might as well blame it on genetics.

Still, he was an associate of Lee's. That fact alone spoke volumes regarding his character, or lack thereof. True, Seth Brady probably knew nothing of the shameful way in which her uncle had neglected his family, but he had to know what Lee was. And that made him guilty by association. He was trouble, just as her uncle was trouble. She said a quick prayer that Seth Brady's injured shoulder would heal quickly so they could all be rid of him.

***

Seth stirred and opened his eyes as Maggie closed the door behind her. He felt so weak and trying to sit up had brought on a bout of nausea. But in spite of his condition his body had responded almost violently to the red-haired green-eyed beauty that he'd found in his room when he opened his eyes. He found that amazing.

"This is hardly the time to be getting ideas like that, Brady," he chided himself. "It would probably kill you in your condition."

Ah, but what a way to go!

Still, in all seriousness, it was best to let go of such thoughts. She was Lee's niece, and Lee was a friend. A man didn't play casual with someone who meant something to a friend. Not that he had ever felt comfortable playing it casual with any woman, unless, that is, that was all that she allowed.

But Magdalyn Fields didn't look like the kind of woman who would settle for casual. There was strength about her, a sense that she was very much her own person. Besides, he had the distinct feeling that he wouldn't be able to keep it casual even if that was all she wanted. A distraction like that could interfere with the job he needed to do.

Chapter Two

Dora Jacobs had just finished setting the breakfast table when Maggie returned to the kitchen with the untouched tray. She saw her grandmother had set four places, and an uncontrollable revulsion swept through her. She could not and would not sit at the same table with Lee, not yet, not while her feelings were in such turmoil. Later, when she had herself under control, she would face him, and she would let him know in no uncertain terms how she felt. For now, she just wanted to withdraw to her room and sort out her thoughts.

She relayed Seth Brady's apology to her grandmother, and setting the tray down on the counter, poured a fresh mug of coffee and set it on the tray.

"No sense wasting this breakfast," she said, her back to her grandmother. She could feel Dora's eyes on her. "I feel kind of tired myself, so I think I'll just take this up to my room, if you don't mind. It might be kind of nice to have breakfast in bed for a change."

"If that's what you want, honey," Dora said. "Lee's going to miss seeing you, though. He's got to run into Indianapolis after breakfast to take care of some things, and he won't be back until tomorrow at the earliest. I know he wanted to see you."

"Tell him I'll see him when he gets back," Maggie said, relieved that she would not have to face her uncle for at least another day. "Is he leaving his friend here? "

"He's going to have to," Dora said. "Mr. Brady is in no shape to travel yet. He'll be all right, but he needs a lot of rest just now."

Maggie started to ask why Seth Brady had not gone to a hospital, but closed her mouth. The answer was obvious. He couldn't afford to go to a hospital where people would ask questions and neither could Lee. She doubted very much if Seth Brady had hurt himself while changing a tire.

Back in her converted attic bedroom, Maggie felt restless. Her grandmother's breakfast was delicious, as usual, but she was unable to concentrate on eating and picked at the food. She finally gave up and pushed the tray aside.

She had been so hungry earlier, and she wished she could blame her sudden loss of appetite on anything but what she knew was the cause—the stranger downstairs in the guest bedroom. She could not get him out of her mind. For a few moments she gave in to the temptation and allowed her mind's eye to rove again over his nearly nude body and handsome face before shaking her head in reproach of herself. Standing, she walked to the window and gazed out over the front lawn.

The Jacobs home sat on three acres of land in the midst of what had once been cornfields and cow pastures, but had since been developed into suburban housing as the old farmers died off and their heirs sold the farms as building lots. Sitting well back from the road, the white frame house was surrounded by old oaks and maples, one locust tree, and a small stand of pines on the north side. Maggie could see the split-level and ranch homes across and down the road, yet they seemed separate, far away, as if she were looking at a picture.

It was peaceful here. That was why she had come home after Tom's betrayal and ultimate death. She had known instinctively that here was the only place she could find peace, the only place where she could weave a cocoon around herself and insulate herself from the pain that was outside, there, in that other world.

She closed her eyes, and for an excruciating second, felt the ache that permeated every inch of her body, the ache that had been a part of her ever since Tom had left her. It was muted now and of shorter duration than it had been at the beginning, just over a year ago, and she knew that meant she was getting well. There had been a time when she had thought she would surely die from the pain. But she'd survived the arrest, the media attention, and finally the funeral and the many details that followed. Then she had escaped and come home to Indiana.

She turned from the window, still feeling restless, and lay across the patchwork quilt that covered her narrow single bed. It was the same bed in which she had slept away her youth. She had been thankful that it was a single bed when she had come home, because it did not seem so empty without Tom. After four loving years of cuddling up to him on cold nights and waking up to his lean hard body hungry for love, she did not think she could have borne the torture of sleeping in a cold empty double bed.

For the first time, she felt that there was an empty place inside her as well, a place that hungered to be filled by the naked stranger. She felt disloyal somehow, as if she were being unfaithful to Tom. Ridiculous, she knew, but the feeling was there and maybe it would keep her from getting carried away. The man downstairs might be the most handsome man she had ever seen, but he was no good. Tom was proof that she was attracted to the wrong kind of man, and it seemed her libido hadn't learned its lesson. She knew in her mind that the man downstairs was the last thing she needed. Now if she could make the rest of her body believe it . . .

She lay quietly, her eyes closed, at first thinking, then just resting, listening to the sounds of the birds outside the open window and the distant noises of her grandmother in the kitchen below until she drifted off into a troubled sleep.

***

Maggie woke two hours later, the breakfast tray still on the bed beside her, the eggs now hardened to the consistency of yellow rubber. She felt groggy and confused and also irritated with herself for having fallen asleep. Why was it, she wondered, that the average person developed such a guilt complex over sleeping during the day? After all, it was Saturday, she didn't have to work, and there really were no other obligations she had to fulfill this morning.

Still, she was angry and a little depressed that she had wasted part of her day, especially since it had started with such promise. But, she thought resentfully, Uncle Lee and Seth Brady had ruined it before it had even gotten started.

She opted for taking another shower in the small bathroom that adjoined her bedroom. It was an attempt to wake up, and afterwards she felt a little more alert. Her mood, however, had not improved. She scowled at herself in the mirror as she dressed in faded comfortable jeans and a short-sleeved black T-shirt bearing the words "Pike's Peak or Bust" and an outline of the famous landmark. She and Tom had visited there the year before he was arrested for bilking his trusting investors out of millions of dollars. He had always gotten a kick out of the T-shirt, pointing at it and saying "bust, most definitely, bust and a great one, too," as if the motto were a multiple-choice question, then laughing loudly at his own joke. She smiled at the memory. Those had been good times, the best of times, before she found out what kind of person he really was. Her smile faded as she wondered morosely if she would ever see good times again.

As she passed the guest room on her way downstairs, she debated with herself for a moment, tempted to knock and ask their guest how he was feeling. Not because she really cared, she told herself, only to see how soon he would be able to move himself to other quarters. But the door was closed, and she could not bring herself to disturb the silence that lurked behind it.

The kitchen was empty. She quickly rinsed the uneaten food down the garbage disposal and placed her dirty dishes in the dishwasher rack. The back door was open, and glancing through the screen, she saw her grandfather surveying his vegetable garden several yards behind the house. It had become his pride and joy since his retirement from active medical practice three years before. Each year it grew in size, providing food not only for their household, but also for assorted friends and relatives in the area. Maggie watched him as he walked slowly back-and-forth along the perimeter of the garden, puffing thoughtfully on his briarwood pipe and gazing appraisingly at the tiny shoots pushing their way through the tilled soil.

He was the only father she had ever known, her own having been killed in an automobile accident when she was only two years old. Her mother had taken her home then, home being Vichy, Indiana, population 10,000 on a good day. And while Dora Jacobs shared motherly duties with her daughter, at least until she too passed away, Dr. Everett Lloyd Jacobs had taken the task of being father to her solely on his broad strong shoulders. As in most other things he tackled, he had done an excellent job.

He took his pipe from his mouth and smiled fondly at her as she came across the yard toward him. "Morning, sleepyhead. Didn't you get enough beauty sleep last night?"

"I guess the older I get, the more I need," she said, kissing him lightly on his suntanned cheek.

"Well, let's see." He puffed on his pipe, but it had gone out. "You were what, thirty your last birthday? By the time you're my age, you'll be sleeping around the clock by that reckoning."

"And, hopefully, I'll be as pretty as you." She grinned at him. "Where's Gran? I didn't see her in the house."

"She drove over to Compton's to pick up a few things she needed for the weekend." He reached into his pocket and extracted a kitchen match, balanced himself gracefully on his right foot and drew the match across the sole of his left shoe. It made a rasping sound and burst into flames. "You know how your grandmother is when she has company in the house. Usually fixes enough food for a small army."

"Has Lee already left for Indianapolis?" Maggie asked. She had noticed the driveway was empty.

"He left right after breakfast. Asked about you, how you were doing and all." Everett Jacobs applied the match to the tobacco in the bowl of his pipe and drew deeply for several seconds. "Said to tell you he was sorry he didn't get to see you at breakfast."

"How sweet." Maggie was unable to conceal the sarcasm in her voice. Her grandfather didn't say anything for several seconds, seeming to concentrate on the pipe tobacco. Then he looked at her, his pale blue eyes serious.

"Don't be too hard on your uncle," he said. "He's got his ways and he's not perfect, but, deep down, he's a good man."

"That's a little hard to believe sometimes."

"Things aren't always what they seem. You learn that as you get older."

"I guess I'm just not as understanding—or forgiving—as you are." Maggie kicked at a clod of dirt that had strayed out of the garden, watching it crumble into powder in the grass. "I hate the way he treats you and Gran, and I hate what he is."

"What do you think he is, Maggie?" Her grandfather stared at her, waiting for her answer.

She looked at her grandfather and opened her mouth to say all the things she had wanted to say since she'd walked into the kitchen this morning and learned that Lee and his friend had slithered in during the night. Then she closed it again.

For the first time, as she stood there in the late morning sun at the edge of the garden, she realized, really realized, that her grandfather was an old man. An old man who had lost his only daughter and whose only son was, at best, a no good bum. He knows what Lee is, she thought, but maybe he needs to pretend. He doesn't need me to rub his nose in the truth. She turned her back to the garden and looked toward the house.

"Oh, I don't know. I guess I'm just a grump this morning, that's all. By the way," she said, trying to sound casual, "what's the diagnosis on Mr. Brady's shoulder?"

"Doesn't seem to be any problem with it," her grandfather said. Maggie suspected he was glad of the change of subject. "He's going to need a bit of rest, he did lose a lot of blood, after all, but he should be all right. Unless infection sets in, that is. He needs watching, which is why I want to keep him here a few days."

"How did you say it happened?" Maggie asked, watching her grandfather closely.

"I didn't," he answered, not looking at her. "Doing some work on the car, from what I understand."

So he and Gran had gotten their stories straight, Maggie thought, and immediately felt ashamed of herself. Maybe that was what they had been told by Lee and Seth Brady. Maybe they really believed it, or maybe they just needed to believe it.

"Speaking of Mr. Brady," her grandfather said. "I guess I ought to be looking in on him. He was asleep earlier and I didn't want to bother him, but I should take a look at that shoulder."

"Why don't you let me go check and see if he's awake?" Maggie said hurriedly. "There's no sense in you having to put your pipe out when he might still be asleep."

Dora Jacobs would not allow smoking inside her house whether she was home or not, and she could always tell when her husband sneaked it in. He often accused her of being related to a bloodhound.

"If he's up, I'll come get you or give you a call out a window."

Everett Jacobs looked at her, an amused expression on his face. He took the pipe from his mouth and tilted his head toward her in a mocking bow.

"Why, thank you, Maggie, that's awfully kind of you to be so concerned with my getting my chance to smoke. I'll wait right here while you go check on Mr. Brady."

He gestured toward the house with his pipe. "Nice looking young fellow, isn't he?"

"I hadn't noticed." Maggie turned quickly and walked toward the house, hoping her grandfather hadn't seen the flush that she could feel warming her cheeks. She heard him chuckle to himself as she walked away.

Chapter Three

Inside the house was cool and quiet, the only sounds coming from outside in the warm summer sunshine. As she walked down the hall to the stairs, she heard distant children's voices shouting in play and the sharp yap of a barking dog. The sounds produced a secure peaceful feeling within her, and she took a deep breath, feeling her mood improve. Maybe life wasn't so bad, after all, not when there was sunshine and children and old pipe-smoking men to love.

As she started up the stairs, she heard a thump and a muffled curse, followed by a groan. She took the remaining stairs two at a time and came face-to-face with Seth Brady. He was leaning against the hallway wall, his face pale, dressed only in a pair of ragged cut-off jeans.

Now that he was out of bed, Maggie saw that he was a tall man, probably at least six inches more than her own five-feet-eight inches. The muscles of his long tan legs were as well defined as those of his gorgeous chest, and his stomach was hard and flat. She couldn't stop her eyes from playing over his body nor could she stop her own body from reacting to what she saw. She reminded herself that the man was injured. This was no time to be ogling him like he was some pin-up.

Beside him on the floor lay her grandmother's milk glass vase. It had apparently been knocked off the hall table. The small bouquet of daisies lay half out of the vase, and a tiny pool of water was gradually spreading over the hardwood floor.

"Are you okay?"

Stupid question, she thought. He certainly didn't look okay.

"I was just trying to make it to the bathroom," he said, smiling sheepishly. "Sorry to be so clumsy. I got lightheaded and stumbled into the table."

Maggie retrieved the vase and slipped the daisies back into it. She inspected it and set it back on the table.

"It doesn't seem to be broken," she said. "No harm done. You shouldn't have tried getting out of bed without help. My grandfather says you lost quite a bit of blood and that you're bound to be weak for a while. You're lucky all you did was knock a vase off a table. You could've passed out and really hurt yourself."

"I guess I'm just not used to having to ask for help to go to the bathroom," he said, still leaning against the wall. He looked at her, his amber eyes twinkling in spite of the fact that he obviously didn't feel well. "But, since you're here, how about it?"

"Maybe I should get my grandfather." The idea of his half-nude body leaning on her for support was disturbing.

"You can wait outside." He smiled. "I just need a friendly shoulder to lean on to get me there."

She stood for a moment, trying to think of a graceful way to decline the request. Nothing came to mind. She shrugged and moved forward, offering him her arm.

"Sure, why not," she said. "Here, hold onto my arm."

He reached toward her, but instead of taking her arm, he slid his own across her shoulders, moving in close and leaning on her. Her first instinct was to draw back. She fought it, telling herself she was acting like a fool. He was hurt and he needed help. That was all there was to it. She just wished her heart would realize that and stop pounding like a scared rabbit's.

As they moved slowly and carefully down the hall toward the second-floor bathroom, her senses of touch and smell seemed to sharpen, the way that a blind person's is said to do. She could smell the man that was Seth Brady, not cologne or aftershave, although that was part of it, but his own unique scent, a scent that was masculine and strong. It was a mixture of sweat and skin and hair, and something else that she couldn't identify, but that identified this particular scent as belonging to a person who was decidedly male. Pheromones, she supposed, as she breathed deeply of that delicious scent, her heart pounding and her breath quickening, as something deep inside of her responded. She wanted to bury her face in his lean muscular chest, wanted to nuzzle into the golden hair, and smother herself in his smell. She fought the urge and contented herself with feeling his weight leaning on her, his hard muscles rippling beneath his tan skin.

They reached the door of the bathroom all too soon. Maggie reluctantly removed herself from his grasp and moved away. He held onto the jam of the door for support and looked at her, his eyes warm.

"Thank you," he said. "Will you wait?"

She nodded. He turned carefully and closed the door behind himself. She waited, leaning against the wall, listening to the sounds of him performing his morning ritual, the toilet flushing and water running in the basin as he washed up. Her body still tingled from his touch, her nipples hard as rocks. Not again, she thought. Maybe it's just loneliness that's causing me to respond to the first attractive man I've come in contact with since Tom went to jail—loneliness and hormones. But why can't I get turned on by a nice guy for a change? Why does it always have to be the bad boys?

The door opened and he came out, still moving gingerly and holding onto the wall for support. A stray tendril of damp hair clung to his forehead and some color had returned to his face. He smiled.

"I feel better," he said. "Nothing like a little cold water on the face. I'm still a little shaky, though."

Without saying anything, Maggie stepped forward and slipped her left arm around his waist, draping his right arm across her shoulders as before. They moved back down the hall to the guest room. When they reached the door, she considered leaving him there to make his way to the bed by himself, but nixed the idea and helped him inside. After all, there were several pieces of furniture inside the room, and she didn't want him to have another accident.

She helped him into the bed, first in a sitting position, then into a reclining one, his handsome head propped on both pillows. She straightened up and started to move away, but he reached out and took her right hand. When she didn't resist, he pulled her gently down beside him on the bed. Releasing her hand, he moved his own to her face. His fingers lightly traced the contours of her cheekbones before moving gently through her hair to the back of her head and pulling her face towards his.

As his lips touched hers, Maggie felt a surge of desire that left her dizzy. She clung to him, returning his kisses with abandon, his lips at first gentle, then growing more and more demanding as his mouth pressed hard against hers, his tongue probing. A tiny voice inside her warned her to pull away, run away. She ignored the voice.

He pulled her roughly further onto the bed, pressing her breasts hard against his chest. He held her tightly for a moment, his lips planting feverish kisses over her face, his tongue tracing outlines around her ear lobes.

"I've wanted to do this since I woke up and saw you," he whispered, his mouth again seeking and finding hers. His hands moved down across the curves of her body, exploring, like a blind man trying to find his way only by touch.

As she felt his hand touching her in places that had remained untouched for so long, the little warning voice asserted itself and she drew back. For a moment he fought her, trying to hold her to him, then he relaxed his grip and let her go.

She stood quickly and backed away from the bed, her breath coming in shallow gasps. My God, she thought, as she looked at him lying there in the bed. I want him, I actually want this man, a man I don't even know. No matter who he is or what he is, I want him. He seemed to read her bewilderment in her eyes.

"Maggie," he started, but stopped, as if he didn't know what to say next. He tried again. "I'm sorry if I frightened you. I shouldn't have gotten carried away like I did."

He had a strange, almost bitter, expression in his eyes. Maggie was suddenly sure that he had not sought or welcomed what had just occurred between them any more than she had. So why had he encouraged it the way he had, flirting with her, touching her? Was it a game with him?

"Forget it," she said, trying to sound casual. "It was nothing, just one of those things."

He looked startled. Then, his eyes hardened and his mouth twisted in an unpleasant grin.

"Just one of those things, eh?" he said. "So you always take advantage of your grandfather's patients who are too weak to fight you off? Naughty Florence Nightingale."

Sudden anger welled up inside her. Why, he was acting as if she had attacked him!

"You hardly seem the type who could be taken advantage of by anyone," she said coldly. "I came up here to see if you were awake so my grandfather could examine your shoulder. I'll get him."

Not giving him a chance to reply, she turned and stalked from the room, her anger blazing. The nerve of him! She had been right from the first about him. Besides being a no-good, he was a cocky Casanova who thought he was God's gift to women. Well, she would show him that one moment of weakness on her part didn't constitute a conquest on his.

***

Seth lay back in the bed as the door slammed shut behind her, cursing himself for his lack of control. He was acting like a horny teenager! Even if he hadn't been injured, there was no time for that. The job had to remain uppermost in his mind. He couldn't afford a distraction like Maggie Fields.

But, oh, he wanted her more than he'd wanted any woman in a long time. He wanted to discover what brought her physical pleasure and do it over and over again, until she begged him to stop. The intensity of his desire surprised him. It wasn't as if he had spent the last few years as a monk! He was hardly sex-starved, but he couldn't stop thinking of what it would feel like to be inside that beautiful redhead.

But the rest of what he was feeling bothered him more than his lust did. To his surprise, he found he not only wanted her, he wanted to know her. What she thought, how she felt, who she was. He hadn't felt that way about a woman in a very long time, had purposely avoided even considering such things. Maybe she had just taken him by surprise, showing up at a time when he was in a weakened state with his defenses down. Whatever, the feeling was there, and it scared the hell out of him.

Maybe it was a good thing she didn't seem to feel the same way. Oh, he was pretty sure he could get in her pants if he wanted to. The way she responded to his kisses told him that. But it was no more than a game to her—just "one of those things."

"Get over it, Brady," he mumbled to himself. "You've got more important things to worry about than a hot chick and a bruised ego."

Besides, even if she had wanted something more than a casual dalliance, he was no good for a woman. Not considering the way he made his living. He'd learned from bitter experience that his way of life could destroy a woman. He wouldn't let that happen again.

Chapter Four

Her restlessness increased as the day wore on. Try as she might, she could not forget the way Seth Brady's kisses and touch had made her feel. Her increasing anger with him and his attitude was also anger with herself for having given into him so easily.

A little before three she decided she had to get out of the house. She grabbed her purse and reached for her car keys, then decided against driving the short distance to the office of the Weekly Sun, the small newspaper where she had worked for the past five months. As she exited the front door, there was a determined bounce in her walk. It was a gorgeous day. She'd be hanged if she'd let the likes of Seth Brady spoil it for her!

She enjoyed the walk, reveling in the smells and colors of the spring flowers blooming in the neighboring yards. It was still a couple of weeks until Memorial Day, yet many of Vichy's residents were already displaying their flags proudly in honor of the Americans—many of them Vichy boys—who had died in the service of their country.

This unabashed public pride was one of the many things she loved about the small town where she had grown up. Denver, where she and Tom had made their home, had been more sophisticated, more exciting, and certainly more scenic in its mountainous setting, but it had never seemed as comfortable as Vichy, not as homey. Maggie guessed she was basically a small-town girl at heart.

She was surprised to see that she wasn't the only one who had decided to do some work in spite of the perfect weather. Jack Brace, the owner and editor of the paper, was sitting at his desk behind the partition at the rear of the small office going over copy for next week's edition of the Sun.

Jack was a portly man, nearing fifty, and his family had owned the Sun for as long as Maggie could remember. Jack had taken over operation of the Sun right out of college after his father was diagnosed with the cancer that ultimately killed him. She had spent many afternoons hanging out here in her adolescence, basking in the smells of ink and paper, and what seemed to her at the time, almost unbearable excitement. She guessed she had wanted to be a reporter from the first time she had stepped foot inside this building on an eighth grade field trip. During high school she had delivered the Sun, and in her senior year Jack had permitted her to write a monthly column on the goings-on at the school from the viewpoint of the students. She doubted if ever in her life had there been such a heady moment as that day when she first set eyes on her words in print.

As she opened the door, Jack looked up and adjusted his bifocals, which had slipped down on his nose. He pushed his chair back from the desk and stretched.

"Hey, Maggie," he said. "What brings you down here on a day like this?"

"I could ask you the same thing."

"I got bored at home. Ethel took the kids shopping for summer clothes and the house was just too quiet. I figured if I stayed there I'd end up wasting the whole day sleeping on the couch."

Ethel was Jack's wife. They had married late in life and had two children, a boy in high school and a girl in the seventh grade.

"I just felt restless. I thought I might do a rewrite on that article about the proposed wastewater treatment plant."

"What for?" Jack picked up a sheaf of papers and gestured with them. "I just finished reading it and it looks fine to me."

"I'm not totally satisfied with it. If it's all right with you, I'd like to do it over."

"It's okay with me. I warn you, though, that if I still like this draft better, I reserve the right to run it."

"Fair enough," Maggie said.

She went to her desk, sat down, and booted up her computer. She knew Jack was right, the piece did not need rewriting, but she had to do something to take her mind off Seth Brady and what had happened between them. She couldn't think of anything more likely to do so than going over an already nearly perfect article on a subject as dull as a water treatment plant. It was kind of like counting sheep to fall asleep. The mere monotony of it took one's mind off everything else.

She worked on the article until ten after four and finally gave it up. Jack was still at his desk, now going over bills. She handed him a revised copy.

"Well, is it Pulitzer material?"

"Without a doubt," she said. "With such a fascinating subject explored by such a great writer, how could it miss?"

Jack smiled and took a few minutes to look over the copy. He was a dear man, Maggie thought, a comfortable plodding man, the kind who looked the part of somebody's daddy, which he was. She wondered what it would be like to be married to someone like him, someone you could count on to come home every night. With someone like Jack there would be no risks taken, no laws broken in a wild gamble to make a fortune, no walk-of-shame, no bleeding out from a shiv wound in a jail shower. With a man like Jack, there would be fewer lonely widows.

He looked up at her and shoved his glasses back up to the bridge of his nose.

"It's okay," he said. "I still think it was fine the way it was, but if you like this better, it's okay with me."

"I just think it's a little more concise is all," she said. She hesitated for a moment, then spoke, trying to sound more nonchalant than she felt. "So, did anything exciting happen last night? I assume you talked to Lester this morning."

Lester Lewis was the town's police chief, commanding a force of nine full-time officers and twenty part-timers. He and Jack had grown up together. During the week, either Maggie or Jack checked police reports for news, but on the weekends, Jack usually touched bases with Lester in an attempt to keep on top of anything even remotely newsworthy. Lester had also been known to call Jack in the middle of the night when something happened, preferring to deal with him rather than the big media people from Indianapolis.

"Sure, I talked to Lester. We had coffee this morning over at the bakery. As a matter of fact, there was some excitement. Not in town, but about five miles out, over on Twin Forks Road. Sorry I forgot to mention it when you came in. Guess I was engrossed in what I was doing."

"What happened?" Maggie asked, dreading what she would hear.

"A burglary. Maybe a shooting."

"Where?" she asked, trying to sound as if she were only interested professionally, when what she really wanted to do was grab Jack and shake the details out of him.

"Like I said, out on Twin Forks Road. There are several real nice homes there and Friday night some burglars tried to hit one of them. The people that live there, name of Smith, were out to dinner when it happened. Anyway, they came home a little sooner than they'd planned and surprised two men inside the house. The guys took off out the kitchen door, and Patrick Smith took off after them with a loaded .38. Lester says he has a carry permit. According to Lester, the county boys think he got one of them. Smith claims he heard one of them yell right after he fired his second shot, and the deputies found a few spots of what looked like blood on the cement down by the pool."

"Did the Smiths get a look at them?" Maggie asked, surprised that her voice sounded as steady as it did.

"Not enough to identify them," Jack said. "There were two of them, both dressed in dark clothes and ski masks. Smith said he couldn't even tell if they were black or white, just that they were probably male, judging by their builds, and that they were both around six feet tall."

He shook his head.

"I guess Smith's wife was pretty shook up, and he had his hands full for a while. He didn't get around to calling the sheriff until almost an hour after it happened. By then the two burglars were probably in the next state. The county put the information out to all the area emergency rooms, but nobody ever showed up with a gunshot wound that couldn't be accounted for. So either Smith missed after all, or the crooks are trying to take care of it themselves."

Or they know a good doctor personally, Maggie thought, her heart pounding. She took a deep breath and tried to organize her thoughts. She looked carefully at Jack, wondering if he had put two and two together and thought of her grandfather, but he was looking at her in total innocence.

No, she decided, he doesn't suspect, at least not yet. Why should he? Her grandfather was a sweet respectable old man, not a man anyone would suspect of harboring felons. Maybe she still had time to figure out what to do to help that sweet old man.

"How frightening for the Smiths," Maggie said, genuine feeling in her voice. "Are they all right?"

"Oh, sure, once Mrs. Smith calmed down, I guess," Jack replied. "Pat Smith is a tough customer himself. We were in Jaycees together a couple of years ago right after they moved here, but he dropped out. Runs a trucking company just outside Indianapolis and has his hand in an import-export business in Florida. I doubt if anything could faze Pat."

Jack smiled as he thought of his old acquaintance.

"Are we going to do a story on it?" Maggie asked.

"Naturally. Front page. Vichy doesn't get this kind of excitement every day. Of course, it won't be much of a story. Just the details of the police report, plus I'll probably give Pat a call and get a quote or two from him. Really not much else to write unless and until the cops catch somebody."

"Well," Maggie said, forcing a smile. "I'll be sure and lock our doors tonight." She turned to leave. "Tell Ethel and the kids I said hi."

Outside, on the sidewalk, Maggie stopped and leaned against the brick front of the building next door. She tried to sort her thoughts and examine the facts. The facts were that two men had been surprised in the commission of a felony and that one had probably been shot. The facts were that the same night Seth Brady had shown up at her grandparents' home, injured, and in the company of her uncle. Coincidence? Maybe, but she seriously doubted it. Still, she had no proof. Not yet.

Even if she found proof, what would she do with it? Turn her uncle and Seth Brady over to Lester and the county sheriff? It would be the right thing to do, wouldn't it? Of course, while she was being a good citizen and turning her grandparents' only living child over to the authorities, she would have to turn those grandparents in, too. It was called aiding and abetting. Maybe they could all get adjoining prison cells, and she could visit them every Sunday.

No, it was better for all concerned to just let it drop. Lee and his friend would be gone soon enough, and she and her grandparents could get back to living their lives in peace.

***

Dora Jacobs was fixing pork chops, baked sweet potatoes, peas, and homemade cornbread when Maggie returned to the house. She washed her hands in the small half-bath off the downstairs hall before busying herself with setting the supper table for her grandmother. She tried to concentrate on the domestic task at hand rather than on the disconcerting news she had just learned.

Dora began fixing a tray as soon as the food was ready, and Maggie slipped out of the kitchen when her grandmother's back was turned. She went to her room and changed clothes, the only excuse she could think of on short notice to avoid being the one to serve Seth Brady. She didn't think she could stand facing him just yet, not with the memory of his warm lips on hers mixed up with the image of a threatening figure in dark clothes and a ski mask.

She knew she should despise him. For that matter, she was convinced that, in fact, she did despise him. But for all that, she still could not rid herself of the feelings he had aroused in her. He frightened her, because she knew that when she was around him, anything and everything might happen. The temptation was too strong. Avoidance was the only course of action that made sense.

As she passed the guest room on her way back downstairs, she heard her grandfather's voice coming from inside. Her grandmother must have commandeered him into delivering the meal. Better him than me, she thought.

The conversation at the supper table was innocuous enough, Maggie talking about this week's paper and her grandfather discussing his fledgling vegetables. Dora passed on the latest town gossip she'd picked up at Compton's grocery. There was no mention made of Lee. The topic of Seth Brady was also ignored until near the end of the meal when her grandfather mentioned that Mr. Brady seemed to be recovering nicely.

"I was a bit worried about him this morning," he said. "He was awfully weak. But he's a strong young man, and he's rallying just fine. Got some color back in his cheeks too."

"Then he should be able to leave soon?" Maggie asked, a hopeful note in her voice.

"Not too soon." Her grandfather frowned. "I don't want to rush things. He could get infection overnight, and then he'd be in real trouble."

He finished off his last bite of cornbread and pushed himself back from the table. "That was real good, Dora. You did yourself proud as usual."

Dora smiled at him indulgently, like a mother with a small boy. Maggie knew her grandfather loved being pampered and cared for, and she knew that her grandmother loved doing it. She envied them that they had each other and that they knew exactly where they stood with each other. They had clearly defined their respective roles a long time ago, and they were comfortable in them. Maggie knew she would probably chafe under such role definition, but there were times when she longed for its simplicity.

She helped her grandmother clear the table, then hustled her out of the kitchen to relax while she rinsed the dishes and pans and placed them in the dishwasher. She had an underlying motive in volunteering to do the cleaning up in that she hoped someone else would fetch Seth Brady's tray. It worked. Dora came into the kitchen with the tray while Maggie was rinsing the dishes. His dishes were cleaned of every crumb of food.

Her grandfather was right. Seth Brady was apparently improving, or at least, his appetite was.

Maggie thought again of him lying in the bed, reaching for her, his lips hungrily searching for hers. She shook her head roughly, frowning. I've got to stop that, she scolded herself, and stubbornly turned her thoughts to an article she was planning on hybrid tea roses. It was, she decided, a much safer topic than the man in the bed upstairs.

Chapter Five

At a quarter till nine the next morning, Maggie woke to the sound of her grandmother's voice calling her for church. She was surprised to find she had slept like the proverbial log in spite of all she had on her mind. She had been certain when she laid down the night before that she would be awake half the night, but instead she'd fallen asleep almost instantly and had slept soundly. It's amazing what the mind can blot out, she thought, when it wants to badly enough.

She showered, applied makeup, and dressed quickly in a simple white linen suit and a light orange blouse that complemented her hair and skin coloring. She gathered her shoulder length curls into a band at the top of her head and fluffed them out in a tousled look, completing the effect with gold color hoop earrings. Not bad, she thought, examining herself in the mirror.

Her grandparents were just finishing their breakfast when she entered the kitchen. There were only three places set, two for them and one for her. She released the breath she had been unconsciously holding. She realized she had been afraid she would see Seth Brady at the table now that he was improving physically.

It was a beautiful morning, a little on the cool side, but sunny. The First United Methodist Church was filled nearly to capacity. Maggie had been a member of the church since her teen years and had attended Sunday school and church services there for as long as she could remember, minus, of course, the years she had spent in Denver with Tom. It was a little like belonging to a huge extended family, the members of which one could be guaranteed of seeing at least once a week, people who did indeed care for you and about you. Maggie has always found peace sitting in the church listening to the minister intone his message. This Sunday was no different. She put Seth Brady firmly out of her thoughts and concentrated on the words of the sermon.

They returned to the house around noon, running a little late due to the usual after church socializing—gossiping, her grandfather preferred to call it. The telephone was ringing as they came in the door, and Everett Jacobs snatched it off the hook in mid-ring.

"Hello?" he said, a little out of breath. "Why, Lee, hello, what's up?"

Probably in jail, Maggie thought spitefully, hoping it was so.

Everett listened for a few moments, then nodded as if his son could see him.

"Sure, I don't see any problem with that," he said. "Your mother will love the excuse to get out of cooking Sunday dinner, too. Just wait there for us. We should be there in an hour, hour and a half tops. We can all stop for a bite to eat on the way back."

"Lee needs us to run over to Indianapolis and pick him up," he said, as he hung up the phone. "He's got to leave the car there. It needs a little work done on it. I figure the three of us can go get him and eat on the way back."

"Mr. Brady hasn't eaten either," Dora said. "We can't just go off and leave him to fend for himself."

"I'm sure he'd make do with a sandwich," Everett said. "We could fix him a light lunch before we leave."

"Why don't you two just go on," Maggie said. She didn't want to stay here alone with Seth Brady, but she didn't want to spend an hour or more enclosed in a car with her uncle either. Feeding Seth Brady seemed the lesser of two evils. "I don't feel much like taking a long car ride right now. I'll take care of feeding our guest and myself. You just go have a nice time."

"Are you sure?" Her grandfather looked at her with that amused smile he had had the day before in the garden.

"Of course. It's no problem." She turned away, feeling herself start to blush. "I'll just go change clothes and then I'll put something on to cook."

She hurried out of the kitchen before he could say anything else. She heard them leave while she was changing into jeans and a lightweight sweatshirt. Suddenly the house seemed too quiet. Maybe I should have gone with them, she thought. Maybe being in the car with Lee would have been better than being alone in the house with Seth Brady.

One thing Maggie missed living with her grandparents was the chance to cook. She had grown to enjoy it during the years she spent married to Tom, but Dora Jacobs was a jealous despot when it came to her kitchen. Mocking the westerns, she often said, "This kitchen's not big enough for the both of us, m'dear," when Maggie offered to help. The most she would allow her granddaughter to do was set the table and help with the cleaning up.

She found the fryer that her grandmother had intended for Sunday dinner. An hour later she carried a tray up the stairs. On it were two plates filled with crispy fried chicken, mashed potatoes with gravy, green beans and buttermilk biscuits. Two glasses of iced tea crowded onto the tray to complete the meal. She had an ulterior motive for deciding to share Sunday dinner with Seth Brady. Maybe she could worm some information out of him about what had really happened to his shoulder.

He was sitting upright in the bed, propped against the pillows and the headboard, reading the Sunday paper. He looked much better, Maggie decided. His color was good and there was a sparkle in his eyes when he looked at her.

"I thought I smelled something delicious," he said, smiling at her. "I was just debating whether I should come and investigate."

"You'd better not try navigating those stairs until my grandfather says you're able." Maggie set the tray on the dresser. "A nasty fall is the last thing you need at this point."

"I suppose you're right," he said. "The trouble is, I feel great. Maybe a little weak, but not too bad. I'm starting to get stir crazy."

"Well, you'll just have to grin and bear it. My grandfather would have your hide and mine if you did too much too soon and had a relapse."

Maggie removed her plate and tea and set them on a small end table beside a comfortable overstuffed chair. She carried the tray to the bed and set it down beside Seth.

"You're going to eat with me?" He sounded both pleased and surprised. "That's great. Thank you."

"You don't have to thank me," Maggie said, embarrassed.

"No, I mean it, really. Thanks. I can use the company."

She shrugged and began spreading butter on her biscuit, trying to cover her discomfort. She couldn't figure him. One minute he was cocky and arrogant, and the next he seemed to be genuinely sweet and considerate. Would the real Seth Brady please stand up, she thought. Whoever that may be.

Of course, just because a man lived on the wrong side of the law didn't mean he couldn't have a good side. More than anyone, she should know that.

They ate in silence for a few minutes until Seth looked up at her, his fork poised over his plate.

"This is every bit as delicious as it smelled," he said. "Be sure and tell your grandmother I said so."

"If I did, she'd think I was bragging since I fixed it."

"You? No wonder it's so good."

He smiled that teasing cocky smile at her, his eyes moving over her body. She felt herself growing warm, and thought again of the day before, of his lips against hers, his muscular chest tight against her breasts. She felt her nipples harden.

"My grandparents had to drive over to Indianapolis to pick up my uncle," she said, anxious to change the subject. "He has to leave the car for repairs or something."

"I'm not surprised," Seth said. "It certainly needed some work after the little accident we had."

"Accident? What kind of accident?" Her grandparents had not mentioned an automobile accident.

"Oh, nothing much." Seth looked away from her and busied himself with his food. "Lee was trying to avoid a dog and ran off the road. The car was still drivable, but it needed some bodywork."

"I thought you hurt yourself changing a tire," Maggie said, her food suddenly forgotten.

He glanced at her, surprised, then looked away again.

"That's right. I did," he said. "A tire went flat when we ran off the road. I was in the middle of changing it when the jack slipped and the bumper caught my shoulder. I should have been more careful, but we were in a hurry. Guess that's how most accidents happen."

So, she thought, her grandparents hadn't worked their story out with Seth and Lee. Her grandmother had probably made it up on the fly. She supposed it *could* be true, that her uncle really had run off the road and Seth really had hurt his shoulder while changing the tire, but she seriously doubted it. Still, there was no point in continuing the conversation. She wasn't going to get anything out of Seth unless he wanted her to. She decided to take a different tack.

"How long have you known my uncle?"

"About two years." He had finished his food and was wiping the chicken grease from his fingers with the linen napkin she had provided on the tray. "We hit it off right away and have been friends ever since."

"Where are you from?" she asked. "And where did you call home?"

He smiled.

"You're right in making that two separate questions," he said "I was born and raised in Philadelphia. After college, I went back there for a while, but I moved away after my wife died. Too many memories. Every once in a great while I go back to visit, but I don't call it home anymore. To tell you the truth, I don't guess there's any place I do call home."

So he was widowed, too. Maggie suddenly felt a kinship with him. It must be true, she thought, remembering what a close girlfriend in Denver had once told her, in her case referring to recently divorced people. The walking wounded do indeed recognize one another.

"I'm sorry," she said. When he looked at her questioningly, she added, "about your wife, I mean."

"Thanks," he said. "I know you mean it. Lee told me about your husband, that he passed away about a year ago. It's not easy, is it?"

She shook her head, feeling tears stinging her eyes.

"No, it's not. Just when you think you got it licked, some little thing happens to remind you. But it does get better as time goes on."

"How did he die? If you don't mind my asking, that is."

"Lee didn't tell you?"

"He just said you were widowed, then changed the subject." He was watching her closely. "I'm making you uncomfortable, aren't I? We don't need to talk about this. It's none of my business, after all."

"It's okay."

Maggie didn't want to talk about the sordid circumstances of Tom's death, but she wanted to see how he'd react when she told him her husband died in jail. Knowing that she had been married to a criminal might lower his defenses even more than a plate of home-cooked fried chicken.

"I met Tom my senior year in college," she said. "He was older than me—almost ten years older actually. He was an investment advisor with his own business and a guest speaker in one of my classes. We talked for a bit after class, and he invited me out."

She smiled, remembering the early times with Tom.

"He wasn't boring like you might expect someone in that business to be. He rode a motorcycle, skydived, and was a spur-of-the-moment kind of guy. He had a pilot's license and owned his own plane. Our second date, he flew us to Chicago for dinner."

"Sounds like he swept you off your feet," Seth said, smiling.

"Small town girl like me? I never had a chance," she said. "We were married a month after graduation. A few months after that we moved to Denver."

"Why Denver?"

"Tom said it was because he'd always wanted to live in the Rockies," she said. "And he loved to ski."

"He said? That wasn't the reason?"

She shrugged. "I suppose that was part of it."

"But?"

"I found out later that one of his clients had gone to the authorities with suspicions that Tom was running a scam rather than a legitimate investment company. Tom paid the man his money, the complaint was dropped, and we moved."

"How did you find out?"

"It was mentioned in the press after he was arrested."

Seth's eyebrows rose. "Arrested? I thought you said the complaint was dropped."

"That one was. He was arrested and charged with fraud and a few miscellaneous charges five years later in Denver. That's when I learned how he really made the money that bought us our luxurious lifestyle."

She heard the bitterness in her voice and took a deep breath. Love, anger, bitterness, and regret made for a disturbing stew of emotions.

"Tom was arrested on charges that he'd bilked his investors out of millions. If the earlier complaint that caused us to move from Indianapolis was any indication, it was the way he'd always done business. But this time he was guilty of more than just stealing from his clients. He'd branched out into money laundering for some people who didn't trust him to keep his mouth shut."

She had been watching Seth closely as she talked. She saw that she had his complete attention, but she was unable to gauge what he was thinking.

"I found out later from the feds that the people who had him killed had reason to worry. He was trying to finagle a deal to avoid a trial and prison in exchange for informing on the people he'd been working for. If he'd succeeded, I guess we'd be living somewhere under the witness protection program. I wouldn't have wanted to, but I probably wouldn't have had a choice. Even if I had left him, I would still have been in danger."

Was that a flash of anger in Seth's eyes? If so, anger at what? Maybe it was the anger that most criminals—TV ones, anyway—seemed to feel when they heard of someone turning "rat."

"The judge denied bail," she continued. "The feds didn't trust Tom to stay in the country, and they were probably right. Tom had his own plane, money in offshore accounts, and contacts that could have gotten him fake ID and a passport. I have no doubt he would have fled to a country with no extradition treaty with the U.S."

"Would you have gone with him?"

The question surprised her. She thought Seth was more interested in the story of Tom's criminal activities than in how it affected her. She thought for a moment.

"Honestly? I don't know. Now I like to think I wouldn't have, but then . . . I was still in love with the man I thought he was, and I was still in shock over his having been arrested. The chances are he could have convinced me he was innocent, but didn't stand a chance of proving it. Or he might have admitted his guilt and convinced me I would be in danger if I stayed. And that might have been true. The people he worked for might have used me to get to him."

She shrugged.

"It doesn't matter one way or the other now. I never had to make that decision. Tom was killed two days after he was arrested—stabbed in the shower with a shiv. No one was ever charged, because the police could never figure out who did it."

"That had to have been hard for you, coming so soon after finding out about the rest."

"It was. It was the hardest thing I ever had to endure."

"I'm sorry. He shouldn't have put you through that."

She stared at him without replying. He had what appeared to be an expression of genuine sympathy on his face. She had expected him to ask more questions about what Tom had been involved in. Instead, he seemed more concerned with how she had been affected.

"Did the feds ever find the money you said he had in offshore accounts?"

Ah, she thought, now he's getting around to what he really wants to know. He probably figures I know where the money is, and if he cozies up to me, I might let something slip.

"Not that I know of," she said. "They questioned me pretty hard after Tom was killed. I think they thought I knew where the money was."

"Do you?"

"If I did, do you think I'd tell a man I just met?" She grinned at him. "Only kidding. No, I don't know where the money is."

"And if you did . . . ?"

"I don't, so there's no point in speculating on what I would or wouldn't do. So, did you have enough to eat?" she said, changing the subject. "How about some dessert? Gran baked a couple of apple pies last night. I don't think she'd mind if we cut into one."

"I'd love some. A la mode, if you've got ice cream."

"I think there's some in the freezer." She gathered her dishes onto the tray with his. She turned at the bedroom door and winked at him. "Don't go away. I'll be right back."

"I'll be waiting," he said.

Chapter Six

When she'd returned to the room, she'd expected Seth to pump her with more questions about Tom and the money. Before she had gone for the pie, he had been very interested in the story of Tom's arrest and the missing money, but then most people would be. That by itself didn't prove he was cut from the same cloth as Tom had been, but that coupled with his friendship with her uncle, certainly implied it. So she had been ready for more questions, especially about the missing money.

Instead he made small talk about books, films, music, and current events. He came across as an interesting and intelligent man, well-educated and well-read. A couple of times she tried to steer the conversation back to him by asking questions about his background and his wife, but each time he gave her a short answer and changed the subject back to a neutral topic.

They were still talking animatedly forty-five minutes later when her grandparents' car pulled into the driveway. She excused herself and gathered the empty saucers and forks. She was just entering the kitchen from the hall when her grandparents and uncle came through the back door. Everett and Lee were in the middle of a heated discussion over the Cincinnati Reds last game, but Lee stopped in mid-sentence when he saw her standing there.

Her uncle had aged. He was what now—forty-eight, forty-nine? She had last seen him just before she and Tom had left for Denver three, no, four years ago. Those four years had left their mark on him. Maggie examined him closely, searching for the rakish charmer who had once mesmerized her.

Lee was still tall and erect, still had the thick head of blue-black hair, the same laughing brown eyes, and the same quick smile. But he looked tired. His skin, which had always been quick to take a deep tan, was badly wrinkled, a combination, she suspected, of overexposure to the sun's rays and overexposure to a dissolute lifestyle. Uncle Lee looked like a man who had spent his life burning the candle at both ends and was now getting close to the middle.

"Maggie!"

Before she could react, he crossed the room and took her in his arms, hugging her tightly.

"God, it's good to see you! Really great!"

He held her back at arms length, looking at her appraisingly.

"You're looking good. She's not too thin, Ma," he said over his shoulder to Dora. Then, smiling at Maggie, "She had me believing you were anorexic. But you look good, you really do."

"Thank you," Maggie said coldly, the dishes still in her hands. "How have you been, Lee?"

"Oh, I'm making it." He shrugged. "No complaints. Can't afford to have any."

He chuckled, then turned serious, his hands still on her arms.

"I'm sorry about Tom," he said. "I really am. I wanted to come out to Colorado to be with you, but I just couldn't get away. It must have been rough on you."

Yes, she thought, it was rough. It was the roughest thing I've ever gone through. But having you there wouldn't have helped any, even if you could have torn yourself away from whatever it is you do.

"Yes, it was. But I managed."

She pulled away from his grasp and walked to the sink. She turned on the faucet and began to rinse the saucers.

"So how long are you here for?" she said, her back to him.

"I'm not sure," he said, a puzzled sound in his voice. Apparently her aloofness had not gone unnoticed. "A few days anyway, maybe longer. A lot of it depends on how quickly Seth recovers."

"Did you fix Mr. Brady something to eat?" Her grandmother interrupted.

"Of course I did. And I have to confess, we got into your pie, too."

"Oh, goodness, I wanted to check it first myself." Her grandmother's needless insecurity about her baked goods was legendary in the family. "Was the crust all right?"

Maggie assured her grandmother that the pie was delicious, finished rinsing the dishes, and placed them in the dishwasher. Lee excused himself and went to check on Seth. Everett Jacobs went with him.

"You could have been a little friendlier to your uncle," Dora said indignantly as soon as the two of them were alone. "Why, you didn't even act like you were at all glad to see him."

"Sorry," Maggie said shortly. "I guess I'm just no good at being a hypocrite. The fact is, I'm not glad to see him. I guess it shows."

"Why are you always so hard on him?" Dora asked. Maggie could see that she was angry and hurt. "Hasn't he always been good to you? What has he ever done to make you despise him so?"

"Gran, I don't want to discuss this. I really don't." Maggie turned and walked to the kitchen door. "I think I'll take a walk. I'll be back in time to help with supper."

She left the room before her grandmother had a chance to respond.

***

The day had warmed considerably, and Maggie wished she had changed into something cooler than the sweatshirt she was wearing. She pulled the sleeves up to her elbows and set off toward the distant row of trees marking the creek line that bordered their property in the rear.

Little Bird Creek was the one spot where Maggie could make herself believe that she was miles removed from civilization. Across its narrow bed, there were still empty fields and pastures, part of the large farms that bordered the state highway on the outskirts of town. Maggie had played along this creek during her childhood, while conjuring exciting adventures of cowboys and Indians, shipwrecks and pirates. She had caught the obligatory dose of poison ivy each and every summer, and earned her share of scraped knees and bruises. Samson had been alive then, the old floppy-eared bird dog that she had loved so much. He was buried in Doc Wilson's pet cemetery now, but in those days he had been her constant companion and playmate.

She smiled now, thinking of him, and sat down on a large boulder at the edge of the shallow creek, her back propped against a gnarled elm. It was cooler here under the trees, the sunlight fighting to break through the canopy of leaves and throwing wavy patterns of golden light across the few inches of water rippling over the stones in the creek bed. A monarch butterfly flitted by. She sat perfectly still as it came closer and closer, then suddenly flew off as if it had sensed her presence. She sighed and stretched her long legs.

Maybe, she thought, I should try to be at least cordial to Lee for Gran's sake, and for Grandpa's, too. He won't be here that long. Maybe that's the least I can do.

She promised herself that she would try to fake it with her uncle. She would be at work part of the time and could probably avoid him some of the rest of his stay. It was just until Seth Brady recovered, which wouldn't be long. Then he would be gone again. And so would Seth.

Her mind drifted back to the day before. She couldn't stop herself from reliving his lips pressing demandingly on hers, his arms holding her tightly, his hands exploring her body. Then she saw the expression on his face that seemed to be concern for her when she told him about Tom. It had looked so real. Was he really that good at faking emotions to get what he wanted? Probably. He had certainly been interested in the money that Tom had hidden offshore.

Damn it anyway! What was wrong with her? She had been attracted to Tom because of his reckless ways and look where that had gotten her. Now she was attracted to a man she had just met who had to be every bit as bad—maybe worse—than Tom had been. She couldn't be attracted to a nice stable guy. No, she liked the bad boys. Or, rather, her body did. Ever since Tom had been killed, she had had no desire for sex and had wondered if that drive was dead forever. Seth Brady had answered that question. She wanted nothing more than to get naked with him, and she despised herself for the feeling.

Somewhere across the creek a bobwhite called. She sighed. Girl, you've really gone and done it now, she thought. She got to her feet and began walking determinedly along the creek line, trying to put him out of her thoughts with physical exercise. An hour later when she returned to the house, she still hadn't succeeded.

***

The house was silent when Maggie returned to it, entering through the kitchen door. She found herself moving about quietly as if afraid of disturbing the illusory peace. She poured herself a large glass of cold water from the glass jug that was kept in the refrigerator, refilled the container, and was starting for the stairs when she heard voices coming from her grandfather's study at the front of the house.

As she crept closer, she recognized the voices as belonging to her grandparents. It sounded as if they were arguing about something, and she moved closer to the door.

"Doggone it, Dora, I still say the girl ought to be told the truth. She's old enough now to handle it. Been old enough for years, for that matter, although I don't suppose there was any need to tell her when she was out West. But now it's different. She's living under this roof again and she's part of the family. She ought to know."

"All I'm trying to say," Dora Jacobs replied, her tone patient and controlled as if she were talking to a stubborn two-year-old, "is that it's not up to us to make that decision. It's up to Lee to tell her if he wants her to know. Remember the promise we made to our son, Everett. We promised to keep his secret, even from family and friends, even though we didn't like it. We got no business breaking that promise now."

"I know, I know." Her grandfather sounded irritated. "I just hate the deception, that's all. For Maggie's sake and for Lee's, too. You saw how she acted toward him today—cold as a February morning. She used to worship the ground he walked on! It's the lies between them that's done it."

"What makes you so sure she'd feel any differently if she knew the truth?"

"She's an intelligent woman," her grandfather said. "She wouldn't hold what Lee's done against him, not if she knew. She'd understand."

"Maybe, maybe not." Dora Jacobs sighed loudly. "I guess I'm not as confident as you are. Which is still all beside the point, the point being that we made a promise to our son and we're going to keep it. Aren't we?"

There was silence for a few moments. Maggie could hear the pounding of her heart in the stillness of the hall. So they knew after all! Her grandparents apparently knew everything there was to know about Lee, and the three of them had been keeping it from her all these years! To no avail, she thought, since it didn't take a genius to figure out that Lee was no good.

She had deluded herself into believing that, while her grandparents might suspect, they didn't really know anything about Lee's life, that they were innocent of any intentional wrongdoing when they sheltered him. What a fool she'd been! And what fools they were to do what they had done. They were good people. She knew that. But for them to become Lee's accomplices in this way . . . she hadn't expected that.

Her grandfather was speaking again.

"Yes, we'll keep our promise, Dora. I don't think it's right and I'm going to speak to Lee about it, but I won't say anything without his okay. I promise you that."

"Good." Her grandmother sounded relieved. "I know how you feel, Everett, I really do, but we've got to keep quiet. Lee's safety could depend on it, you know that. He could be in danger if we say anything to anyone, even Maggie."

She heard her grandfather mumble something that sounded comforting. She could picture him standing there in his study, in front of his big oak desk, holding her grandmother in his arms and soothing her. She ran quietly up the stairs to her room, her grandmother's words ringing in her ears.

Chapter Seven

In her room, Maggie yanked the too-hot sweatshirt over her head and slipped on a yellow T-shirt. Grabbing her car keys and purse, she headed back down the stairs, moving quietly as she passed her grandfather's study. She had to get away from the house for a while. Otherwise, she would probably say or do something she would later regret.

It was several minutes before her ancient white Toyota stopped sputtering and dying long enough for Maggie to put it in reverse. Since she walked most places now that the weather was nice, the car hadn't been started in over three weeks. It died again in the driveway as she shifted into drive.

"Come on, Christine, that's it, baby," she crooned to it as she turned the key again. The engine hesitated for a moment, and then roared into life. Maggie smiled and patted the dashboard affectionately.

It didn't take the car long to work the cobwebs out of its system. Soon she was past the city limits and moving along at a brisk clip. The car handled well and Maggie took the sharp country curves at a pace that she knew was illegal, and for that matter, not too smart. But the speed and the road took all her concentration. For the moment, that was what she needed.

It was a beautiful day. The countryside was glorious, the trees thick with new foliage and spring wildflowers in full bloom. Maggie passed a rich green pasture where a herd of Jersey dairy cattle grazed peacefully, new calves still awkward on their legs huddling close to their mothers. Farther on, she passed another pasture grazed by quarter horses that raised their heads in curiosity as she drove by.

A half-mile beyond the horses, she passed a farmhouse sitting close to the road, a white frame two-story with a large front porch. There were several cars in the drive. A large group of people were pitching horseshoes and eating from the covered dishes that sat atop the folding tables at the front of the porch. Maggie smiled and waved at a group of children who shouted at her as she passed.

Nearly five miles beyond the farmhouse, the road dipped into a cool tree-shaded ravine through which ran the sluggish Twin Forks River. Maggie realized with a start where she was. Five hundred yards ahead was a sharp ninety-degree bend in the road, the scene of more than one auto accident over the years. Just beyond that, a one-lane bridge crossed the river. Half a mile beyond the bridge, the road on which she was traveling intersected with Twin Forks Road, and two miles north of the intersection was the Smiths' home.

The Toyota took the bend with ease, and Maggie heard a clack as the tires crossed the seam joining the road and the bridge. She slowed to a stop at the intersection and sat for a few moments staring at the steering wheel. She'd had no conscious intention of driving anywhere in the vicinity of the Smiths' house. There were a lot of miles of country road to lose oneself in, so why had she ended up at this particular intersection?

The answer was obvious. While her conscious mind had been supposedly relaxing, distracted from its concerns by the requirements of driving and the scenery, her subconscious mind had been working overtime. The fact was that her subconscious mind could not let go of Seth Brady and how she had felt in his arms. Nor could it let go of her uncle and what his presence meant to her grandparents.

The fact was that she was convinced Lee and Seth had something to do with the bungled burglary of the Smiths' home. She hadn't planned to come to the scene of the crime, but since she was so close, why not drive by? What could it hurt?

Driving by proved to be a disappointment. She found the address easily enough, marked as it was with a large black metal mailbox atop a wooden post. On the mailbox, the Smiths' name and house number were painted in white. The house itself was obscured by a thick grove of trees.

Maggie slowed as she approached the lane leading to the house. Looking down it, she saw that it curved several yards into the trees, blocking any view of the house from that angle. Over the tops of the trees she could see a portion of the apex of the slate roof, but that was all. It didn't look as if the house sat very far back from the road, yet thanks to its positioning, it might as well have been miles away.

Maggie let out her breath in a loud sigh of exasperation and accelerated the Toyota. She had just moved past the grove of trees and a fence that apparently marked the boundary of the Smiths' property when a black Lincoln Navigator with tinted windows came around the curve in front of her, riding the center line. The driver, whose outline could barely be seen through the windshield, swerved just in time to keep from colliding with the Toyota. It all happened so quickly, Maggie had no time to react.

"Idiot!" Maggie swore at the driver of the Lincoln, her heart racing.

She had slowed in a delayed reaction to the close call. Now, as she approached the curve, she glanced in the rearview mirror. The Lincoln's brake lights were on. It had slowed and was turning into the Smiths' drive. She assumed that the car belonged to the Smiths until she saw the recognizable colors of its Illinois license plate. The Smiths apparently had visitors.

She rounded the curve and lost sight of the Lincoln. She drove on slowly, her curiosity piqued. Of course, it was probably nothing to get excited about. The Smiths were, after all, rich and influential people. People like that had friends who drove expensive cars and lived in places other than hick towns in Indiana. Nothing unusual about that.

Still. There was something about the car that she couldn't quite put her finger on, something that didn't feel right. "Sinister" was as close as she could come to describing it. The car had a sinister look to it, maybe only because of the tinted windows or the fact that it had almost run her off the road, but still it was there. It bothered her.

She pulled to the side of the road and sat there, drumming her fingers on the steering wheel and thinking. On her right was another grove of trees, but no fence and not much undergrowth. Somewhere on the other side of the trees was the Smiths' house. About a quarter of a mile past where she sat, she could see the roof of a house and a barn, but the trees prevented anyone who lived there from seeing her. On her left was an empty field. She could simply shut off the motor, lock up the car, and walk through the trees and take a look. Why not? After all, it was a nice day for a walk in the woods.

Then, again, what good reason did she have to go creeping through the forest to spy on people who obviously valued their privacy? There was always the possibility she would get caught. At the least, it would be embarrassing. It was even possible that the Smiths would be entitled to press charges of trespassing against her, depending on whether or not the trees outside the fence line were on their property.

Even if she didn't get caught, what good would it do? Probably all she would see would be the house, and if she were lucky, maybe the Smiths visiting with their out-of-state friends. It was hardly worth the risk just to satisfy her reporter's natural curiosity. Actually the whole idea seemed just a little bit silly.

She switched off the ignition and removed the key. It wouldn't be the first time she'd done something silly, and she doubted it would be the last. She locked the car doors and set off through the trees, her heart pounding.

There was little undergrowth due to the thickness of the foliage above her, so the walking was easy. As she wove her way through the trees and up a slight incline, she breathed deeply of air fragrant with the smells of green growing things. Overhead the trees rustled in the breeze, and somewhere in the distance, she heard the faint sound of cattle lowing. She realized it would be a pleasant walk if she weren't so nervous. It could even be a romantic walk with the right person beside her.

In less than ten minutes, Maggie saw that she was approaching a fence. It was a low wooden affair, well maintained, and she climbed it quickly. If the Smiths did catch her and charge her with trespassing, she could hardly say she didn't realize it was private property. In fact, if she were caught, she had no idea what she would say.

It was a large two-story brown brick Tudor that the Smiths called home. She crept forward carefully through the remaining trees, trying to keep them between herself and the house at all times. She berated herself for having worn such a brightly colored T-shirt, but there had been no reason for her to know ahead of time that camouflage clothing would be more appropriate.

At the edge of the tree line separating the woods from the Smiths' yard, there were several sickly looking shrubs, probably the remnants of a hedge. Maggie eased behind the thick trunk of an old maple, the base of which was concealed by the shrubs. She peered carefully around the trunk of the tree, holding her breath, half expecting to hear someone shout at her. But the only sound coming from the house was that of a radio tuned to an oldies station. It sounded as if it were coming from an open upstairs window.

She had approached from the side, but near the rear of the house, and she could see only the nose of the Lincoln parked in the front drive. Sitting in the grass to the side of the drive was a battered blue van. It looked out of place in the plush surroundings. Probably it belonged to a servant, she thought, maybe a gardener.

From her vantage point, she had a clear view of the glittering kidney-shaped pool and nearly all the patio and deck that bordered it. There was no one in sight. The Smiths and their visitors were apparently inside the house. Maggie held perfectly still, afraid that they might at this very moment be looking out a window or the patio doors.

As she looked at the pool, she thought of what Jack had told her the day before. Lester had told Jack that the deputies found blood on the cement by the pool. Was it there that Seth had received his injury? Had he and Lee fled through the woods near where she stood hidden now? Maybe they had even parked where her car now sat.

She shuddered involuntarily as she imagined that night, the shouts, the frenzied escape, the sound of the shot as it tore through the flesh of the man who had held her close and kissed her so passionately. She knew she still had no real proof that Seth and Lee had had anything to do with the burglary, but she also knew that she didn't need any. It had been Seth and Lee who had broken into this house. She was as certain of that as if she had witnessed it herself.

There was a sudden flash of white behind the patio doors; a second later, the doors opened and three men stepped onto the deck. She drew back further against the maple. She recognized one of the men from a picture that had appeared sometime last fall in the Sun. The picture had been of a group of men playing in a golf tournament given for charity. Maggie realized that the man must be Patrick Smith.

He was the tallest of the three men. He appeared to be in his late forties and was well over six feet tall with the emaciated build of a runner, thinning blond hair and a deep tan, the kind associated with winters spent in

Florida. He was dressed in white shorts and a white short-sleeved golf shirt. His clothing must have been the flash of white Maggie had seen behind the door. He was carrying a tall drink glass, as were the two men with him.

They were shorter, with olive skin and black hair. They were both dressed in dark suits and white shirts. The younger one appeared to be in his early thirties, with the bulky build of a weightlifter. The other one was in his late fifties or early sixties, with thick silver hair and an aristocratic bearing. The rays of the sun glinted off the large diamonds adorning his fingers. They looked Middle Eastern, but what were they doing here in the middle of nowhere and how did Patrick Smith fit in with them? Even more important as far as she was concerned, how did Seth and Lee fit in?

She watched as the three men went to a circular white wrought-iron-and-glass table near the edge of the deck. The sun had not reached there yet so the table was still in shade. They sat down, placing their drinks on the table. The older man loosened his tie and opened the top button on his shirt. He mumbled something to Patrick Smith who answered him, shaking his head emphatically. They were talking too low for Maggie to catch the words, but the intense expressions on their faces gave evidence that the conversation was of great importance. The younger man sat quietly, sipping his drink now and then. Five minutes passed. Suddenly the older man jumped to his feet, nearly knocking over his drink. Leaning over the table, he shook his finger in Smith's face.

"You bungled it," Maggie heard him say, his voice raised in anger, his face flushed. Then he said something else and in a lower tone, most of which she couldn't make out, although she thought she heard the word "police."

Smith shoved his chair back as if he was about to stand, his face contorted in anger. Maggie saw the younger man tense. It was obvious whose side he was on in the argument. She saw Patrick Smith glance his way, then settle back in his chair.

"Okay, okay, so what do you want me to do?" Smith said in exasperation, staring stubbornly at the older man.

The man stared back, not saying anything, still leaning on the table. Slowly he eased back down into his chair. Reaching into his jacket pocket, he pulled out a white handkerchief and wiped his face. Even from a distance, Maggie could see the sweat glistening on his skin. He carefully folded the handkerchief and placed it back in his pocket, then took a long drink from his glass. The flush was gradually receding from his face. It was clear to Maggie that he was making a conscious effort to calm himself. Finally he smiled an unpleasant and obviously forced smile at Smith and resumed the conversation in low tones that failed to carry to Maggie's hiding place in the trees.

The three men talked for another twenty minutes with only an occasional word reaching Maggie's ears. Her legs were starting to cramp and her lower back was throbbing, but she was afraid to shift position, fearful that a sudden flash of yellow or the red of her hair might attract their attention. The music had stopped and the announcer was giving the news on the unseen radio. It had grown warmer, and Maggie felt sweat trickling between her breasts. A fly buzzed around her face, brushing her right ear; she fought back the impulse to swat it.

Finally the three men stood, their business apparently concluded. They left the way they had come, through the patio doors. Maggie stood still for several more minutes, afraid to move in case they might be standing just inside the doors.

After what seemed an eternity, she heard the sound of a door closing and voices coming from the front of the house. Groaning with relief, she flexed her aching legs and back. Then moving quickly and quietly, she headed back through the woods toward the spot where her Toyota sat. The two men would very likely leave in the same direction from which they had come, and she did not want them to see her or her car still sitting in the area. After almost running her down, they would be sure to remember the car. If they were engaged in some nefarious activity as all appearances implied, they would be sure to become suspicious of her. In spite of the heat, a shiver ran down her back at the thought of what these men might be capable of doing to someone they considered a threat.

She quickly unlocked her car and slid behind the wheel. There were several long agonizing moments during which the car's engine perversely refused to start before it roared into life. Maggie threw it into gear and hesitated for a second. She didn't have much time before the Lincoln would be rounding the curve behind her. They had been at their car when she started back through the woods, and she doubted that the two men and Patrick Smith would have had a long farewell at the door.

She had one chance to bluff it out and not arouse their suspicions. Quickly she made a U-turn, heading the car back toward the Smiths' drive. She turned up the radio, and rolling down the window, leaned her arm out of it and assumed what she hoped was a nonchalant expression.

She had not had a moment to spare. The Lincoln rounded the curve ahead of her, the driver moving more slowly and carefully this time. Maggie began singing along with the music. She was positive they would recognize her. Her only hope was that they would make the assumption that she was simply returning from wherever it was she had been and that it was purely coincidental that they were again passing at almost the same location. As the Lincoln passed her, she glanced its way, realizing that it would look odd if she ignored it altogether. It didn't slow. She rounded the curve and lost sight of it.

She drove quickly past the drive to the Smiths' house and took the fastest and most direct route home. Her thoughts were racing. As she zipped along the nearly deserted country roads, they kept coming back to one point. How did Seth and Lee fit in? If Patrick Smith was mixed up in something illegal, what were Seth and Lee doing breaking into his home? Did they work for Smith's visitor? It was obvious there were problems of some sort between the older man and Smith. Perhaps Lee and Seth had been sent by him to find out what Patrick Smith had bungled. Only they had bungled, too, and Seth had been shot.

Then, again, maybe she had been watching too many late movies. Maybe Smith and the two men were simply engaged in some sort of perfectly legal business transaction and something had gone wrong. Maybe Seth and Lee really had had car trouble, and Seth really had been hurt when the jack slipped.

And maybe there really was a Santa Claus.

She pounded her hand hard against the steering wheel, tears stinging her eyes. She always came back to the same conclusion. Seth and Lee were involved in something criminal and dangerous. True, her evidence was shaky. But she knew deep down that they had been the men who broke into the Smiths' home. She had been sure of it before and had even felt sorry for the Smiths. Now the scene she'd just witnessed between Patrick Smith and his two visitors confused her even more. Patrick Smith no longer looked like an innocent victim. But if he wasn't an innocent victim, then what did that make Seth and Lee?

Chapter Eight

She had found no answers by the time she reached the house. Everett Jacobs was in his study with the door shut and her grandmother was in the kitchen, putting food on the wicker tray. Too late Maggie realized she was going to be drafted into delivering the tray to Seth.

"I'll run this on up," she said, as her grandmother started to voice her request. "I'll be right back down to set the table."

She hurried out of the kitchen, wondering how she would face Seth. Her feelings for him were in a jumble. On the one hand, she turned into a quivering mass of animal lust every time he looked at her in that way he had, and especially when he touched her. Just thinking of the kiss they'd shared the day before started her loins throbbing with want. Underlying that want, like a measured drumbeat to a melody, was the suspicion that he was involved in criminal activity during the commission of which he had been shot. No, not suspicion, she thought, certainty. She was certain he was one of the burglars at the Smiths' house.

What was worse, that certainty changed her feelings for him not one iota. What did that say about her character? Was it an indication that she craved exciting men so much that her so-called values flew out the window?

The guest room door was ajar. Maggie knocked lightly on it, balancing the tray against the jamb.

"Come in, "she heard Seth say, her heart skipping a beat at the sound of his voice. She pushed open the door.

He was sitting on top of the bedspread, dressed only in the cut-off jeans. His color was good. Maggie thought he had improved even from this afternoon. In fact, if it hadn't been for the bandage on his shoulder, she wouldn't have known anything was wrong with him. No one who looked that good without a shirt, she thought, could possibly be very ill.

He had been reading one of her grandfather's magazines; he laid it on the bed open to his place.

"Hello," he said, his eyes warm. His expression was one of affection, rather than the teasing flirtatiousness she had seen before. She found that even more disconcerting. "My stomach was just telling me that it must be close to dinner time."

"You look like you're feeling better by the hour," she said. "Do you want to eat in bed or would you rather sit up?"

"I do feel better," he answered. "Put the tray on the table and I'll sit in the chair to eat. That is, unless you're going to join me again."

"No, I'll be eating downstairs," she said, the thought of being alone with him again bringing warmth to her cheeks—and elsewhere. "Do you need anything? Maybe something else to read or even a TV? I've got a small one in my room that I never use."

"No, thanks," he replied. "Your grandfather was kind enough to bring me plenty of magazines. That should hold me until bedtime, which I think won't be too long from now. I'm still a little tired."

"Well, if you change your mind, just give a yell." She turned to the door, then stopped, a thought forming. "It was a beautiful day. It's a shame you had to be cooped up. I went for a drive in the country."

"I bet it was nice. I wish I could have gone with you."

A picture of the two of them in a sun-dappled forest popped unbidden into her mind, followed by an image of the two of them nude, making love on a carpet of pine needles. She knew she was blushing and pushed the thoughts from her mind.

"Maybe when you're well, you could," she said. "If you're here long enough. Today I drove out to Twin Forks Road, a few miles outside of town. It's really a lovely drive."

Even if she hadn't been watching him closely for his reaction, she couldn't have missed it. He froze for a couple of seconds, his Adam's apple working as if he were trying to get his breath.

"You drove out to Twin Forks Road?"

"Yes. Are you familiar with it?"

"No." He looked away from her and out the window. "No, of course not. This is the first time I've been in the area. I think Lee has mentioned it, though. That's why it sounds familiar."

He looked back at her, concern in his eyes.

"Lee told me there are some pretty bad curves on that road, Maggie," he said. "Be careful. Okay?"

"Of course, I'll be careful," she said. "I know the roads around here pretty well."

"I'm sure you do." He tried to smile, but the worry in his eyes belied the smile on his lips. "It's just that I wouldn't want anything to happen to you."

They looked at each other for several seconds. Suddenly, Maggie was sure that if she stayed in this room one moment longer, he would get out of the bed and take her in his arms. She couldn't take that chance for the simple reason that she knew she would welcome it.

"Oh, I'll be fine," she said, turning to the door. "Enjoy your dinner."

***

Seth sat for several minutes after Maggie left. His appetite was gone. What had she been doing on Twin Forks Road? Could she be telling the truth, that she had simply gone for a drive in the beautiful spring weather? Maybe it was just a coincidence that she had ended up where she did.

Still, he'd had the distinct impression that she'd been testing him when she mentioned the road. If that were true, he knew he'd failed the test. He didn't need a mirror to know his shock and concern had been written all over his face. Even a casual observer would have known that he had recognized the name of the road and that it had upset him.

How much did she know? Lee had said that she knew nothing about his life, but that he believed she suspected him of criminal activity. Lee had just told him that afternoon that it was an issue he was going to have to face soon. She was also a reporter. That meant she knew about the police report that Lee had discovered Patrick Smith had made. Had she put two and two together and come up with four? If so, what must she think of him?

Seth realized suddenly that he very much cared what she thought of him, but more important than her opinion of him was her safety. Let her think him a terrible person, he thought. She'd be right. Just don't let anything happen to her. Above all else, she had to be kept safe.

He turned to the tray and began to pick at the food. He was going to have to talk to Lee. If they couldn't get out of here and get this job wrapped up soon, then she was going to have to be told the truth. Maybe when she knew the truth, she would stay away from Twin Forks Road and Patrick Smith.

Chapter Nine

Maggie overslept the next morning, having spent a restless night. She quickly showered, applied makeup, and dressed in a lightweight blue pantsuit and plaid blouse. She was thankful she had overslept so she didn't have time to sit down and have breakfast with her grandparents. She knew Dora would notice how tired she looked and question her about it.

There had been a time not so long ago, she thought wistfully, when the sleeplessness would have been caused by thoughts of Tom, his lies, and how much she missed him. How quickly that had changed! Of course, the feelings of betrayal she'd felt when she learned the truth about his secret life would probably never go away, and in spite of them, she would probably always miss him and love him. But now the flesh and blood man lying in the guest room bed was shoving those feelings and memories to the back of her mind.

Tom would have liked Seth Brady, she suddenly realized. They were two of a kind.

As she walked to work, she thought about the situation with her family. She had decided one thing while lying awake in her narrow bed. For the time being, she would try to act with her grandparents as if nothing was wrong. What else was there to do? Turn them into the authorities for harboring a criminal whose misdeeds she couldn't even prove? Face them with what she had overheard — eavesdropping, her grandmother would call it, and she would be right — and demand they toss their only living child out of their home? There weren't many options, and the available ones were not very attractive.

Jack was already at his desk, a steaming cup of coffee in his mug that said "The Big Dog" on it in inch-high red letters. Della Henderson, the Sun's secretary, was at her desk also and looked up as Maggie came in.

"Good morning, dear," she said, her voice motherly. Della wasn't more than ten years older than Maggie, but she was one of those people who seemed to have been born old and who stayed that way the rest of their lives. "How are you this morning?"

"Fine, just fine," Maggie lied. "Yourself?"

"Oh, I'll be all right." A slight whining note entered Della's voice. "A little pain in my lower back is all. I suppose I must have slept wrong. I'm sure I'll be just fine."

The usual morning amenities with Della having been concluded, Maggie moved to the rear of the office, nodded good morning to Jack, and poured a hot mug of black coffee. Her mug was white with a large black "M" on it, a gift from Jack. Della had a similar mug sporting a "D" on her desk that she used for tea.

Maggie spent a few minutes cleaning out her desk, a task she performed at least once every two weeks. She tried to put her mind in the proper frame to work. Mondays and Tuesdays were always full, as were Wednesday mornings when the paper came out. The end of the week moved more slowly, winding down to the weekend. The pace was always predictable.

Maggie had found a certain comfort in that when she had come to work there five months before. The large daily paper where she'd worked in Denver had been more exciting, but she had known she would not have been able to handle the pace, at least not so soon after Tom's disgrace and death. The long hours, the sudden catastrophes and tragedies, would have been too much for her with her own tragedy tearing at her heart. A healing time had been in order. So she had come home, ultimately winding up at the paper where she had started her career while still in high school. And now, perversely, excitement seemed to have followed her.

Her desk tidied and a second cup of coffee warming her stomach, Maggie gathered her voice recorder, notepad, and pens. Waving goodbye to Jack and Della, both of whom were on the phone, she set out for the Monday morning meeting of the Vichy Garden Club, which was held in the basement hall of the Civic Center.

During the winter months, the ladies met monthly, but with the coming of spring, the meetings increased to weekly. Jack had been more than glad to turn their coverage over to Maggie when she came to work for him; he said he'd always felt like the unwanted weed in the garden. She was surprised to find she enjoyed them. The ladies ranged in age from thirty to nearly eighty, and Maggie had known many of them all her life. Dora Jacobs was a member also, but usually made no more than two meetings a month. Maggie knew she had not planned on coming today.

Women were still trickling in when she arrived. She set about filling a small plate with fresh fruit and homemade croissants still warm from the oven. Finding a chair at the rear of the room, she settled back, enjoying the food. The room was filling up fast; it looked like it would be a good turnout for the meeting.

"Is this seat taken?"

Maggie looked up into a pale face, framed by short coal-black hair done in a wedge cut. The woman was petite, probably not much over five feet tall, and slightly built. Maggie guessed her to be about thirty-five years old, although the lines of strain around her eyes made her look older. She looks like she's had a sleepless night, too, Maggie thought, as she nodded her head at the chair.

"No, it's not taken. Please sit down."

Maggie returned to her food and her thoughts. After a few minutes, the woman leaned closer and spoke in a low voice.

"I saw you yesterday." She sat back in her chair and looked at Maggie.

Maggie could see from the woman's expression that a reaction was expected from her. She just wasn't sure what it should be. Saw me where, she thought to herself. Church, out driving, what? And so what?

"I'm sorry." She tried to keep the irritation out of her voice. "You have me at a disadvantage."

"In the woods," the woman said, leaning closer again. "Watching my husband and his business associates." The last was said with more than a trace of sarcasm. "I'm Lydia Smith."

The radio inside the house, Maggie thought. It had been Lydia Smith who had been listening to it. She berated herself for not having been more careful.

"I can explain," she began, wondering just how she was going to do that. Maybe she could claim her presence in the woods was related to a story on the burglary. Before she could speak, Lydia waved her hand impatiently.

"No, never mind that now. There isn't time. We both know why you were there. It was to spy on my husband and his friends."

"I don't know why you'd think that," Maggie began lamely.

"I saw you," Lydia whispered forcefully between clenched teeth. "I recognized you. I'd seen you in town before and I knew you worked for the paper."

She glanced around at the women nearest them. Satisfying herself that none were listening, she looked back at Maggie.

"I have to admit it was a surprise seeing you there. Cops, I would have expected. Cops, I always expect. Not reporters. At first, I thought it had to do with the incident the other night, but then I figured if that was it, you would have knocked on the front door."

She doesn't know my connection to Seth and Lee, Maggie realized with relief. She thinks I was after a story.

"If you saw me, why didn't you tell your husband?"

Lydia Smith glanced around them again and lowered her voice even more. "For one thing, I didn't want to see you get hurt. Or maybe worse."

A chill ran down Maggie's back. Was Lydia Smith implying that her husband and his friends might have done her harm if they'd caught her watching them?

"For another, I need help. I don't have anyone else to ask." She laughed bitterly. "That's pretty bad, isn't it? To have to ask a total stranger for help and protection from your own husband."

"I still don't understand."

"It's all falling apart at home and I'm scared. I don't have any relatives and the sort of friends I do have can't be counted on under the circumstances. I want help getting away."

"What kind of help?"

"A place to stay, to hide out, until I can get out of town. And help getting out. That's all. I don't need money. I've got some hidden away. My contingency money, I guess you'd call it."

She looked down at her hands in her lap. She looked tired, Maggie thought, tired and desperate.

"My husband keeps pretty close tabs on me," she said. "Real close. He knows I'm here. I told him I was going to come get some information about joining the group. That's why I need someone to help me when I make my move."

"Mrs. Smith, I don't know that I can do what you ask," Maggie said. "I'm not sure I care to get involved in whatever problems you and your husband have. Besides, if what you imply about your husband is true, it sounds like it could be dangerous for me to get involved."

Lydia looked around again. The room had become more crowded in the time they'd been talking. It wouldn't be long before they would be unable to carry on their conversation without being overheard. She turned back to Maggie.

"If you help me, I'll give you a story. A pretty hot story, too. One that can take you out of this burg if that's what you want."

Three laughing women excused themselves and scooted past them down the row, settling into the chairs on the other side of Lydia Smith. An older lady who had just come in called Maggie's name and waved. She was a friend of Dora Jacobs, and she began making her way toward them.

"Just think about it, okay?" Lydia Smith said, pleading in her voice. "Please."

She slipped a folded piece of paper into Maggie's hand.

"Here's my cell number and a place we can meet in person to talk more. Think about it and call me, please. One way or the other, let me know what you decide, so I'll know where I stand."

She cast a final furtive glance around the room before taking Maggie's hand in hers.

"Please do this for me. You're the only chance I've got. Without your help, I'll probably end up like Elton."

"Elton?"

"Never mind." Lydia's cheeks reddened. "Forget I said that. Maybe I'll tell you later. If you decide to help me, that is."

Just as her grandmother's friend reached them, Lydia let go of Maggie's hand, stood, and left the hall. Maggie and the woman exchanged pleasantries before resuming their seats as the meeting of the Vichy Garden Club was called to order.

Maggie surreptitiously unfolded the paper Lydia Smith had thrust into her hand. On it was a telephone number, followed by the name of a health spa located in the new mall at the west edge of town. If Lydia were concerned about being followed by her husband or his cronies, the choice of the spa for a meeting place was brilliant. It was for women only. Depending on the time of day, they could be assured of privacy, and it wouldn't look odd if they showed up at the same place. While Maggie wasn't a member, she knew complimentary visits were offered to potential members. Obviously Lydia knew it, too.

Well, Maggie thought, tuning out the reading of the last meeting's minutes, the Garden Club meetings were certainly becoming interesting. If this type of cloak-and-dagger shenanigans continued, Jack would want his old assignment back.

As she listened to lectures and discussions on mealybugs and soil acidity, half of her mind concentrated on the information she was jotting down, while the other half thought about what had transpired with Lydia Smith.

There was no doubt in her mind that Lydia was a frightened and desperate woman. It must be terrible, Maggie thought, to be that frightened of your own husband, so frightened that you had to beg a stranger for help leaving him.

If Lydia was to be believed, she had been right in her assessment of Patrick Smith and his two visitors. Lydia had said whatever he was involved in was "falling apart" and she had mentioned the police. Smith's visitor had accused him of bungling something. Were the two statements connected? It was reasonable to think so. And if so, where did Seth and Lee fit in?

Lydia had also promised Maggie an exclusive story if she would help her. Maggie had thought that part of her professional life had died along with Tom, that she would be forever content with being a small-town reporter covering Garden Club meetings and the like. Now she was surprised to find herself excited by the prospect of a big story. If her suspicions and Lydia's promises held even a grain of truth, it would be a big story, one that would be grabbed up by the national news services and the broadcast media. But what would she do if that story had to also include the names of her uncle and the man who now occupied her every thought?

Chapter Ten

From the Garden Club meeting, Maggie went to the high school where she was filled in on the plans for the graduation ceremony scheduled to take place the Friday after Memorial Day. She arrived back at the office around eleven and quickly typed up the Garden Club and school pieces, then headed out for lunch.

She opted for a turkey sandwich and salad to go from Millie's, taking it to a bench in the little park across from the diner. The park was actually more of a town square. It occupied a small city block and contained the usual benches, two World War I cannons and a bandstand where local groups sometimes performed in the summer. There were several people in the park, but Maggie was able to find a bench to herself. She needed some alone time to think things out.

She felt betrayed by her grandparents, but that wasn't all or even most of the problem. She had always known what Lee was, at least since she had been an adult, and she had always supposed that her grandparents had to at least suspect. It had been a shock to find that they knew exactly what he was up to and that they had conspired to keep his secret from her. They were his accomplices, and it was difficult for her to think of them that way. Still, it hadn't been a total surprise.

Seth Brady was the real problem. Seth with his golden body and laughing amber eyes had walked into her life and turned it topsy-turvy. She wanted him more than she would have imagined she could ever want anybody.

She wadded her empty sandwich wrapper into a ball and dropped it into the empty bag. Looking out at the busy noontime street and the familiar faces she'd known all her life, she wondered how this could have happened to her. Was it some genetic flaw in her own personality, a flaw that refused to allow her to be satisfied with a safe small-town man—a man like her boss? It had been Tom's recklessness and his craving for adventure that had first drawn her to him while she was still in college. He had excited her. When she was with him, she felt glamorous and alive.

That excitement had never completely worn off, but there had been times during the marriage when she had found herself wishing he were a little more stable, that he would finally grow up and settle down. She had wished it when she watched him walk the walk-of-shame into the Denver courthouse, but she had never wished it more than she did when she received the news that he had died on the dirty floor of the jail's shower room.

Yet, in spite of all that, here she was, a little over a year later, falling for a man cut from the same cloth as Tom Fields. She was like a moth being drawn to a flame, the flame being dangerous men.

"Earth to Maggie, Earth to Maggie," she heard a male voice say and looked up into the face of the town's police chief.

Lester Lewis with a thin, wiry man in his late 40s with thinning red hair and pale freckled skin. He had been a police officer in Vichy for as long as Maggie could remember and had become chief six years before when old Chief Manning retired. He was well liked by the townspeople; even more important, he was respected.

"Hello, Lester," Maggie said.

She had always liked Lester and felt comfortable around him. Now she suddenly felt guilty, and not, she admitted to herself, without justification. Where does it all end, she wondered. One lie, one cover-up, leads to another, and pretty soon one's whole world view is changed.

"How have you been?" Lester sat down on the bench beside her and stretched his long legs.

"I've been just fine," Maggie lied, her heart racing. "How about yourself?"

"Oh, age is starting to catch up with me, but I'll make it." He lit a cigarette. "So, anything newsworthy going on in Vichy that I should know about?"

"You tell me." Maggie tried to keep her tone light. "You'd know before I would."

"Sometimes I think the cops are the last to know." He shook his head in disgust. "I tell you, Maggie, the world's going to hell in a handbasket."

"Come on, Lester," she said. "It's not so bad here and you know it."

"I admit it's not the big city and thank God for that," Lester said. "But, anymore, the craziness isn't confined to the big cities. Would you believe they've got teen gangs fighting now over in Anderson? It's not much more than twice the size of Vichy."

"That is frightening."

"Yeah, well." He smiled at her. "What can you do? Just keep plugging away, I guess."

She smiled back and decided to do a little probing. "Jack tells me there was a burglary the other night out on Twin Forks Road. Any new developments yet?"

"Nothing I've heard." Lester took a drag off his cigarette. "Of course, the county Mounties don't always tell me everything."

"Jack said Mr. Smith shot one of the burglars."

"Yeah, Smith thought he heard one of them yell after he fired."

"You would think the burglar would have shown up at a hospital by now if he was injured."

"Only if he was badly enough injured," Lester said. "Could be Smith only grazed him. Or maybe he knows a crooked doctor that patched him up.

Maggie felt her face grow hot. Fortunately Lester was looking out across the park and didn't notice. She struggled to get herself under control.

"The county's having more than their share of excitement this week. I just heard this morning they found a body in a wooded area out on Strimple Road. Some farmer's kid was out hunting and came across it."

"Maybe it's the burglar who was shot." Maggie felt her hopes lift.

"Doubtful," Lester said. "This guy took one to the head. Instant lights out. If it had been the burglar Smith shot, he'd have been laying by the pool."

So much for wishful thinking, Maggie thought.

"Of course, it's always possible he was involved with the break-in," Lester continued. "No identification on him, but his fingerprints got a hit. He was a small-time crook out of Indianapolis. Name of Elton Jackson."

For the first time in her life, Maggie thought she was going to faint. Her vision and hearing blurred, and she felt dizzy. The dead man's name was Elton, the name that Lydia had inadvertently let slip this morning. With a name like Elton, it could hardly be a coincidence. Patrick Smith was involved in murder.

She took a deep breath, thankful Lester was still looking out at the park.

"So what do the deputies think he was doing in our area?" She was surprised her voice was steady.

"They say they have no idea," Lester said. "From the evidence, it doesn't look like he was killed where he was found. They're leaning toward the possibility that he was killed over in Indy and the body dumped here."

Or maybe he was killed on Twin Forks Road and carted a much shorter distance to be disposed of, Maggie thought. What should she do? Should she tell Lester about Lydia Smith? Or would that be putting the woman in too much danger? Maggie suddenly felt a responsibility to her. The woman had come to her for help; she couldn't betray that trust without Lydia's knowledge. Besides, it would be better if Lydia were safely away from Twin Forks Road before the authorities became involved.

Lydia Smith's safety aside, there were still Seth and Lee to consider. Until she knew what Lydia had to tell her, she couldn't take the chance that their involvement, whatever that might be, could become known.

Lester stubbed out his cigarette and glanced at his watch.

"Maggie, it's been good talking to you, but duty calls. As usual, there's paperwork to be done." He stood up. "Stop over to the house sometime. Viola was just asking me the other day if I'd seen you lately."

"How is she doing?" Viola Lewis had been fighting the good fight against ovarian cancer for nearly nine months. Maggie had last visited her a month before, and she hadn't looked good.

"Ah, Maggie, she's tough. Tougher than I am, that's for sure." Lester shook his head. "She just keeps fighting, but I don't know. Nothing seems to work for long. We're going to California in a couple of weeks to meet with a doc who's starting a clinical trial for some new chemo drug."

"Tell her I'll come by to see her before you go," Maggie said.

"She'd like that."

"I'll call first." Maggie knew from Lester that Viola had bad days and worse days—no good ones at this stage of the disease. She stood and gave him a hug. "Let us know if you get any news about either the burglary or the murder."

"You'll know when I do," Lester said and started off toward the police station.

Maggie dropped back down on the bench, feeling drained. She had put up a good front and she didn't think Lester was suspicious. But what would happen when he learned what Lydia Smith had told her? One thing was certain. Eventually he would have to know that Lydia knew something about Elton Jackson's murder. Keeping quiet about burglary suspects was bad enough; she couldn't keep information about a murder from the authorities forever. Once Lydia was safe, Lester would have to be told. And he would probably be disappointed in her that she hadn't confided in him right away. She could only hope he would understand.

The big question was whether or not Lydia could connect Lee and Seth to her husband. If they worked for a rival as Maggie feared, their names might be known to her. The very fact that Maggie had not mentioned their visit to anyone, not even at work, would make Lester very suspicious of her.

She wondered if anyone in town knew about their houseguests. She had been with her grandparents at church on Sunday, and she knew they hadn't told anyone then. Their silence, as well as her own, only now struck her as curious. There had been an unacknowledged conspiracy among them to keep the men's presence a secret. That in itself was proof that her grandparents knew the real cause of Seth Brady's injury.

At the thought of Seth, Maggie felt very afraid. If Lester or anyone discovered the truth, what would happen to him? Prison, probably—prison for both him and her uncle. But, God forgive her, she realized she didn't care what happened to her uncle. Deep down, she guessed she felt he deserved whatever he got for the way he had treated his parents. She worried only for her grandparents—and for Seth. Above all, God help her, for Seth.

Chapter Eleven

"I thought I'd let Mr. Brady join us at the dinner table tonight," Everett said, drawing deeply on his pipe. "See how he feels. He's still a bit weak, but he's starting to get antsy staying upstairs like an invalid."

Maggie and her grandfather were on the front porch, Everett in the rocker, she perched on the wooden glider, her feet drawn under her. He had been sitting there when Maggie arrived home from work at five. She had stopped to talk and had stayed.

At the mention of Seth's name, she felt her pulse quicken.

"Do you think that's wise? I mean, are you sure he's up to it?"

"Only one way to find out," her grandfather said. "He'll probably need a little help with the stairs just to be on the safe side, but I don't think he'll have any problem other than that. It will probably be good for him, maybe help him get his strength back faster."

"You're the doctor." She stood. "Speaking of dinner, I suppose I better go get cleaned up for it."

"You look fine." Everett smiled. "No need to go to any extra effort because we have a guest."

"That's not it." Maggie felt her cheeks grow warm. "It's just been a hectic day, that's all. I feel yucky. I think I'll take a shower and put on something cooler."

She hurried through the front door before he had a chance to reply. Her grandfather was no fool. He had spotted her attraction to Seth Brady almost before she had. Maggie wondered if her feelings were that evident to everyone and hoped with all her heart that they were not.

She showered, then wrapped a fluffy beige towel around her body and began applying her make up. She took more care than usual, not even trying to deny to herself the reason why. She wanted to look good to Seth Brady. Maybe it was just foolish feminine pride, but she wanted him to be as attracted to her as she was to him.

Not that anything could come of it, she reminded herself. She wanted him and she thought she might even like him, but she had to be a realist. He might be the man she wanted, but he wasn't the type she wanted. She had to keep that fact uppermost in her mind. He would be gone soon, and then she would erase him from her mind and her heart. At least, she would try. But when he left, she wanted him to leave with his memory of her as vivid and poignant as she knew hers would be of him.

She started to put on a lightweight summer dress, a shade of green that matched the emerald color of her eyes, but decided against it. She never dressed that nicely for supper, and she knew the change would draw comments from her grandmother as well as her grandfather. Instead, she chose a beige jumpsuit that was a couple of years old. It was one of her favorite outfits and fit snugly on her body, clinging in all the right places. She ran a comb through her hair, which she left hanging loose, then did a quick appraisal of herself in the mirror. She was satisfied with what she saw.

Seth seemed to handle the trip downstairs quite well. He was animated and cheerful, and it was obvious to all of them that his appetite hadn't been affected by his injury. Dora Jacobs had outdone herself, having fixed a large tender roast cooked with carrots and chunks of red potatoes with the skin still on, peas with pearl onions, and homemade corn muffins. Seth had more than one helping of everything and heaped praise on Dora for her cooking. She watched her grandmother swell with pride and thought that Seth's charm had been as unaffected by his injury as his appetite had been.

Dora had had Maggie set the big oak table with the good china and silver. Maggie knew that for her grandmother this was a very special occasion indeed. Her child was home for dinner, and that was a rare event in itself.

Lee was cordial and friendly to Maggie, but she noted a reserve in his manner that hadn't been there when he'd greeted her the day before. She knew she had hurt him with her coolness and sensed that he was afraid of being too demonstrative in case she might snub him again. But she'd promised herself that she would try for her grandparents' sake, and so she was civil, even friendly to him. He seemed to relax as the meal wore on.

Everett sat at one end of the table, as usual, with his wife at the other. Lee occupied the chair on his father's right. Maggie and Seth sat next to each other on the other side of the table.

Without the leaf, the table was not large. Maggie found being in such close proximity to Seth both unnerving and exhilarating. She was aware of his every movement, of his muscles rippling under his thin cotton T-shirt as he reached to accept a bowl of vegetables from her grandmother, of his hard thighs as he shifted position in the chair, of his strong hands gripping the silverware. Her excitement at the nearness of him seemed to stimulate her own appetite, sublimation, she supposed, of her deeper desires. She ate ravenously of her grandmother's delicious spread. She wondered if Seth's insatiability stemmed from the same source as her own.

Dora cleared the table with Maggie's assistance and then brought in her good dessert plates, apple pie, a white stoneware crock of vanilla ice cream, and a plate of cheese for those who preferred it. Maggie wondered at herself for even being able to consider dessert after the meal she had just consumed.

Dora cut the pie, placed the wedges on the dessert plates, and passed them around the table.

"Whichever you want," she said, "ice cream or cheese, just help yourself. There's plenty for everyone."

"It's ice cream for me." Seth scooped a large dip from the crock. "It's a real weakness with me. My idea of heaven would be to die and go to the great Baskin-Robbins in the sky."

As he settled back in his chair, he reached for his water glass with his left hand and winced in pain as he twisted his injured shoulder, jerking his arm and knocking his napkin to the floor between his chair and Maggie's. She bent to retrieve it at the same time as he did; their heads collided with a light bump.

"Ouch," Seth said, laughing. "Sorry about that."

He turned and gently smoothed her hair back from her forehead with his right hand, examining her closely.

She looked into his gentle concerned eyes and was suddenly unaware of anyone else at the table, conscious only of his amber eyes and his fingers lightly stroking her forehead.

"I don't think there's any damage done," he said softly. "Fortunately. The last thing I would want to do is hurt you."

"No need to worry." Maggie managed to get the words out in spite of suddenly feeling breathless. "I've got a hard head."

"Runs in the family." Everett laughed, and the spell was broken. Seth removed his hand from her forehead and, smiling sheepishly, bent down and retrieved the napkin.

Maggie glanced quickly around the table. Dora was looking at her, concern on her face. She knows, Maggie thought. The way I feel about him must be written all over my face. She knows and she's worried for me.

Her grandfather, on the other hand, looked amused by the whole incident. Lee seemed to be the only one at the table unaware of what had just passed between her and Seth. He concentrated on his pie, and Maggie wondered if his studied unconcern wasn't just a little too forced.

She smoothed her hair back into place and concentrated on devouring her pie à la mode. She said little during the remainder of the meal, her body still tingling from Seth's touch.

Later, while clearing the table and rinsing the dishes, she thought of his words. "The last thing I would want to do is hurt you," he had said. Was he referring to the bump on the head or to a far more real and imminent danger?

Chapter Twelve

Tuesday at the Sun proved to be more hectic than Monday. Maggie was thankful for the diversion since it gave her the excuse of being too busy to call Lydia Smith. She knew she would end up helping the woman, but she wasn't yet ready to face the issue. Because once she heard Lydia's story, she might finally know the truth about Seth. What was worse, she might have to do something about it.

Her mind repeatedly wandered back to his touch and his words of the night before. She was more certain than ever that her attraction to him was returned in kind; she also had the suspicion that he didn't welcome it anymore than she did. Still, it was there, and it was getting more and more difficult to deny it.

She was even more convinced of her suspicions that evening at dinner. Seth was rapidly regaining his strength, and he joined them at the table again. Everett had driven Lee to Indianapolis that afternoon to pick up the car. Lee had not yet returned, so Seth sat opposite Maggie at the table. Several times she looked up from her food to catch him looking at her, a tender expression on his face; yet every time he quickly looked away as though loath to be caught with his feelings so exposed. There was a tension between them that was almost unbearable in its intensity.

Maggie sensed that her grandparents were aware of that tension, yet their reactions to it were very different. Her grandfather seemed amused by it and even to encourage it by his sly innuendos and general attitude, while Dora seemed sullen and concerned. Maggie couldn't help but compare their opposing attitudes to her own confused feelings.

After dinner, Seth and Everett took their coffee to the front porch while Maggie helped Dora clean up. Several times Maggie thought her grandmother was about to bring up the subject of Seth, yet they finished rinsing and stacking the dishes in the dishwasher without the subject being broached. She was thankful for the reprieve.

While they were wiping the countertops, she heard the front screen door slam and the voices of Everett and Seth in the front room. Then there was silence. Maggie guessed that her grandfather had gone into his study to read as was his usual custom before bed. Seth had apparently gone upstairs. Maggie found she was slightly disappointed he hadn't stopped in the kitchen to say good night, but decided it was just as well.

It was too early to go to bed and she didn't feel like joining her grandmother in front of the television in the living room. Her thoughts would not stop spinning around, running first on one track devoted to the topic of Seth and the way he made her feel, then skipping to another track named Lydia Smith and what she knew, then back again to Seth.

She poured herself a glass of lemonade and decided to try relaxing in the cool night air on the front porch. It would be quiet and peaceful there. Maybe she would be able to sort out her thoughts, something she badly needed to do.

She had closed the screen door quietly behind her and was halfway to the glider, lost in thought, when she became aware of the shadowy figure. Seth was sitting at the top of the steps, his back propped against a support post and his legs stretched out before him along the edge of the porch. Maggic's first instinct was to turn back into the house, but it was too late. He was already aware of her presence.

"Sorry," she said. "I didn't know anyone was out here."

"Don't apologize," he said, bending his legs and stretching his arms out to rest on his knees. "It's your home, after all. Besides, I'm glad for the company. It was starting to get too quiet out here."

"I thought I heard you come in."

"I did for a few minutes. Then I changed my mind and came back out. I just wasn't ready for sleep yet."

"I know what you mean," Maggie said. "It's too nice an evening to spend it sleeping."

She moved to the wooden glider and sat down. For several minutes, they sat in companionable silence, listening to the repetitive call of a whippoorwill in the field behind the house and watching the intermittent flickering of a few early fireflies. Down the road, a dog barked hysterically until a gruff voice silenced it.

Maggie sipped her lemonade and tried to relax, telling herself it was ridiculous to be so nervous just because they were here together in the dark. After all, he was right. This was her home and she certainly had a right to be here. Her eyes had adjusted to the dark and now she stole a look at him.

He was staring out into the dark, his body tense, his hands clamped tightly around his kneecaps, as if whatever thoughts were playing through his mind were disturbing to him. He looked as if he were in more need of sorting out his thoughts than she had thought herself to be. She had just decided to do the gracious thing and leave him to his private musings when he spoke.

"I love it here," he said. "I really do."

He turned his head and looked at her. His eyes were in shadow.

"This may sound strange, but I feel more at home here than I have anywhere for a very long time."

Maggie opened her mouth to reply, but closed it again. What was there to say? His statement had not required an answer, and anything she might say would sound shallow and inane. She rocked slightly in the glider, unaware of her movement; the glider squeaked low in protest. Seth suddenly got to his feet and held his hand out to her.

"Walk with me," he said.

"Are you sure you're up to it?" She got to her feet without hesitation and took his hand.

"I think it will be just what I need."

They stepped off the porch and moved through the cool grass to the road. As they stepped into the washed-out light of the streetlamp, Maggie self-consciously pulled her hand away. She felt a slight pressure from Seth's fingers, as if he were reluctant to lose physical contact with her, then he relaxed his grip and let her go.

They walked for a while in silence, passing lighted houses where families gathered around the flickering light of the television, the children finally freed from the nightly chore of homework now that the school year was nearly at an end. They passed the home of the hysterical dog, and he began yammering from the backyard until the gruff voice again quieted him. At the intersection of Henry Gray Road, they crossed the street and headed back toward the house. Seth finally broke the silence.

"I'll be leaving soon," he said. "I don't want to. I'm almost starting to hope for a relapse."

"You don't mean that."

"No, I guess I don't," he agreed after a moment's hesitation. "I despise being ill. It doesn't set well with me. And there are things I have to do, things that can't be put off any longer. They're too important. But that doesn't make me any happier about leaving."

She was silent for a moment. Then she spoke hesitantly.

"I'll be sorry to see you go. It's been kind of nice having you in the house."

"Do you mean that?"

"Of course." She didn't look at him as she spoke, afraid that how she felt would show in her eyes.

"It means a lot to me to hear you say that," he said. "More than you can imagine."

They had reached the front of her grandparents' yard and turned in under the trees. A large maple sat several yards back from the sidewalk. It was an old tree, having been there when the house was built. Maggie had spent many happy childhood afternoons clambering about in its low hanging branches.

Now, as they passed into its shadow, Seth reached out and drew her to him. She didn't resist. His strong arms enveloped her, holding her tight against his warm heaving chest. She could smell his heady man-smell and feel the straining of every muscle in his body as he held her to him.

Then his mouth closed on hers and she gave herself over completely to the wave of desire that swept through her as their tongues probed and explored. Their bodies pressed closer together as if they were trying to meld into one, and she felt his penis stir and harden. She pressed herself against it, her head growing light with need. At that moment, she wanted nothing more from the world than to have him inside her, loving her.

"My God, I can't get you out of my mind," he groaned, drawing in ragged gasps of air, his lips planting feverish kisses over her face and neck. "God knows I've tried. I'm obsessed with you. I think about you every moment I'm awake and dream about you when I go to sleep."

"Seth, don't," she started to protest, but he cut off her words with his lips.

Again she gave herself over to her desire, returning his kisses with an abandon that startled her, then frightened her, slowly returning her to the present. She became aware of the lights and the noises of the people in the world around them, remembering finally that it was still early and someone might walk by at any minute. She pulled away and looked at him, still breathless and weak.

"Please, Seth." She heard a pleading note in her voice. "We've got to stop. This is crazy."

"Don't you think I know that?" He still held her by the shoulders and was staring into her eyes, his expression almost one of wonder. "I didn't expect to feel this way about anyone ever again. What's more, I didn't want to. Can you understand that?"

"Easily," she said. "I was sure after Tom's death that I'd never care for anyone again and that was fine with me."

"And now?"

"Now I'm confused." She pulled away from him. "Maybe it's just the fact that it's spring and you're an attractive man and I've been alone too long. Whatever it is, I care for you. More than I should and more than is good for me."

"Maggie, I would never hurt you." His hand touched her shoulder. "I promise you that."

"Are you sure that your lifestyle permits you to make promises like that?"

He looked at her strangely.

"I'm not sure we're talking about the same thing," he said. "But maybe you're right. Maybe I can't promise that I won't hurt you. I wouldn't mean to, but the end result would be the same."

He turned away and leaned his arms against the trunk of the old tree, his head hanging down between them.

"Damn, I'm sorry, Maggie. I'm sorry for letting myself get out of hand."

She looked at him standing there, unhappiness and regret etched in his very posture. Suddenly she was very, very tired. Tears stung her eyes, tears of bitter regret that she had ever laid eyes on this man who was no good for her and yet was rapidly becoming so precious to her.

"I think I should go in now," she said and turned before he could stop her. She heard him say her name once as she walked away, but she kept her head down and continued walking. As soon as she reached the privacy of her room, the flood broke and she cried for many things, but most of all for the futility of loving the wrong man.

Chapter Thirteen

Maggie wasn't surprised when she found herself unable to fall asleep. Part of it was Lydia Smith and her pleas for help. Maggie knew she was going to have to make that phone call. She was going to have to sit down with Lydia and hear her story, even if hearing it confirmed what she suspected about Seth's involvement.

She could probably hide Lydia out, and she could probably arrange for her to get out of town safely. But once she heard what Lydia had to say, she would have to act on the information. Lester, the deputies, somebody would have to be told or Lydia would never be safe. For that matter, she thought, I might not be either. Patrick Smith might very well find out she had helped his wife. She shuddered to think of how he would repay that act of kindness.

And if she confirmed Seth's involvement, it meant she would also confirm her uncle's. She was afraid if he went to jail it would kill her grandparents. They were old people; Lee might easily be locked up for the rest of their lives. Suddenly she felt an unexpected emotion. It was love for her uncle, something she had denied to herself for so many years. She finally admitted to herself that it wasn't just for her grandparents' sake that she didn't want to see anything bad happen to him.

All these thoughts flitted through her mind as she lay tossing on her single bed, but the overriding reason for her insomnia was Seth Brady and her feelings for him. She tried to put him and his kisses out of her mind once her tears subsided, but that proved impossible. Over and over her mind replayed every touch, every word that had passed between them since he'd arrived in her life four days before. She told herself to forget about him, that to love him would only invite heartbreak.

But as she lay sweating in the cool breeze that blew through her open window, listening to the night sounds, part of her still hoped that love stories did have happy endings. Maybe her love for him and his for her would be enough to give him the strength and courage to change his life. Such things did happen. If a prince had once been able to give up a throne for the woman he loved, surely Seth would be able to give up a life of crime.

Yet as soon as those thoughts crossed her mind, she rejected them. This wasn't a fairytale. Problems didn't disappear with the wave of a magic wand, and people in the real world seldom lived happily ever after. For that matter, she was being more than a little presumptuous in assuming that Seth would even want to change his life for her. There was no question that he found her physically attractive, but there was a good chance that was all there was to it. Just because he wanted to sleep with her didn't mean he was falling in love with her. For that matter, maybe she was letting her own desire for his body delude herself into thinking that she was in love.

Stop acting like some lovesick horny teenybopper, she told herself sternly, and get some sleep. Twenty minutes later, she gave it up. With a sigh, she threw back the covers and pulled her cotton robe on over her nightshirt and slid her feet into her slippers. Maybe a little warm milk would do the trick. She slipped quietly out her bedroom door and down the stairs to the second floor.

The house was quiet except for the occasional creaks and groans old houses are prone to make. As she passed her grandparents' closed bedroom door, she heard the faint sound of snoring. Dora had complained about her husband's log sawing for years. She often said it was a good thing they lived in such an old house with such thick walls or nobody would be able to sleep anywhere in the house. Her grandfather usually replied to the complaints with the observation that there were plenty of other beds in the house that his wife could sleep in. Yet they still slept together. Dora believed that a woman's place was beside her man, especially at night, even if it did mean occasionally giving up a good night's sleep.

Maggie moved on down the hall toward the stairs. As she came abreast of the closed guest room door, she heard a muffled cry. Seth sounded as if he were in pain or frightened. Without thinking, she hurried to the door and pushed it open.

The blue curtains were pulled back and clear cold moonlight streamed in through the open window, bathing Seth's sweating face in an eerie blue-tinged glow. His eyes were shut, but the muscles of his face twitched and strained as he tossed his head from side to side. He mumbled something unintelligible, too low for her to make out the words, but he seemed to be begging someone not to do something.

She quickly closed the door, not wanting her grandparents to hear. He was having a nightmare, and she wanted to be the one—and the only one—to bring him out of it. She crossed the room to the bed and sat down gingerly on the edge.

He lay covered only from the waist down as on the day she had first set eyes on him. Maggie felt sure that he was nude under the spread. Beads of sweat glistened on his forehead. Whatever creatures and events inhabited his dreams, they were bad.

Maggie touched him gently, her fingers lightly stroking his damp brow. She wanted to take him in her arms and comfort him, but she was afraid of frightening him in his sleep. He groaned as her fingers touched his forehead, then he began to relax, his muscles gradually loosening, his face smoothing. Then his eyes opened and he grabbed her arm hard. Frightened, she tried to pull away, but he held tight. Fight or flight, Maggie thought, and with Seth, it's definitely "fight." She should have known better than to have surprised a man like him in his sleep.

As his eyes locked onto hers and he came fully awake, he released the pressure on her arm, but didn't let go.

"Why—what are you doing here?" he said, his voice hoarse.

"You were having a nightmare." Maggie drew her free hand gently down the side of his face and around to the back of his neck where she began to massage his knotted muscles. "I heard you cry out."

He swallowed and ran his tongue across his dry lips. He was fully awake now, the after affects of the nightmare subsiding.

"I'm sorry," he said. "Did I wake everyone?"

"You didn't wake anybody. I was having trouble sleeping and was on my way downstairs when I heard you."

She continued to massage his neck, feeling the warmth of his body traveling through her fingers and into her own body. He released his hold on her arm, and she moved that hand to the other side of his neck. Her fingers moved more and more slowly, then slipped down onto his uninjured shoulder where they continued their gentle massage.

"If you want, I can wake my grandfather. I'm sure he could give you something to help you sleep."

"No," he said quickly, his voice low and husky. "I don't need anything to help me sleep. All I need is you."

His right arm moved upward, his fingers twining through her hair. Grasping the back of her head, he pulled her lips down to meet his. She could taste the salt from his sweat on her lips as she returned his kiss with a passion that seemed to feed on its own intensity. He pulled her roughly onto the bed beside him, his lips never leaving hers, and slid her robe off her shoulders.

She kissed him with a passion equaling his own while a tiny voice inside screamed at her to flee, to run away from this man who had become so important to her before it was too late. She ignored the voice. Maybe when she talked to Lydia Smith she would have confirmation that he was really the no-good she feared he was. But she hadn't heard those words yet; tonight she could still pretend. Tonight would be hers.

As his hand moved under her nightshirt and began edging its way up, the tiny voice grew into a shout of warning. She pulled away and stood, pulling her robe back on.

"I'll be right back," she said. She turned at the door. "Don't start without me."

She heard Seth chuckle as she slipped out the door.

She practically tiptoed past her grandparents' door. The last thing she wanted to do was wake them and ruin what was promising to be a very good night. She hurried up the stairs to her room and went straight to her dresser. She pulled the condom three-pack from the back of her underwear drawer. It had been a going-away present from a girlfriend in Denver.

"Take it," Andrea had urged when Maggie tried to give it back, positive she would never have a use for them. "The expiration date is two or three years out. When you're ready to use one, you'll know you're healed."

Back in the guest room, she laid the box on the nightstand and dropped her robe on the floor. Kneeling on the bed, she slipped her nightshirt over her head. She heard the sharp intake of his breath as he looked at her naked body kneeling over him in the moonlight.

"God, you're beautiful," he said, a catch in his voice.

Rising on his elbow, he grasped her bottom and pulled her astride him, taking her erect nipple in his mouth, teasing it with his tongue, while his hand massaged her bottom. She moaned as wave after wave of sensation washed over her until she could stand it no longer.

Tangling her fingers in his hair, she pulled him off her breast and guided him to the other one. Groaning, he ran his tongue around her nipple, then sucked deeply on it, his hand slipping between her thighs, stroking. As his fingers touched her, a fire coursed through her, starting at her center and rushing through the rest of her body. She pressed herself against his hand, trapping it, her body moving of its own volition against the delicious pressure of his fingers.

After a time, he lifted his mouth from her breast and ran his tongue lightly down her chest. He slid further under her, teasing her navel with his tongue, then slid even further down and buried his face in the thick auburn hair at her center, his tongue probing and stroking. The world exploded for Maggie. As wave after orgasmic wave washed over her, she bit her lip to keep from screaming, her hips moving in a rhythmic undulation against his tongue.

As she moved against him, Seth felt an immense pleasure—and pride—at the joy he brought her. The taste of her filled his mouth and he ate hungrily of it, knowing that he could never get enough. His penis swelled and throbbed, and he was torn between wanting to go on tasting her and wanting to feel her body surrounding him.

She made the choice for him. Pulling away from him with a gasp, she slid under the spread and lay alongside him, pressing against his hard body. She had been right. He was nude under the spread.

He raised himself over her and kicked the spread to the foot of the bed. Kneeling between her legs, he shook a foil packet from the box and tore it open. He slipped the condom on quickly, held his kneeling position for a moment, marveling at the play of moonlight and shadows on her bare body. He lifted his eyes to her face, his gaze tender. She felt caressed by that look. Then, he shifted his body between her legs and entered her.

Maggie cried out softly as she felt him slide into her, filling her with his hardness. She grabbed his bottom tightly, fingers digging into his skin, pulling him to her as she lifted herself to meet him. He held back, setting the pace, moving slowly and rhythmically, his eyes occasionally drifting down from hers to view their joining. She twisted and turned, trying to pull him deeper into her, but still he moved slowly, teasing, bringing her closer and closer to the brink, until suddenly she was there and the world exploded again.

His pace picked up and his eyes locked on hers. He was out of control now. She thrust against him hard and fast, her hands pulling his butt toward her, delighting in the pleasure she was bringing him. A nerve at the side of his mouth spasmed, and he groaned and shuddered as he erupted within her.

"Maggie," he moaned, "Maggie," and clasped her to him, his body trembling.

She held him close on top of her, loving the feel of his weight on her. He nuzzled his face in her hair, whispering her name over and over. She kissed his shoulder and the side of his neck, her hands roaming across his back and butt, her fingers memorizing the feel of him.

They lay under the moonlight in the big soft bed, resting, holding each other tightly, then made love again, their bodies arching and straining. Afterward, they lay exhausted in each other's arms, resting until the moment when their hunger for each other would rise again and they would make good use of that third—and last—condom.

Maggie felt totally at peace. It had been too long since a man had physically loved her and the release was more than welcome. But it was more than just good sex with an incredibly sexy man. She was on the verge of falling in love with Seth. No matter what she learned in the next few days, she was falling in love with him. What she was going to do about that, she didn't know.

Chapter Fourteen

Maggie slipped out of the guest room just as dawn was beginning to steal over the town, and hurried stealthily down the hall and up the attic stairs to her room. Knowing that even an hour's sleep before she readied herself for work was out of the question, she turned on the shower and slipped under the warm spray. She soaped herself slowly, running her hands caressingly over her body, the memory of Seth's embraces still fresh, as if her skin were some sort of photographic film that had recorded the touch of his fingers for posterity.

He had touched her gently at first, as if afraid she might break, then as their passion had increased, he had grown rougher. Now, as she cleaned herself, she saw a small reddened area on her upper left arm, an imprint made by his finger as he momentarily lost control of himself and gripped her tightly in his moment of release. She smiled, remembering, and ran her finger over the small bruise.

She applied her makeup absentmindedly, her mind playing over the events in the guest room, then dressed carefully in a pale green summer dress and a short-sleeved white linen jacket. She looked at herself critically in the mirror, wondering if the change in her showed. She saw that it did. There was no trace of fatigue on her face or in her eyes; instead, her skin positively glowed and her eyes sparkled. She had seen the look before on the faces of friends. It was the look of a woman in love.

Was it also the look of a woman who had just made a huge mistake?

Slipping past her grandparents' bedroom, she thought she heard movement inside and hurried toward the stairs. The guest room door was still closed. She wondered if Seth was asleep or awake, remembering, like her.

She didn't want to face her grandparents just yet; she was afraid they might intuit the events of the night just by looking at her. She quickly scribbled a note to her grandmother on the slate board that hung by the telephone to tell her she was leaving for the office early and stepped out the front door into a glorious May morning. The sun was already warm on her skin, and what seemed like a million songbirds were singing.

The streets were almost empty of people as she walked briskly down them, passing an occasional sleepy-eyed paper delivery boy or girl and the trucks on their way with supplies to the town's stores and restaurants. Through the open windows of the houses she passed, she could smell freshly brewed coffee and frying bacon and hear the authoritative voices of the announcers on the morning news shows.

She walked two blocks past the empty office of the Sun to Millie's where she picked a window table and ordered bacon, eggs, home fries, and a side order of biscuits and gravy. She consumed every morsel of it, thanking her ancestors for her metabolism as she did so.

Pushing away her empty plate, she settled back with a second cup of coffee and tried to bring her thoughts back down to earth. Okay, she thought, you're falling in love with the guy. Not much doubt about that.

He's almost perfect except for one little detail. He's a crook. So what now?

What were the options? Accept him and try to live with and ignore what he does for a living? Try to convince him to change, even if that meant facing prison for what he had already done? Or walk away from him—no, run away from him—and never look back? How about none of the above, Maggie thought, feeling her euphoria slip a notch.

Of course, there was always the chance, slim though it was, that she had been wrong from the start about him. She didn't think so, but it was possible. The reporter in her told her that she needed more facts. She needed to be sure now more than ever. If he were what she feared, then she would have to pick one of those three lousy courses of action; but if she had been wrong, maybe it all could still work out.

She pushed her chair back and stood. She would call Lydia Smith this afternoon as soon as the paper was out. And this evening, she would talk to Seth. She would demand answers to her questions. She deserved that much.

Now that she had made a decision, she felt even better—if that were possible—than she had when she entered the restaurant. She paid her check and left the waitress a generous tip.

***

Jack was in by the time she got back to the Sun. She smiled cheerfully at him as she poured herself another cup of coffee.

"Good morning, boss," she said. "Beautiful day, isn't it?"

Jack glanced up from the proofs on his desk.

"Good morning." He looked at her curiously. "Yes, it is, I guess."

"You guess?" She was amazed that anyone could ignore the fantastic day outside. "It's spring, Jack. How could you miss it?"

"It's been spring for a while now. Did you just notice?" He smiled "Never mind. Don't answer that. Whatever the reason, I'm glad you're in such a cheerful mood. I get more work out of you that way."

"Slave driver." She grinned at him, then turned and headed for her desk and the last minute details that preceded the weekly birth of the Sun.

Della arrived a few minutes later. The three of them hardly had time to stop and catch their breath for the rest of the morning. The conversation-deterring sound of the old press filled the office, Jack running it as usual. He had grudgingly taught Maggie the basic operation of the machine, but he had yet to relinquish control of it. Most small town papers farmed out their printing to a central location, but the Sun was Jack's baby from the reporting to the printing. Maggie doubted they would farm out the printing until the old press breathed its last.

The first folded papers were stacked neatly on the front counter when the walk-in customers began arriving just before noon. By one, all the local stores had had their stacks delivered to them, and the subscription editions for out-of-town readers had been labeled and tucked neatly under Della's arm on their way to the post office.

Maggie rested for a moment at her desk, relishing the peaceful quiet of the office now that the press had stopped. It was time for lunch; judging from the way her stomach had just rumbled, her body knew it, too. But first there was a phone call to make.

She fished the paper Lydia Smith had given her out of her purse and spread it on the desk. She thought it best not to call from the paper in case Patrick Smith checked his wife's call log, so she used her cell phone to dial the number.

"Yes?" A male voice answered sharply.

"Hello," Maggie said. "May I speak to Lydia Smith, please?"

"Who's calling?" The male voice asked. He sounded suspicious, Maggie thought.

Somebody who wants to know what you're up to, she thought. Somebody who hates your guts for hurting the man she's falling in love with.

"Candace's in the Apple Tree Mall," she replied, picking the name of a trendy dress shop located in the same mall as the health spa Lydia had designated as their meeting place. "We have an item in that Mrs. Smith ordered."

"Hold on." The phone was practically dropped on a hard surface. Maggie winced. Patrick Smith certainly needed lessons in telephone etiquette.

"Lydia," she heard him shout. "Some damn dress shop on the phone."

Several minutes passed, then Lydia picked up the phone.

"Hello," she said. Maggie thought she could detect a trace of nervousness in the woman's voice. "This is Lydia Smith."

"Mrs. Smith, this is Maggie from Candace's in the Apple Tree Mall." Maggie thought it was probably safe to talk openly to Lydia, but just in case Patrick was standing next to his wife and listening, she decided to keep up the pretense. "The item you requested is in and can be picked up whenever you like. Or we can deliver it, if you prefer."

Maggie heard a man mumble something. She would have bet a month's wages that Patrick Smith was standing at his wife's shoulder listening.

"No, thank you, I'll pick it up when I'm in town." Lydia's voice was businesslike. "I was planning on coming to town tomorrow anyway to work out at the spa. I'll stop in then, say around four?"

Lydia was good at this, but then, with a husband like Patrick Smith, she probably had had plenty of practice.

"You did get a size 6, didn't you?"

"Yes, it's a six," Maggie replied. "I think it will fit you perfectly."

"Great," Lydia said. "Thank you so much for calling."

The phone went dead. Maggie stared at it in her hand. Well, she was in for a penny, in for a pound, as her grandmother would say. She was going to find out the truth about Patrick Smith, and by extension, the truth about Seth. She might not like what she heard. Lydia had promised her it would be a big story. Maggie prayed the story wouldn't have Seth and Lee as major characters.

***

She stopped at Millie's for lunch and ordered a sandwich and iced tea to go, heading for the park as she had on Monday. Again, she found a bench all to herself, and again she sat, eating, lost in solitary thought. But there all similarity to Monday's lunch ended. Monday she had been depressed and apprehensive; now, only two days later, she was filled with a mix of emotions.

She finished her food, carried the empty containers to a nearby trashcan, and returned to the bench. There were few people enjoying the park with her, most having returned to their air-conditioned offices by now. She leaned back against the bench, sipping her tea and stretching her long legs.

She wondered what Seth was doing right now at this very moment. She wondered if he was outside like she was, enjoying the beautiful spring weather. Most of all, she wondered if his thoughts were as full of her as hers were of him. She closed her eyes and replayed the caresses of the night before, his lips sucking her nipples, his fingers and tongue stroking her clitoris, his lean hard body pressed against hers, the feel of him inside her. She felt her body start to tingle and grow warm with the memories.

Suddenly she heard loud feminine laughter nearby and sat upright, startled, her face reddening in embarrassment, certain her thoughts had shown on her face. But it was only a chubby blonde woman, laughing at something her friend had just said to her as they walked along the outskirts of the park, shopping parcels in hand. Maggie smiled self-consciously and settled back on the bench, sipping her tea and trying to put all thoughts of the night before from her mind.

She would talk to Seth tonight. He had to tell her the truth now. If what she feared were true, he might not want to tell her, might not want her to think badly of him or involve her in something dangerous. She remembered the look on his face when she told him she had gone for a drive on Twin Forks Road. He had been taken by surprise and he had seemed concerned for her safety.

But he had to tell her. If they were to have any chance together, she had to know the truth. Yet what if she pushed too much? She might anger him and lose him. He had to be going through a difficult period now, stuck between his nefarious involvements and what might be growing between them. He was intelligent enough to realize that he couldn't continue with both, that he would have to make a choice and have to make it soon. What if he chose to run from her? He might even be able to justify it to himself on the grounds that he was protecting her. Maybe she should wait just a little longer.

No, she decided, as soon as the thought crossed her mind. From the way Lydia Smith sounded on Monday, they didn't have the luxury of time. Lydia had said things were falling apart. When they collapsed, they just might bury Seth in the rubble.

***

Seth surprised himself by sleeping until nearly noon. He supposed his fatigue could be attributed to the trauma his body had sustained from the gunshot wound, but he suspected it was more likely due to the paces he had put it through during the night. Remembering the feel and smell and taste of Maggie, he felt himself growing hard.

My God, he thought, what's wrong with me? I'm acting like a randy teenager! After the busy night they'd had, he would have thought his body would have been sated, that he would have had enough of her. His smile faded as he admitted to himself that it was unlikely he would ever have enough of her.

He swung his feet to the floor and sat on the edge of the bed, elbows resting on his knees. He was still in shock at what had happened between them. His emotions had been dormant for so long that he had pretty much given them up for dead. Then he opened his eyes Saturday morning to a vision of red hair and emerald green eyes and felt his heart jumpstart itself back to life.

Was it possible he had a second chance at happiness after all? It scared him a little to think of the responsibility that entailed. But if he had a chance, this time he wouldn't screw it up. Or would he? Could he really make that promise? Once Maggie found out what his life was really like, she might run screaming in the other direction.

No, he was deluding himself if he thought this amazing interlude could grow into anything more. Drugs, guns, murder—that life had killed the first woman he'd loved. He couldn't take that chance with another, especially now that he was involved in so much worse.

Chapter Fifteen

The afternoon seemed to drag on forever. Wednesday afternoons were always a slow time for the employees of the Sun, but this particular Wednesday afternoon seemed to be interminable. Finally, she couldn't take it any longer and begged off a half hour early, claiming a sudden headache. It wasn't a lie. Her head had started to pound, both from the lack of sleep and from the stress of wondering how Seth would react to her questions.

As she approached the house, she saw a blue sedan in the driveway; apparently Lee had returned from Indianapolis. The house was quiet when she entered. Dora was in the living room napping in her favorite chair, an open magazine in her lap. Through the screen door, Maggie saw her grandfather and Lee side-by-side in chairs in the back yard, glasses of iced tea in their hands. A father/son moment, she thought, and was happy for her grandfather.

She walked to the bottom of the stairs and stood for several minutes looking up. Was Seth waiting for her, she wondered? Was he ready to take her in his arms and love her the way he had the night before? She couldn't let him distract her from the questions she had to ask. She knew if he touched her, all those questions would seem unimportant, but they had to be answered.

And she wasn't going to get those answers by standing here at the bottom of the stairs. She began to climb.

She was raising her hand to knock at the closed door of the guest room when she heard the sound of running water coming from the hall bath. Seth must be showering. She hesitated for a moment, then opened the door of the guest room and slipped inside, closing it quietly behind her, deciding to wait inside until he was done.

Looking at the unmade bed, her thoughts strayed back to this morning. It had only been hours since Seth had held her in his arms and made love to her, yet it seemed ages had passed. Surely she must be wrong about him. A man who could be so gentle and loving could not be guilty of the things she imagined, but she had to know for certain.

Sighing, she turned and started toward the chair by the dresser when her foot caught against something. Looking down, she saw the corner of a suitcase protruding from under the bed. She hesitated for only a moment, then bent down and pulled the well-worn brown canvas bag from its hiding place and laid it on the neatly made bed. She took a deep breath and wiped her sweaty palms across her skirt, then clicked the double latches on the suitcase and opened the lid.

At first glance, the contents look normal enough. Maggie let her breath out in a sigh of relief. What in heaven's name had she expected, she wondered, a machine gun in a violin case, a pinstriped suit with a white carnation in the lapel, what? She laughed nervously at herself, her hands trembling as she carefully removed the folded T-shirts and underwear, laying them neatly on the bed.

She was starting to feel embarrassed and more than a little guilty. Here she was spying on the man she had just spent the night making love to! Thanks to Tom, was she so jaded that she could no longer trust? She had already planned to ask Seth to tell her the truth about himself. Why did she feel the need to have corroborating evidence of whatever he might tell her? Sneaking and spying was not the way to start or conduct a relationship. Besides, she thought, as she laid the last pile of underwear on the bed, there's nothing here anyway.

She picked up a stack of clothing, having carefully memorized its position in the suitcase, and started to repack when something caught her eye, something that didn't look quite right. The suitcase was too shallow. It looked normal enough from the outside, but there was less room than there should have been on the inside. Maggie laid the underwear on the bed again. Reaching in, she began prying at the floor of the suitcase with her nails. It took only a few seconds to lift up the false bottom.

She stood there for what seemed an eternity, staring down at the exposed portion of the suitcase. Then she roused herself and replaced the cover of the false bottom. She quickly repacked the clothing, then closed the case and replaced it under the bed, taking care to leave one corner sticking out in exactly the same position as she had found it.

She'd been right in her suspicions after all. The two guns and extra clips hidden under the false bottom of Seth's suitcase proved it. Maybe it was true that lots of people carried guns for lots of reasons, but the fact that it was hidden so cleverly indicated beyond a shadow of a doubt that the man she had spent the night with used those guns for no good purpose. Seth and Lee had been the burglars that the Smiths had surprised. Her grandfather had knowingly and willingly treated a gunshot wound suffered in the commission of a felony.

The door to the room opened and Maggie spun around, startled. Seth was standing there, his hair damp from the shower, his face freshly shaved. When he saw her, he looked surprised and started to smile. Just as quickly, the smile faded.

"I didn't expect to see you here," he said, his eyes looking everywhere but at her.

"I—uh, I just thought . . . ," she started, then stopped.

She had come into his room with the intention of waiting until he was done with his shower, then demanding answers to the myriad questions she had. Now she knew she already had the answers—or at least, the most important one. The guns hidden in Seth's suitcase pretty much confirmed what she suspected about him. She still had questions, but she was no longer so sure she wanted to know the answers. She needed time to process what she'd found.

"I just wanted to see how you were feeling." The lie sounded lame even to her ears.

"Stronger," he said. "Better."

He was acting oddly, Maggie suddenly realized. She had been so flustered that he'd almost caught her going through his things that she hadn't registered his aloofness. She wouldn't have been surprised if he had grabbed her and kissed her the minute he saw her. A part of her was relieved that he hadn't, because she didn't know how she would react to that after what she'd just seen. Instead he was almost acting as if she were a stranger he barely knew. Was he afraid that she might have been searching his room? Or was he pulling back because of what had happened the night before? Maybe he was the kind of man who bedded a woman, then never called her again.

It's for the best if he is, she thought. Distance is the best thing that could happen between us now. But why didn't it *feel* like the best thing?

"Well, okay, then," she said. "I'll let you get dressed."

He moved away from the door, still not looking directly at her. She hurried out the door and up the stairs, not stopping until she was in her own room, the door locked behind her. When the tears came, she didn't try to stop them.

***

Seth slammed his fist into the pillow and welcomed the pain that exploded in his injured shoulder. It didn't hurt as much as forcing himself to be cold toward Maggie had hurt. When he'd opened the door and found her standing next to his bed, all he'd wanted was to take her in his arms and into that bed. But he'd made a promise to himself that morning. He was going to stop what was happening between them before it was too late and she got hurt. He couldn't—and wouldn't—risk anything happening to her.

He'd be leaving soon anyway. Now that he was healed enough to get back to the job at hand, he would be in and out of the house, but once the job was finished, he would leave for good. If he could just keep Maggie at arm's length until then, everything would be okay. He would get over her, she would get over him, and no one would get hurt.

But, dammit, he didn't want to get over her! He wanted her sexually, but he also wanted to *know* her. He wanted to wake up with her every morning and go to bed with her every night. He wanted to take her to restaurants, have long conversations over coffee and a morning paper, care for her when she was sick. Hell, he wouldn't even mind making a baby with her! He hadn't felt like this since the early days with Diane.

Diane. If only he had changed the direction his life was heading back then, Diane might still be alive. She had wanted him to give up the life, but he had kept putting it off. He'd been hooked like an addict on the excitement and the danger, and his addiction had killed his wife.

Could he give it up now? Could he give up the excitement and the danger for Maggie? Could he be satisfied with a boring mundane job? Would she have him if he did? She'd seemed a little distant to him just now. Maybe she was regretting their impulsiveness of the night before. Maybe all she had wanted was a one-night stand and some hot sex to make her forget her dead husband. She didn't seem like the type, but then he really didn't know her, did he? Or maybe she had been distant to him because he had been distant to her.

A lot of maybes here, Brady, he thought, a lot of grasping at straws. For his own peace of mind, he would have to find out if there was still a chance for them, but not until after the job was done. He couldn't make any decisions about his life until then. Of course, that was assuming he survived the job. Being shot had made him realize there were no guarantees of that.

***

Maggie begged off supper that night. When her grandmother called her cell phone to tell her the food was ready, she pretended she had been asleep.

"I came home early with a headache, Gran," she had said. "I'm going to sleep a while. If I get hungry later, I'll fix myself something."

She did fall asleep shortly after and woke around eight in the evening. Her stomach was rumbling, but the last thing she wanted to do at that moment was go downstairs and take the chance of running into Seth. She kept a few snacks in her room to munch on when she watched TV, so she made do with a small bag of peanuts and a granola bar. Afterwards, she washed off her makeup, brushed her teeth, and changed into her pajamas. Those simple chores seemed to require a huge effort on her part, as if her limbs were mired in muck. She crawled back in bed, pulled the covers over her head, and went back to sleep.

Something woke her hours later. She came wide awake, her heart pounding. As she lay still, listening to the silence, she wondered if she'd had a nightmare that she'd forgotten as soon as she opened her eyes. Then she heard a car start. It sounded like it was in the driveway below her window.

As she pulled back the covers and stood, she noticed the clock showed it was half past four. She moved quickly to the window as she heard the car's motor change its sound as it shifted gears. Looking out, she saw the blue sedan's lights flick on. The car backed out of the driveway to the left, stopped, and pulled forward. As it moved under the street light to the right of the drive, Maggie saw there were two people in the car. Seth Brady sat in the passenger seat.

Maggie slipped on her robe, opened the door, and went down the steps to the second floor. She was careful to move quietly so as not to disturb her grandparents. The door to the guest room stood open. The bed had been stripped, the sheets wadded into a bundle atop it. It didn't look as if its former occupant intended on coming back.

Knowing she would never get back to sleep now, she started down the stairs to the first floor, intending to put coffee on. She had descended only a few steps when she heard low voices coming from the kitchen. Her grandparents were up. She hesitated for a moment, then continued down, placing her feet carefully on each step, hoping to get close enough to hear what they were saying before they knew she was there. Eavesdropping again, she thought, but so what? It's the only way I have any hope of finding out anything around here.

As she neared the bottom of the steps, she realized her grandmother sounded like she was crying. All the resentment she felt at being treated like a child and kept in the dark faded, replaced instead with concern. All thoughts of stealth forgotten, she took another step and heard the loud squeak that had been a part of that step for as long as she could remember. The voices in the kitchen ceased immediately.

"Maggie?" Her grandfather said after a moment of silence.

"It's me," she said. "I heard a car outside."

As she entered the kitchen, her grandmother turned away from her and busied herself at the sink. Maggie noticed Dora taking quick swipes at her eyes as she busied herself with filling the pitcher she always used to pour water into the coffeemaker. Her grandfather was sitting at his usual place at the table.

"I saw Lee's car pulling out," Maggie said. "It looks like Seth is gone, too. What's going on?"

"They had to leave," her grandfather said, his eyes looking everywhere but at her. "I'm sure they're sorry they didn't get to say goodbye, but it was kind of sudden."

"Are they coming back?"

"Oh, I'm sure they will." Everett stood and stretched. "How's that coffee coming, Dora? I haven't been up this early in a long time and could sure use the caffeine. How about you, Maggie, or are you going back to bed?"

Maggie shook her head. "I couldn't get back to sleep now."

Dora finished pouring water into the coffeemaker. She filled the filter basket with coffee and turned the machine on. She turned and looked at Maggie. Other than a slight redness to her eyes that could be passed off as sleepiness, all signs of her crying were gone.

"You ready for breakfast then?" she said in a cheerful voice that sounded forced.

"What I'm ready for are some answers."

Maggie was shocked at herself. She hadn't expected to blurt out how she felt, but there it was. Maybe it was about time it was all out in the open.

"What is going on with Lee and Seth?" She looked at her grandfather. "I don't believe for a minute that Seth hurt himself while changing a tire. What are they up to and what have they gotten you involved in?"

"Maggie . . . ," her grandfather started, but Dora interrupted.

"What has gotten into you, Magdalyn Marie?" Growing up, her grandmother only called her by both her first and middle names when she had been caught doing something wrong. "You have no business accusing your uncle or your grandfather of whatever it is you're accusing them of."

"Gran . . . ," Maggie started, but Dora shook her head emphatically.

"No. You go on back upstairs now and either go back to bed and get out on the right side this time, or get yourself ready for work. Breakfast will be ready when you are."

She turned back to the sink, indicating Maggie was dismissed from the kitchen. Everett had suddenly found his shoes interesting. Maggie stood for a few seconds, staring at them both, then gave it up. They might be old and growing fragile, but they could be tough when they wanted to be. Especially Dora. If her grandmother didn't want to answer her questions, she wouldn't, and she wouldn't allow her husband to answer them either.

Maggie turned and left the kitchen.

Chapter Sixteen

While walking to work, Maggie decided to put Seth, her uncle, and whatever they were up to out of her thoughts and concentrate on work. The meeting with Lydia Smith was set for that afternoon. After talking to Lydia, Maggie had little doubt her thoughts would be back on Seth and her uncle, but until then, worrying about something she could do nothing about would be pointless.

As for what had happened between Seth and her— well, it had been a one-night stand to remember, but that's all it was. She was going to have to accept that. He had been distant to her the day before, making it very clear that he didn't want anything more. In a way she was grateful. If he had been loving and attentive, she knew she would have been putty in his hands. The last thing she needed was to become seriously involved with the wrong kind of man. She had done it once and once was enough.

She spent the first hour at the Sun editing announcements people had dropped off for next week's paper. Jack held a brief staff meeting. He tried to do that every week after the paper was out—sometimes on Wednesday afternoons, sometimes Thursday mornings. After it was over, Maggie headed out for an interview she'd scheduled the week before with a local sculptor who created amazing statues by using a chainsaw and other tools on sawn-off tree trunks. She spent the next hour with the thirty-five year old man, asking questions and watching him work. He was a strong, good-looking man, and she enjoyed watching his muscles flex as he coaxed a man-sized eagle out of a chunk of oak. He worked at a local tire store, his art a sideline for now, but he told her he hoped one day to be able to support himself and his family with his carvings.

And that's the trouble with finding a man, Maggie thought. The good ones are already taken. All that's left are the ones who will get you in trouble or break your heart—or both. She sighed, took a few pictures of him working, and thanked him for his time.

She stopped for an early lunch at Millie's. Only a few tables and stools were occupied. Maggie nodded and spoke to most of the people, some she had known since childhood and others she had met only since coming home. She decided on the counter and picked the end stool closest to the door. She had just ordered her sweet tea and turkey club sandwich when Lester came in. She caught his eye and patted the stool next to her.

"Have a seat," she said. "I hate to eat alone."

"Don't mind if I do," Lester said. "Although you're probably just wanting to pump me for news."

"Anything to pump you for?"

"Nope. Been pretty quiet. Just the way I like it."

"What about the break-in at the Smiths?" She tried to sound casual, but wondered if casual was a mistake. She was a reporter, after all. Reporters shouldn't be casual when trying to get information about a crime, should they? "Anything new there?"

"Not that I've heard. I saw Blake Thomas last night at the VFW. You know him?"

"Not personally, but I know he's a detective with the county."

"He's working the burglary. I asked him about it last night and he said they got zilch. They sent a sample of the blood that was by the pool off for DNA analysis, but he doesn't think they'll get anything. Guess there wasn't all that much and most of what there was had already soaked into the concrete. Even if there is enough to test, it won't lead them to anyone unless the guy's DNA is already in CODIS."

Maggie knew CODIS stood for Combined DNA Index System, an FBI program that stored DNA information contributed by forensic laboratories around the country and used to run comparisons between DNA samples taken from individuals and DNA samples found at crime scenes.

"Even if the DNA is in the system," Lester continued, "he doesn't expect to hear anything soon. Nobody died or got raped at the Smiths. A burglary where only the burglar got shot is low on the list of priorities."

Maggie tried not to let her relief show on her face. With any luck, the county wouldn't get a hit on Seth's DNA until well after he was gone from her grandparents' house. There wouldn't be anything to link him back to them unless he was caught later and confessed where he'd been treated for the wound. Like Lester said, no one had died or been raped at the Smiths, so finding the burglar long after the crime had occurred wasn't going to be a high priority for any law enforcement agency. By the time the results came back, Seth would likely be in another state.

"What about the body found on Strimple Road? Elton Jackson, wasn't it?" she said. "Anything more on that?"

"Not that I've heard. Thomas said the Indianapolis cops are scouting around trying to find out if somebody did him in their town, but so far, nothing. Or at least nothing he told me about."

"Well, there goes my headline story," Maggie said, forcing a laugh.

"Yep. Guess you'll have to beat the bushes for another one."

"Oh, something always turns up," Maggie said. "Human nature being what it is."

"Unfortunately."

"Even if you did have news about the body, I doubt I'd be able to wrestle the story away from Jack. He likes to do the exciting ones and leave the humdrum stuff to me."

They spent the rest of the meal in small talk. Maggie found she was actually enjoying the conversation now that she could relax about the DNA. Her grandparents were going to be okay. The DNA might never be analyzed due to the sample being too small, but even if it was, Seth and Lee were gone. They were out of harm's way. Seth and Lee probably deserved to be caught, but the fact was she didn't want them to be and not just for her grandparents' sake.

But while she was relieved that the danger to all of them was over, she still ached inside. She wished that she had never laid eyes on Seth Brady, but most of all, she wished she had never opened the door to the guest room when she heard him cry out. She'd had a taste of what it was like to be loved by him, and it had only whetted her appetite for more.

***

Maggie got to Eve's Fitness Club and Spa a little before 3:00. She wanted to be there before Lydia arrived to scout out a good place for the two of them to talk. She also didn't want to be seen by any flunkies assigned by Patrick Smith to follow his wife.

Eve's was restricted to women only, which was doubtless the only reason Patrick had permitted his wife to join. Maggie wasn't a member, but knew she could get a guest pass to try it out. The only problem was that an employee might then follow her around pointing out the benefits in an attempt to get her to join. She solved that problem by asking for the manager, proffering her credentials, and informing the woman she'd like to do an article on the spa. For the next twenty minutes, she interviewed the manager and a couple of employees about the spa, and as expected, was offered a guest pass. When the manager offered to have one of the employees accompany her, she said she'd rather spend some time on her own getting the feel of the place and maybe talking to a few of the members.

She changed into workout clothes and asked a question or two of other women in the locker room before heading for the exercise equipment. The club offered a good selection of exercise machines, a steam room, sauna, whirlpool, massage therapy, manicures, pedicures, and facials. It also had a juice bar with no outside windows. It might be the perfect place to talk to Lydia without worrying about her guard seeing them.

Maggie used a few of the machines and talked to some of the other women working out on them. She did think it would be an interesting article for the paper, but she also wanted to be sure the employees saw her talking to customers. She didn't want them to take particular notice when she talked to Lydia.

Lydia arrived a few minutes before four. Maggie could tell Lydia had seen her, but the woman didn't approach her. When she came out of the locker room, she headed for a treadmill not far from where Maggie was doing free weights. Maggie continued talking to other customers, making sure Lydia could hear what she was saying and figure out her cover.

Twenty minutes later Lydia headed for the locker room and Maggie followed. Four other women were dressing to leave when she entered. Lydia disappeared into the showers; Maggie followed a few moments later. Three stalls were occupied. When she stepped out of the shower a few minutes later, Lydia was just stepping out of hers, a towel wrapped around her body. Lydia glanced at her and tilted her head slightly toward the steam room. Maggie followed her inside. Walking behind the woman, Maggie could see the purple and yellow of fading bruises across her upper back and the backs of her thighs. Lydia had said that her husband was dangerous. Had he done this to her?

The steam room was empty except for the two of them.

"You made it." The relief was evident in Lydia's voice. "I wasn't sure you would."

"I told you I'd be here."

"I know you did, but . . ." Lydia shook her head. "My husband scares people. I'm not used to being around people who don't know him well enough to be scared off."

"Surely you don't think people in this town are involved with him," Maggie said.

Lydia laughed, but there was no humor in the sound. "Of course I think that! He makes sure to have people under his thumb wherever he is. People either work for him or they're scared of him. The only reason I decided I could trust you was that you haven't been in town long enough for him to get to you."

"Is that why you won't go to the police?"

"You got it."

"I can't believe Lester Lewis is dishonest, and I don't think he's scared of anyone," Maggie said.

"Maybe not, but you can bet someone in his department is in my husband's pocket. I don't know who is and who isn't, so I'm not taking any chances. Same thing with the county cops. Patrick takes special care to have eyes and ears in any police department he comes near."

Maggie was starting to wonder if Lydia Smith had mental problems. The woman sounded paranoid. Then she flashed back to the scene she had witnessed from her hiding place behind the tree in the woods bordering the Smiths' home. Patrick Smith was involved in something and it didn't look legal. Maybe Lydia was paranoid, or maybe she was just smart.

"So what do you want to tell me?" Maggie asked.

"Not so fast. Not until I know you'll get me out and away from him."

"You can come with me now," Maggie said. "Get dressed and leave with me. I'll drive you wherever you want to go."

"We wouldn't make it to the county line," Lydia said. "The only reason Lou—that's my bodyguard—

doesn't follow me in here is because it's women only. That's why I joined it. For that matter, it's why Patrick let me join. He doesn't want me around any men other than the ones who work for him, because he knows they're too scared of him to do anything with me."

"He's that jealous?"

"Oh, it's beyond jealousy! He's crazy as a loon! I'm lucky if a day goes by that he doesn't accuse me of something."

She stopped talking for a few moments. Up to this point, Lydia Smith had come across as a tough-talking broad used to making demands. Now Maggie saw her rigid posture slump and her chin quiver. Lydia pulled the towel tighter around her body and took a deep breath.

"And," she said, "I'm really lucky if a week goes by that he doesn't knock me around for something he thinks I did or thought."

"He beats you?" So the bruises were courtesy of Patrick Smith.

"He hits me. Often. Beats me? I only get a real beating a couple of times a year. Believe me, that's enough."

"Has he put you in the hospital?" Maggie asked, thinking that if Lydia had required treatment, the police would have been involved and she could run down the reports.

"A couple of times I needed a hospital," Lydia said. "But just like with the cops, Patrick has a couple of doctors in his pocket, too. The kind who'll do what he asks and keep their mouths shut."

Maggie flushed, thinking of her grandfather doing what his son asked and keeping his mouth shut. The difference was he did it out of love for his son and not for fear or money like the doctors Patrick Smith knew. That was different. Wasn't it?

"Okay," she said. "If we can't just walk out of here, what do you propose we do?"

Lydia turned to her. "I've got it figured out. I overheard Patrick talking to a couple of his men yesterday. There's something big going down tomorrow night. He told them to plan on being up all night and to be ready to hit the road by six."

"So do you want me to come pick you up, or should I meet you somewhere?"

"It's not that simple," Lydia said. "Patrick always leaves someone with me. I don't know from one time to the next who it will be, but it's never been more than one guy. I've never given any of them a problem, so they're usually pretty relaxed with me. Most of the time I fix dinner for them or something for them to snack on. This time I'll add a few Ambien to the food. That should knock whoever it is out."

The door to the steam room opened. Two overweight women in towels entered, chatting with one another.

"Oh, hello," the first one through the door said. "Room for two more?"

"Of course." Maggie stood. "In fact, you can have my spot. I've sweated about as much as I can stand."

The women laughed. Maggie left the steam room; Lydia stayed inside. Maggie heard the steam room door open as she quickly rinsed the sweat from her body. She dressed slowly, waiting for Lydia to finish her shower. The locker room was still empty when Lydia came in.

"Let's talk fast before someone comes in," she said, glancing around her.

"I've been talking to other members, so it's not going to look funny to anyone if I'm seen talking to you," Maggie said. "Besides, your guard can't see us here."

"If I know my husband," Lydia said. "He's paid someone here to keep tabs on me."

Maggie wondered again if Lydia was paranoid and hoped she was. The thought of any woman having to live with a husband like the man Lydia was describing was too disturbing.

"Anyway," Lydia continued. "You'll have to come get me. Patrick never leaves a car when he goes on his little trips. You know the woods where you hid that day? On the other side of it is a road. Just past the edge of the woods, there's a vacant house and a barn. Pull behind the barn. You won't be seen from the road."

Maggie flashbacked to the day she'd sneaked through the woods to spy on Patrick Smith and his visitors in the Lincoln. She remembered seeing the roofs of a house and barn farther up the road from where she had pulled off. At the time, she had noted that the house's occupants wouldn't be able to see her from their windows. Apparently there had been no occupants to worry about.

"Be there by seven-thirty. Patrick will probably want me to fix dinner for them before they leave. I'll slip Ambien in the food for whoever's watching me, so he should be snoring by seven. It will still be light enough for me to come through the woods. I'll be there by eight. No later."

"What if you're not? Should I come to the house? Or should I call?"

"God, no, don't come to the house! I don't want you to get hurt!" Lydia was silent for a few moments, thinking. "I'll call you if I'm running late, but if Patrick's plans get cancelled, I won't be able to. If I'm not there by eight, just leave. I'll get in touch with you later and we'll set up another time."

"How do I know you're telling me the truth about your husband?" Maggie said. "I might be getting myself in the middle of something I have no business being in."

"I understand. I promised you a big story in exchange for helping me and now you want a taste of what that story is." Lydia's tone was cynical.

"No, it's not that . . . ," Maggie started, but Lydia waved her hand at her in a silencing gesture.

"It's okay. I don't blame you for watching out for number one." She looked around at the empty locker room again as if she suspected her husband's spies might be hiding in a locker.

"There's no time to go into all the details, but I can give you a taste. Patrick moves things—drugs, people, weapons, you name it. He's not small-time either." Lydia sat up straighter, and Maggie was pretty sure she spotted a little pride. "He deals with drug cartels, organized crime, and crazy-ass militants holed up in compounds out West. His trucking company and his import/export business are the perfect cover."

She stopped for a moment and took a deep breath. She didn't look so proud now.

"But I think he's gotten in over his head this time. Those guys you saw the other day? They're Middle

Eastern. I don't know from where exactly, but I don't think they're friendly to this country. I think Patrick got greedy and now he's in bed with terrorists. And he doesn't know how to get out."

"Are you serious?" Maggie was shocked. Terrorists in her hometown? Surely Lydia was delusional. Still, she had seen the men for herself. They did look Middle Eastern and Patrick hadn't looked like he was in charge.

"Yeah, I'm serious." Lydia sounded sad. "I've got to get out of there, Maggie, and I've got to get out of there as soon as possible. Will you help me?"

Maggie looked at the desperate woman staring back at her, her eyes pleading with Maggie to help her escape. There was no question that Lydia was a tough broad, one that had probably known about and been proud of her husband's criminal activities before she married him. His abuse had probably been a surprise, but apparently she had endured that for some time, maybe because she was too afraid to leave him. But now that she suspected her husband of being involved with terrorists, she was more afraid to stay. Maybe she was paranoid and delusional, but Maggie didn't think so. As hard as it was for her to believe terrorists had come to her corner of the world, she believed Lydia Smith was telling the truth.

"I'll be there," Maggie said.

Chapter Seventeen

Maggie found it hard to sleep that night, her thoughts bouncing from Seth to Lydia to her grandparents and back to Seth again. He and Lee had not returned, and her grandparents claimed not to have heard from them. She wasn't sure she believed them. They both seemed jumpy and worried like they knew something that she didn't. Then again, maybe they were just worried about what their son was up to now. And with good reason, Maggie thought. When he'd reappeared in their life, he'd been in the company of a man with a gunshot wound. That by itself was enough to worry any parent.

She finally fell asleep sometime after one. When she woke, the sun was just beginning to show above the horizon. She showered and dressed for the day, going over in her mind the plans for Friday evening. She had decided that after she picked up Lydia, she would drive her to Cincinnati. Indianapolis was closer, but the dead man found on Strimple Road had been from there. Patrick Smith probably had a lot of connections that close to home. For that matter, he might have them in Cincinnati, too, but it was the best Maggie could come up with. She would check into a hotel with Lydia and would spend the night trying to convince her to go to the federal authorities. She wasn't sure she would succeed. Lydia was a woman more interested in taking care of number one, but she also seemed genuinely concerned about what her husband's Middle Eastern contacts might be planning. Whether her poorly developed sense of civic duty would override her sense of self-preservation remained to be seen. If it didn't, Maggie had decided to call the feds herself.

All that remained was a good cover story for her grandparents. They didn't need any more worry than they already had.

"Morning, honey," Dora Jacobs said when Maggie entered the kitchen. "Sleep well?"

"Not too bad," Maggie lied. She poured herself a cup of coffee. After taking a couple of careful sips of the steaming liquid, she began setting the table. "You'll never guess who called last night."

"It wasn't Mr. Brady, was it?" Her grandmother had been dropping slices of bacon onto a griddle and now she stopped, a strip of bacon dangling from her hand.

Maggie was surprised. She hadn't expected her grandmother to hazard any guess as to who her fake caller was, but Seth? *I guess we were pretty obvious after all,* she thought.

"No! Of course not. Why would you think that?"

Dora just looked at her, her eyebrows raised. *Do you think I'm stupid,* the expression said. Maggie decided not to pursue the topic.

"It was Andrea." At Dora's puzzled look, Maggie continued. "My Denver friend. You've heard me talk about her."

"Oh, yes, I have. Sorry. I guess I forgot." Dora dropped the bacon she had been holding onto the griddle's surface and continued adding more. "I imagine you were pleased to hear from her."

"More than pleased," Maggie said, forcing enthusiasm into her voice. "I don't remember if I told you, but she travels a lot on business."

Andrea was a stay-at-home mom whose vacations consisted of hitting the Colorado ski slopes, but Maggie was pretty sure she'd never gone into detail about her friend to her grandmother.

"She flew into Cincy yesterday and isn't leaving until late Saturday. She called to see if we could get together before she leaves."

"Is she coming here?"

The emotion on her grandmother's face looked like alarm. What the heck is going on, Maggie thought. It wasn't like Dora Jacobs to be alarmed at the prospect of company. The woman was at her best when hosting guests, be they for dinner or for the weekend. Normally she would already be brainstorming what she needed to buy at the grocery and which set of bedding should go on the guest room bed. Instead the prospect of Maggie's friend visiting seemed to be the worst news she'd heard in a long time.

"No, she's not coming here," Maggie said. "I'm going to head down to Cincinnati after work and spend the night with her."

"Oh, that's wonderful!"

Maggie knew she wasn't imagining the relief in her grandmother's voice. While she would have expected her to be happy that she was getting out with friends, this was more than just relief that her granddaughter was going to do a little socializing instead of shutting herself off from the world. Dora sounded like she was thrilled that Maggie was leaving town.

It's a good thing she doesn't know the real reason why, Maggie thought. Learning that her granddaughter was helping an abused wife escape from a nutcase husband with ties to organized crime and terrorists would put her in an early grave!

But why was Dora Jacobs so pleased that Maggie would be in Cincinnati instead of here in Vichy? Had she been in contact with Lee and Seth? Were they part of whatever it was that Patrick Smith was involved in? Did they work for a third party who was in competition for the Middle Eastern men's business, or did they work for another of Smith's clients—maybe someone who didn't take kindly to what Smith had gotten himself involved in? And if any of that were true, why would Lee tell his mother about it?

She wasn't going to get any answers to those questions and the million others she had about what her uncle had been doing all these years and how Seth was involved. She poured a second cup of coffee and resolved to focus on what she knew—Lydia Smith was in danger, she needed help that Maggie could provide, and she had information that just might save a lot of American lives. She might not be able to do anything to change the direction Lee's and Seth's lives were going, but she could change Lydia's.

***

Maggie thought Thursday at the paper had been hard to get through, but Friday was torture. It seemed as if the cosmic clock had crawled to a stop and five o'clock was never going to come. She busied herself with rewriting a couple of articles for next week's paper, trotted across town for an interview with a local teen who had just gotten a spot on a televised talent show, talked to the manager of the local Walmart about a recent increase in shoplifting incidents, and finally was reduced to cleaning out her desk for the second time that week. Through it all, her thoughts were on the looming evening and Lydia Smith.

She was worried for the woman. Would Lydia be able to act with her husband as if nothing was out of the ordinary? If Lydia had painted an accurate picture, Patrick Smith was a paranoid nutcase. Would he spot something in his wife's actions that would tip him off that she planned to leave him? Maggie didn't want to think about what he might do to Lydia if he became suspicious.

At four-thirty, Maggie gave it up and told Jack she was done for the day. He told her to have a good weekend, his attention on an article in the professional journal that was open on the desk in front of him.

"You're early," Dora said when Maggie entered the house.

"Nothing going on at the paper, so I thought I'd get on the road. I want to make Cincinnati before it gets dark."

"I'll fix you something to eat before you go."

"You don't have to," Maggie said, even though her stomach was rumbling. She wasn't sure she could sit at the table with her grandparents while keeping up the pretense of a night visiting a Colorado friend who was just passing through. "I can grab something on the road."

"Nonsense. Everett and I don't mind eating early. You go shower and pack. The food will be ready when you are."

Maggie hurried to her room, showered and threw a few things in her suitcase. She didn't plan on being with Lydia in Cincinnati more than one night. No matter what, she would find a way to get in touch with the local FBI on Saturday. She hoped by then she would have convinced Lydia to talk to them, but regardless, Maggie was going to call them. She thought it was possible they would insist that she also stick around for questioning, so she threw in an extra change of clothes in case she had to stay the entire weekend.

Her grandfather was sitting down to the simple meal of grilled cheese and tomato soup when Maggie came into the kitchen.

"Your grandmother tells me you're heading to Cincy for the weekend," he said.

"Probably just for the night," Maggie said. To cover her bases in case she did have to stay over, she added," Unless we're having too good of a time, of course."

"I'm glad you're getting away for a bit."

He had a serious look on his face, not the kind of look Maggie would have expected him to have when talking about her spending a night away from home with a girlfriend. Her grandfather would normally have been cracking jokes about not drinking too much and being sure to watch out for smooth-talking men. Was she imagining it or did he look as glad as her grandmother that she was leaving town? She started to ask if they'd heard from Lee, but decided against it. She knew they wouldn't tell her even if they had, and she was tired of hearing their lies. She knew they believed they had to do it to protect their son, but it still hurt to know she was excluded from family secrets.

The three of them managed to make small talk while eating. Grilled cheese and tomato soup had always been Maggie's go-to comfort food, but she hardly registered the taste, quickly chewing the sandwich and washing it down with spoonfuls of the rich, red soup. When she started to help her grandmother clear the table, Dora waved her away.

"Go on now," she said. "I can get this. I know you're anxious to get going."

Or are you anxious to get me going, Maggie thought, but didn't say. She already knew the answer. She kissed them both on the cheek, promised to have a good time, grabbed her suitcase, and headed out the door. It was a quarter till six.

***

It was exactly six when Maggie pulled in behind the barn next to the vacant farmhouse. She pressed the buttons to lower all the car windows, then turned off the car. For a few minutes all she heard was the ticking of the cooling engine, the leaves rustling in the wind, and the musical backdrop of the birds in the woods. When a crow cawed a harsh protest about something, she jumped hard enough that the seat belt and harness tightened across her, and she realized just how tense she was. She unfastened the seat belt, removed the keys so the warning ding wouldn't sound, and stepped out of the car, leaving the door standing open.

For the next ten minutes Maggie paced behind the barn and around the car, trying without success to still her racing heart. She tried to take her mind off Lydia and what horrors she might be enduring in the house by peering through the cracks in the barn's walls. It was an old building, empty of everything except dust floating in the beams cast by the sun on its journey toward the horizon. She quickly moved across the barnyard to the house and walked around the back and one side hidden from view of anyone passing on the road. She peered in the windows and found it no more interesting than the barn. The rooms were devoid of furniture, the wallpaper in one room was peeling, and the paint in the others was in serious need of refreshing. As she hurried across the open barnyard to the car, she glanced at her watch. She had only been there a short time, yet it seemed as if she'd been waiting for hours.

She had just reached the car when she heard distant voices. The sound seemed to be coming from the direction of the Smiths' house, but she couldn't distinguish what was being said. A minute later, she heard the sound of more than one car starting, followed by the crunch of gravel under tires. She let out the breath she hadn't been aware of holding. Patrick and his men were leaving a little later than Lydia had said. Still, she should be coming through the woods in less than an hour. It would be none too soon as far as Maggie was concerned.

Time slowed even more than it already had. Seven o'clock came and went. No more sounds drifted from the direction of the Smiths' house, and even the crows had quieted. Maggie wondered if Lydia's guard was nodding off. What would happen to the man? Would he end up like the man named Elton? If Patrick was the kind of man Lydia had described, Maggie doubted he would be forgiving of an employee so easily tricked by his wife.

As seven-thirty approached, Maggie's tension became almost unbearable, but as seven-thirty came and went, it ratcheted up further. She felt like screaming. Lydia had told her that under no circumstances was she to call or come to the house, but as her imagination conjured up images of Lydia beaten and bleeding—or worse, Maggie knew she had to have a look. She wouldn't call and she wouldn't go all the way up to the house, but she had to have a peek. She had spied on the house from the woods before and Patrick Smith had been none the wiser. She could do it again.

She climbed the fence running along the property line of the abandoned house and began making her way through the woods. It took her longer approaching from this direction than it had from where she had parked the car a few days before. The trees were thinner here, allowing more sunshine to reach the forest floor. Thorns from wild blackberry bushes snagged her clothing, and once she tripped and nearly fell when her foot snagged in some kind of vine trailing across the ground. Although she didn't notice any poison ivy, she had little doubt she had already walked through some and would probably pay for it in the coming days.

Finally she reached a part of the woods where the trees were thicker and the undergrowth thinner. She picked up her pace and was soon within view of the Smiths' home. All looked quiet. No cars sat in the drive or at the side of the house that she could see. The sounds she had heard earlier must have been Patrick and his men leaving, but if that was the case, where was Lydia? She should have been able to sneak out by now. Had her guard decided he wasn't hungry and refused to eat his Ambien?

She moved closer. The line of sickly shrubs she had hidden behind on her first trip to the Smiths extended to her current position. She had just started to move toward them, intending to crouch behind them and watch the house for a bit, when she heard the crack of a twig close behind her. Before she could turn, strong arms encircled her, pinning her own arms to her side. A hand clamped hard across her mouth, cutting off the scream that had started to build. She twisted and stomped down and back with her feet, but her attacker deftly avoided her attempts to crush his arch. Her twisting and squirming did nothing to loosen his grip. She felt herself giving up and that made her more angry than scared. She bucked back against him and felt the hand across her mouth loosen slightly. She took the advantage and sunk her teeth into his thumb. She heard him curse, but before she could bite again or scream, he pressed his bleeding hand back across her mouth.

"Quiet!" He spoke in a harsh whisper. "Now!"

He may have spoken in a whisper, but his tone made it clear he meant business. He was too strong for her. She was not going to get away, no matter how much she struggled or bit. As he began dragging her back through the woods, away from the Smiths' property line, she began to cry.

Chapter Eighteen

Maggie wanted to struggle against the strong arms that were holding her captive, but it was all she could do to keep her footing as her attacker dragged her back through the woods and away from the Smiths' home. They seemed to be heading in the general direction of the barn and her car. She wondered if he had followed her from there. Had the house not been empty after all? She hadn't been able to look in every window, because she hadn't wanted to risk being seen from the road. Was it one of Smith's men? Maybe Patrick had posted a lookout in the vacant house or even somewhere in the woods.

She dismissed the idea as quickly as she thought of it. She hadn't been spotted by anyone other than Lydia on her first foray into the woods to spy on the Smiths. Patrick didn't know about that little escapade so why post a lookout now? Besides, if the man holding her worked for Patrick Smith, he would have forced her into the house, not dragged her away from it with an admonishment to be quiet.

Not that any of that really mattered, she thought. What mattered was whoever it was had her now, and it didn't look like she was going to have an easy time getting away. But if he gave her an opening, she was going to scream, run, fight—whatever it took. She wasn't going to give up easily.

The man was breathing heavily by the time they reached the thicker undergrowth that Maggie had struggled through on her way into the woods. He stopped and held her for a few seconds before he removed his hand from her mouth and released her arms, moving his hands to her shoulders to turn her around. She opened her mouth to scream and prepared to knee her attacker in the groin, then stopped.

"Seth? What . . . I don't . . . What are you doing here?"

"Not so loud." Seth's voice was low. He glanced in the direction of the Smiths' house. "Sound carries out here. Wait till we get back to your car."

He took her hand and led her through the undergrowth, sticking to the spots that had been trampled down by her earlier passage—and his, she assumed. In a few minutes, they climbed the fence and were back behind the barn. Seth motioned for her to get in the car. He went around to the passenger side and got in.

"Roll the windows up," he said, still in the low voice he'd used in the woods.

Maggie put the key in the ignition, turned the auxiliary power on, and did as he instructed. It was hot inside the closed vehicle, but she barely noticed. She turned to him, her anger growing at the scare he'd given her.

"What are you doing here?" she said at the same time as Seth said, "What the hell are you doing here?"

They stared at one another for several seconds. Seth's fists were clenched. He was angry, but more than that, he looked scared. What is he scared about, Maggie thought? Is he afraid I'm going to mess up whatever he and Lee are up to? If half of what Lydia had told her about Patrick was true, Seth and Lee would be better off if they had to give up on whatever hairbrained scheme they had cooked up. Patrick Smith did not sound like the kind of man you wanted to cross.

Then again, if Lee and Seth were willing to cross him, what did that say about them? Maybe her uncle and the man she'd so stupidly made love with were even worse than Patrick Smith.

"You first," Seth said through gritted teeth.

"Oh, no! Not on your life!" Maggie's voice rose. "Why are you following me?"

"I wasn't." Seth took a deep breath. He unclenched his fists and just as quickly clenched them again. "At least not until I got here and saw you going into the woods."

"You didn't know I was here?"

He shook his head. "Lee dropped me off here. He went around to the other side of the property to work his way in from there."

Maggie stared at him. It was just her luck that at the same time she was to help Lydia get away, Seth and Lee had decided on an encore performance of their botched burglary.

"Decided to try again, huh?" she said.

Now Seth looked puzzled. "What do you mean?"

"You know exactly what I mean! You and Lee are the would-be burglars from last Friday night. Patrick Smith shot you by the pool and Lee brought you to my grandfather for treatment."

Seth's mouth fell open and stayed there for a second before he closed it and swallowed hard. "How did you . . . ?" he began, but she interrupted.

"It doesn't take a genius to figure it out, Seth! If the local cops knew what I know, you'd be locked up instead of sitting here giving me a hard time!"

"If you weren't here, I wouldn't be giving you a hard time! Why are you here, Maggie? What are you up to?"

"What business is it of yours?"

"Damn it!" Seth stared through the windshield, the muscles of his jaw working, his hands clenching and unclenching. After a few seconds, he took a deep breath and turned to her. "Okay, so don't tell me. Just get out of here. Go home and go home now."

"I will not!" A little voice inside Maggie's head cautioned her against arguing with a man capable of breaking into houses and who knew what else, but she ignored it. He was not going to run her off so he and Lee could break into Patrick Smith's house. They probably thought the coast was clear because Smith and his men were gone, but Lydia was still inside. The woman had been hurt enough by her husband; Maggie was not going to leave her to be hurt by Seth and Lee.

"Maggie, please!" A pleading tone had entered Seth's voice. She had expected him to argue, but she hadn't expected that. "You'll be in danger if you stay here. The man on the other side of those trees is no one to mess with. You've got to leave."

"I know Patrick Smith is no one to mess with," she said. "That's why I can't leave his wife in that house."

"What?" Maggie had thought Seth looked surprised when she'd told him she knew about his gunshot wound, but that had been nothing compared to the look on his face now. "His wife? You know Lydia Smith?"

"I wouldn't say I 'know' her, but she has asked me for help. And I intend to give it to her."

"Help? What kind of help?"

"Help in getting away from her husband," Maggie said. "What else?"

"Start at the beginning," Seth said. "I want to hear it all."

The look on his face brooked no argument. Maggie debated with herself on whether to tell him, but one glance at the clock on the car's dash convinced her. Lydia might be lying inside the house hurt or worse, and she couldn't waste any more time arguing with Seth. She took a deep breath.

"I was at the Garden Club meeting," she began.

***

Maggie told Seth how Lydia had approached her and what she'd said about Patrick and his men having something big planned tonight, but she left out the part about his being involved with terrorists. She still had trouble believing terrorists were here in rural Indiana, but more than that, she didn't trust Seth. If Patrick was involved with drug cartels and human smugglers, what did that make Seth and Lee? Maybe Patrick had botched a job for someone, and Seth and Lee were here to mete out some twisted form of underworld justice. She couldn't see them being involved in terrorism, but until she did know what they were doing here, she decided to keep that information to herself.

When she finished, Seth sat silently for a minute or so before pulling out his cell. He hit a speed dial number and a second later said, "Lee? We've got a problem. Maggie is here. Wait . . . Wait, let me finish."

He relayed what Maggie had told him, then listened for several minutes to Lee. Occasionally he'd mumble, "Umm-hmm," or "yeah," but said nothing that would tell Maggie what was being discussed. She clenched the steering wheel hard to keep her hands from wrenching the phone out of his. She wanted to scream into the phone and demand answers from her uncle, but she knew that would get her nowhere. Worse, it would delay her getting to Lydia. With every second that passed, Maggie's certainty that Lydia was in danger grew. So she forced herself to be patient and wait for Seth and Lee to finish their stupid phone conversation and get down to business.

Finally Seth hit the button to end the call. He took a deep breath and sat staring out the windshield, tapping the cell phone on his thigh. Maggie couldn't take it any longer.

"What?" she said. "What is going on? Tell me!"

"Lee and I will take care of getting Lydia Smith out of the house," Seth said. He didn't look happy about it. "You need to go home and wait for us there."

"Like hell I will!" Maggie shook her head. "I promised Lydia I would help her and I will. She doesn't know you and Lee. For that matter, I'm not sure I know you either! I'm not risking her safety by leaving her to you two."

"We're not the bad guys here, Maggie," Seth started, but she interrupted.

"Save it," she said. "I'm not leaving."

He let loose an exasperated sigh. "Okay, okay, so don't go home. Just promise me you'll stay here in the car and wait for us. We'll bring her to you."

"Seth, I am going to the house and I am going to get Lydia out of there. I'm not going to go home and I'm not going to wait here. End of story."

"Maggie, for God's sake, it's not safe!" He grabbed her arm and turned her toward him. She was shocked at the look on his face. It was a mixture of anger and fear, but mostly fear. And unless she was very much mistaken, it was not fear for himself, but fear for her.

"I'm going with you," she said, refusing to let his fear deter her. Maybe it wasn't safe for her to go to the house, but if it wasn't safe for her, it wasn't safe for Lydia. She had to do something to help the woman.

Seth stared at her for several seconds. "Okay," he finally said. "I can see I'm not getting through that thick skull of yours. I'd probably have to lock you in the trunk to make you stay here, and it's a little hot for that."

"But . . . ," he said when she started to interrupt, "you will stay in the woods until Lee and I make sure it's safe for you to come in the house. Agreed?"

Maggie hesitated for a second, and then nodded. She could live with that. She would be close enough to the house at that point that she could hear Lydia scream for help if help was needed. Not that she really thought Lee and Seth would do anything to harm Lydia. She couldn't see either of them doing anything like that, but just in case . . .

"Agreed," she said and opened the driver's door. "Let's go get her."

Chapter Nineteen

The return trip through the woods to the Smiths' home was easier than the first one had been. With Seth going first, they followed the path they had made through the undergrowth and were soon within a few yards of the shrubbery that delineated the edge of the woods. Seth stopped, motioning for Maggie to do the same. He removed his cell phone from the pocket of his jeans and hit a speed-dial number.

"We're in place," he said.

In the quiet of the woods, Maggie could hear Lee's voice coming through the phone. Seth gave her a look that said, "Thanks a lot."

"Yeah, well, you tell her that. I tried, believe me. She's promised to wait in the woods until we give her the all clear."

"Your uncle is not happy with me," he said as he disconnected the call.

"What a shame." Maggie didn't bother to hide the sarcasm in her voice.

"Stay here." Seth said. "When we're sure it's clear, I'll come to the patio and wave."

Maggie nodded. Although she felt like she should be going in with Seth for Lydia's sake, a part of her was relieved that she didn't have to be the first one through the door. While the empty drive made it appear that Smith and all his men were gone, that didn't mean they all were. Lydia had said her husband usually left someone to watch her. Since the purpose of leaving a guard was to make sure she didn't leave the house, the guard wouldn't need a vehicle. He could be waiting and watching for someone to come into the house as much as he was watching for Lydia to leave.

As soon as the thought occurred to her, she was afraid for Seth. She opened her mouth to ask him not to go, but quickly shut it again. Someone had to help Lydia. Besides, just a few minutes before she had been afraid he and Lee might do something to harm the woman. Now she was afraid they would be harmed? Was there no middle ground here?

She reached out and touched Seth's arm as he started to move away.

"Be careful," she whispered.

He looked at her for a few seconds and she had the feeling he was about to say something, but instead he only nodded. Turning, he moved through the woods toward the back of the Smiths' house. When he reached the shrub line, he stopped. A few seconds later, she saw her uncle moving around the rear of the home toward the patio. Seth moved out of the trees and crossed quickly to the rear corner of the house. The two men converged on the patio doors from opposite sides. Seth tried the knob, but the doors were locked. Lee pulled something from a pack he had around his waist and bent to the knob. A lock-pick gun, Maggie thought. So her uncle and the man she was falling in love with were technologically savvy criminals, not just smash-and-grab thugs. She wondered if they were into computer hacking and identity theft as well. The thought made her feel a little sick, so she pushed it to the back of her mind. Getting Lydia out was the important thing. The rest could be sorted out later.

It only took Lee seconds to unlock the door. He pulled a gun from the small of his back, while Seth took one from an ankle holster hidden under his jeans. He pushed the patio door open just enough for the two of them to slip inside.

Maggie stared at the house until her eyes began to smart and realized she had been watching without blinking. Her hands were clenched into fists and her entire body was rigid. She blinked several times and breathed deeply, forcing herself to unclench her fists and relax her muscles. Lee and Seth knew what they were doing, she reassured herself. They're obviously not novices. They'll be okay.

Seth was shot, a pessimistic little voice nagged at the back of her mind. She tried to ignore it.

After what seemed hours, but was only minutes, the door opened wide and Seth stepped out. He made no attempt at stealth as he waved her in. Either there was no guard in the house or the guard had been taken care of. Maggie hoped she wasn't going to have to see something she would never be able to forget. She wriggled through the shrubs, ignoring the poke of the branches, and moved toward the door.

***

"Where's Lydia?" Maggie said as soon as the patio door shut behind her.

"Upstairs," Seth said, taking her arm and leading her to the foyer. "She's in the master bedroom."

"Is she okay?"

"We're not sure."

When Maggie entered the bedroom, she saw Lydia on the bed. Her eyes were closed, but her chest moved up and down. A handcuff was around her left wrist; the other cuff was attached to a piece of chain. Maggie followed the chain to the headboard of the bed. The chain's other end was wrapped around the thick post of the headboard, below the crosspiece. Another set of handcuffs secured the end of the chain to itself. Even if Lydia had been conscious, she would have had no hope of freeing herself.

Lee was bent over Lydia's wrist holding a small key. He inserted it into the cuff attached to her wrist and Maggie heard a click as the cuff popped open. He slid it off the unconscious woman's wrist. So, Maggie thought, a lock-pick gun *and* a handcuff key. Everything the well-accessorized burglar needs.

"Was there anyone else in the house?" She realized she had used the past tense. Some part of her had already accepted that if there had been someone else in the house, that someone was probably dead.

Seth shook his head. "Just her."

Lee straightened and turned to face Maggie. He glared at her, not bothering to hide that he was angry at her presence. At the same time, he looked scared. She guessed his feelings for her mirrored hers for him. They were each angry with the other—although for different reasons, but they still cared for each other. He didn't like her intruding on his "jobs," but he still didn't want her harmed. She was disgusted by his treatment of his parents and the path he'd taken in life, but at the same time, she didn't want him hurt. Why did life and feelings have to be so complicated?

"Is Lydia okay?" Maggie decided to preempt any scolding he was ready to give her.

"She's been drugged," Lee said. He motioned to the nightstand and Maggie saw a medication vial sitting next to the lamp. "Ambien. I'd say she was forced to take more than the prescribed dose."

"Is that dangerous?"

"I guess it depends on how much she's had. Her pulse is strong. The fact that she's chained to the bed makes me think that Smith didn't give her a huge dose. He must have been afraid she'd wake up before he got back."

"She'd planned to use it to drug her guard," Maggie said. "She was going to put it in his food."

"Smith apparently couldn't spare a guard for her," Lee said. "Probably why she's drugged and chained to the bed."

"We need to get her out of here before he gets back."

Lee nodded. He looked at Seth.

"How are the woods you came through? Think we could get her to Maggie's car?"

Seth shook his head. "The undergrowth is as thick as it is on the side you came through. I doubt even the two of us could manage the deadweight of an unconscious woman."

For a second Maggie wondered how Seth knew what the woods were like on the other side of the house. Then, she realized that must have been the way they'd approached the house the night he was shot.

"So the only choices are to either leave her here or bring a car to the house." Lee didn't look happy about the options.

"No!" Maggie spoke up. "We are not leaving her here. She needs medical care and she needs to get away from her crazy husband."

"Okay, okay." Lee raised his hand. "We're not going to leave her. Seth, take Maggie and go for her car. I'll stay with Lydia."

"I don't like leaving you here alone in case Smith comes back," Seth said.

"He's not likely to be back this early."

"You both stay here," Maggie said. "I'll get the car."

The two men looked at one another, then Lee nodded. "Okay, but be careful. If you see any cars in the drive when you pull in, put it in reverse and get the hell out of here."

"Sure," she said, turning to go.

"Maggie, I'm serious." Lee's anger was gone and only concern showed on his face. "Promise me. If you see a car in the drive, you head for home. Seth and I can take care of ourselves."

"I have no doubt," she said, the sarcasm back in her voice. She looked at her uncle for a moment before nodding. "I promise."

"While Maggie's getting the car, we need to wipe the security tapes and disable the cameras trained on the drive." Lee said to Seth.

"We've got more than that to do here."

An unspoken message passed between the two men as they looked at one another. Maggie started to ask what they were up to, but decided she really didn't want to know. She turned and headed for the stairs.

Chapter Twenty

The drive was empty when Maggie pulled in. She hadn't expected it to be any different. If Patrick Smith and his men weren't going to be gone a long time, there would have been no need to drug and chain Lydia. Whatever was going down tonight in Smith's world, it required time and all of his men.

She pulled her car to the side of the house, as close to the patio as she could get. She slid the door open, stepped into the kitchen and crossed to the living room. Lydia Smith was lying on the couch, still unconscious. Maggie crossed to her and felt the pulse in her neck. It was strong and regular. She guessed Lee was right—Patrick Smith had probably not given his wife a lethal dose of the sleeping pill. Still, she'd feel a lot better once Lydia was in the hospital.

"Lee? Seth?" she called out.

They had said they needed to scrub the security tapes so Smith wouldn't know who had been in his house and taken his wife. Where would be the most likely place for the recording equipment? Maggie started down the hall that led off the living room to the other rooms on the lower level. The first door on the left opened into the dining room; Maggie saw a swinging door on the other side of the room that she guessed led into the kitchen or a butler's pantry. The door to a small half-bath opened off the right side of the hall. Just beyond it was a door to a set of stairs leading down. Maggie listened for a moment, but didn't hear anything coming from the basement. She closed the door quietly. She didn't relish the idea of descending into a basement belonging to a man like Smith, but if she didn't find Seth and Lee anywhere else, she'd check there.

At the end of the hall was a closed door. As she reached for the knob, she heard the low murmur of voices inside. She opened it and saw that it was an office. A desk stood against the far wall, the centerpiece of built-in shelves holding monitors and two rectangular boxes that looked similar to the DVR she'd had in Denver. As she watched, views from the various cameras stationed around the house played across the screens. Seth was at the desk going through the drawers. Her uncle was standing in front of a wall safe on the left wall. A hinged door stood open. Based on the shape and size of the door, Maggie guessed a picture was on the other side. Not the most original way to hide a safe, she thought, not that she was a safe-hiding expert. Lee was staring at the safe, an odd expression on his face. Scared, Maggie thought. He looks scared. That surprised her. She would have expected a look of anticipation or excitement or just plain greed when a criminal found a safe, but fear?

"This is just great," she said, not bothering to hide the disgust in her voice. "I'm surprised you bothered to get Lydia downstairs before you started tossing the place. Do you think we'll have room for her *and* the TVs and stereo in the car?"

"Maggie . . . ," Lee started, but Maggie waved him silent.

"You are a piece of work, Lee!" She felt herself getting angrier by the second. "I can't believe you're looking for stuff to steal while that woman out there . . . ," she stabbed her finger in the direction of the living room, ". . . needs medical help!"

"You don't understand," Lee started.

"Oh, I understand perfectly! You're a poor excuse for a human being, *Uncle* Lee! I'm ashamed to be related to you!"

"Hey, you two! We don't have time for this." Seth came from behind the desk. "We need to get Mrs. Smith and get out of here."

"Any luck?" Lee said to Seth without taking his eyes from Maggie.

"Nothing. The recorder's erased and disconnected."

Lee muttered something under his breath. Based on the look on his face, Maggie guessed it was a curse word. What had they been looking for? There were plenty of valuable items in the house—electronics, some art that looked pricey, probably jewelry and cash, although she supposed they might already have that in their pockets. But they seemed to be looking for something in particular, not just anything to steal. So they weren't "common" criminals who stole televisions and computers, but what exactly were they? Were they some kind of "specialists" hired by someone to steal a particular item? Maybe something related to the deal that Smith had going with the Middle Eastern men? Then, again, did she really want to know? For the first time in a year, Maggie wished she had never left Denver.

Lee closed the hinged door and Maggie saw she had been right. It was a painting—a seascape. Avoiding Maggie's eyes, he headed for the door.

"Let's go," he said.

In the living room, Seth picked up Lydia. Maggie saw him wince as he lifted her. His shoulder was still bothering him, but as the younger of the two men, he was the stronger. She hurried ahead of him to open the patio door. He was out of breath by the time he reached the car sitting only a few yards from the patio. Maggie started to open the front passenger door, figuring they could belt Lydia in upright, but Lee shook his head.

"Let's lay her in the back seat," Lee said. "We want her out of sight in case we pass any cars on the road."

He went around the car and opened the rear driver's side door. As Seth lowered Lydia to the seat, Lee crawled in and, taking her by the shoulders, pulled her into position on the back seat. When she was settled, he closed the door and turned to Seth.

"You go with Maggie. I'll meet you at Dad's place," he said.

"No!" Maggie couldn't believe her ears. It had been bad enough that Lee had brought Seth to her grandfather to be treated for his gunshot wound, but now he wanted to take the wife of a nutcase who abused his wife and consorted with terrorists there? Didn't he realize how much danger he was putting his parents in? Besides, Lydia needed to be in a hospital. "You can't take her there! She needs a hospital."

"She can't go to a hospital," Lee said. "Not unless it's absolutely necessary and I don't think it is. Dad can examine her and make that call."

"And you don't care if you put him in danger?"

"Maggie, we can't talk about this now." Lee's frustration with her was starting to morph into anger.

"We are going to Dad's and that's it. No more discussion."

Before she could reply, he turned and moved back across the patio, heading for the woods on the other side of the house.

"Come on," Seth said gently, taking her arm. "Let's get out of here."

Maggie jerked her arm out of his grasp. She was seething. She didn't want to take Lydia to her grandparents' house, but she knew they were pushing their luck staying where they were any longer. Her grandfather was a doctor and he was closer than the nearest hospital. She would let him look at Lydia, but after that, they were calling an ambulance and having the woman transported to a hospital, both for her own good and for the good of the two people she loved most in the world.

"You want me to drive?" Seth said.

She shook her head. She hadn't had any control over any of the other decisions that had been made in the last hour, but she was not going to turn her keys over to him. Childish, maybe, but it made her feel a tiny bit better. She got in and started the car.

***

"She should be fine," Everett Jacobs said as he entered the living room. "You called it right, Lee. She's been given too much Ambien, which is why she can't be roused, but her vitals are good. She just needs time to sleep it off."

It had been full dark when they reached her grandparents' house. Seth had carried Lydia into her grandfather's study and laid her on the futon rather than try to carry her up the stairs to the guest room. Maggie had been surprised to see the futon unfolded and made up with sheets, a pillow, and blankets. Lee had apparently called ahead while on the way there.

Dora was bustling around. She had put coffee on and was making sandwiches. Maggie had offered to help, but her grandmother had waved away her offer, all the while refusing to meet her granddaughter's eyes. At the same time, she was solicitous and even downright motherly toward Lee and Seth. She had protested that Seth was going to hurt himself when she saw him carrying Lydia into the house, and after he had delivered the woman to the study, had insisted on inspecting his shoulder wound. In spite of telling herself she shouldn't care, Maggie had stolen glimpses over her grandmother's shoulder. The stitches had held and there was no blood, so even though it had obviously hurt him to carry the weight of the unconscious woman, there didn't appear to be any damage. She hated herself for it, but she couldn't help being relieved that he was okay. At one point he saw her looking and gave her a tentative smile. She refused to respond and turned away.

"We need to call an ambulance," Maggie said now. "She'd be better off in a hospital and so would all of us."

She motioned to herself and her grandparents, ignoring Lee and Seth. Like Lee had said, they could take care of themselves. She certainly wasn't going to worry about them.

"She'll be fine, Maggie." Her grandfather patted her shoulder and smiled. "I'm a doctor, remember?"

"And you're in danger as long as she's here."

Maggie had had it. Everyone seemed to be conspiring to keep things from her. She couldn't picture her grandparents being involved in anything criminal, yet they seemed to be aware of the truth about Lee and Seth and more than willing to aid and abet them. She knew, in the eyes of the law, that made them as guilty as Lee and Seth. But that was just the legal worries. They could wait. Patrick Smith and his crew were the more immediate danger.

"We scrubbed the security video," Lee said. "Smith will have no way of knowing who took his wife, so he'll have no idea where to look for her."

"Are you sure about that?" Maggie glared at him. "Can you be positive you got all the recorded video from all the cameras in the house? What if he had another setup—a backup just in case someone like you came in and erased what was in plain sight?"

"That's not likely," Lee said, but a look of uncertainty passed across his features.

"We weren't there all that long," Maggie said. "Did you search the entire house for recording equipment or were you too busy looking for stuff to steal?"

Before he could answer, she continued. "What about the basement? If I were in Patrick Smith's line of work, I'd have a backup system in the basement or the attic or in a hidden room somewhere where no common criminal could find it and steal it."

She had emphasized the word "common" and saw that it registered with both Lee and Seth. They looked at one another.

"I think it's time, Lee," Seth said.

Lee stared at him for a moment, and then nodded his head.

"Yeah," he said. "I guess it is. Way past time, for that matter."

Dora Jacobs was standing in the kitchen doorway. For a second, she looked as if she were about to speak, but didn't. Everett was nodding in agreement, a look of relief on his face.

"Maggie, we're not who you think we are," Lee said. "Mom and Dad have told me that they were pretty sure you thought I've been involved in criminal activities over the years. You're right. I have been. Just not in the way you think. We're FBI."

A part of Maggie's brain knew she looked ridiculous standing there with her mouth hanging open, but there was nothing she could do about that until the rest of her brain processed what she had just heard. Lee and Seth were feds, not crooks? But why the secrecy? It had to be a lie, a story they had cooked up to get her grandparents to help them. The thought brought a sense of relief. Believing her grandparents had been willing to condone and even assist criminal activity had been almost too much to bear, even if it was explainable by the fact that they loved their son. But if they thought they were helping the "good guys," then they were innocent of any intentional wrongdoing. That would make a difference in the eyes of the law, wouldn't it?

"I don't believe you," she said, lifting her chin defiantly. If Lee and Seth were the good guys, then why couldn't Seth have gone to a hospital when he was shot instead of coming to her grandfather? "If you're both feds, then why the secrecy?"

"The Bureau has known for some time that Smith is involved with the transport of drugs, weapons, even some human smuggling, but we've been unable to do more than snag a few of his low level operatives. We want him. Seth and I infiltrated Smith's organization in Indianapolis several months ago. We got plenty of evidence to bust a lot of his employees, but had trouble tracing any of it directly to him. The Bureau was close to ordering arrests on the ones we could get in the hopes of getting one or more to testify against him in exchange for a deal, when we learned something that changed everything. That's when we came here."

Lee took a deep breath.

"I'm sorry about the lies, Maggie, but we had to keep a low profile. Smith has people everywhere. We're not sure about the Vichy police, but we know he has at least two county officers on his payroll. He's lived here long enough that there's probably more, including some from the state. It's been the same everywhere he's lived. Getting eyes and ears inside local police is top on his list of priorities when he moves into an area . . . and he continues to pay those people even when he moves somewhere else. I guess he never knows when they'll come in handy."

So Lydia wasn't paranoid after all, Maggie thought—assuming Lee was telling the truth, that is. My God, how did such a man ever end up here anyway? For some reason, she only pictured criminal masterminds living in places like New York or Los Angeles or Chicago. Guess even a crook can enjoy quiet country living.

"You say you learned something that brought you here. What could be important enough to get shot over . . . ," she glanced at Seth, ". . . and what is important enough to endanger Gran and Gramps like this?"

"That's a long story," Lee said.

"Then maybe you'd better get started telling it," she said.

Chapter Twenty-One

"You know," Lee said. "I've rehearsed this moment in my mind many, many times in the past years, especially after you were older. I've wanted to tell you the truth, but I always backed off. Dad and Mom thought it was safer for you and for me if I didn't tell you. I always ended up agreeing with them, but I still thought about it a lot."

As Maggie stared into her uncle's troubled brown eyes, a slideshow of forgotten memories raced through her mind, vivid scenes of looking up at her beloved uncle—the viewpoint that of a little girl holding her hands up to this man, sleepy evenings cuddled in the warmth of his arms, the surprise gifts he pulled from his pockets to her squeals of joy. Then the slideshow grew dark and she saw the disappointment on her grandparents' faces, the hurt and love in their eyes when they spoke of their son. Was there ever a good enough reason to cause that kind of pain—and worry, if Lee was telling the truth about being a federal agent— to those you professed to love?

"I've always had a wild streak in me." Lee walked to the window and looked out. Maggie thought it was more to give himself time to organize his thoughts than to get a look at what might be outside in the darkness. "A craving for excitement. Dad says he doesn't know where it came from, but it's there. Katherine had it, too, to some extent, though not as bad as me. So do you."

He turned to face her and leaned against the wall beside the window, his arms folded.

"There's something else that you, your mother, and I have in common, and that's good values. I know where those came from. I guess we should all thank God that we had these two wonderful people . . . ," he smiled at Dora and Everett, ". . . to counteract the wildness. Otherwise, we would all have ended up in trouble."

"Get to the point, Lee," Maggie said. "I don't need to hear your justification for why you treated Gran and Gramps the way you have over the years."

"Maggie . . . ," her grandmother started, but Lee waved her silent.

"It's okay, Mom. She's got a right to be angry. And she's right. I can apologize and try to come up with excuses later." He turned back to Maggie. "Whether you believe me or not, Maggie, Seth and I are federal agents."

"So let me get this straight," Maggie said. "You sneaked into the area a few nights ago, attempted to burglarize Patrick Smith's house, Seth got shot, and you came to Gramps for help rather than go to a hospital. Since when is that accepted police procedure?"

"Since never," Lee said. "Not that it doesn't happen occasionally. When the stakes are high enough—as they are here."

"We did it because of the information Elton passed to us the last time we met with him." Seth had been silent during the exchange between Lee and Maggie. Lee gave him a look that Maggie interpreted as gratitude. Apparently her uncle was more than willing to turn over some of the storytelling burden to Seth.

"He'd overheard something that wasn't intended for his ears. Elton Jackson wasn't exactly a model citizen, but he did draw the line at certain things. Like terrorism and nuclear materials."

"What?" Maggie hadn't expected that. Lydia had claimed her husband had gotten involved with terrorists, but she hadn't said anything about nuclear materials.

"Smith is a mover. For the right price, he'll move just about anything from one place to another—drugs, people, money, weapons. You name it and give him enough money, he'll move it."

"That's what his wife said."

Lee and Seth glanced at one another.

"What else did she say?"

"Only that she thought that this time he'd gotten involved with terrorists and was in over his head. She thought he'd tried to get out of whatever he'd gotten involved in, but couldn't. Based on what I saw, I'd say she's right."

"What do you mean—what you saw?" Seth's tone was sharp.

"Remember I told you I took a drive out that way," Maggie said, enjoying the look on both Lee's and Seth's faces. "I was a few yards from the Smiths' drive when a black Lincoln Navigator with tinted windows and Illinois tags nearly ran me off the road on the curve. I saw it turn into the Smiths' drive and got curious, so I parked just down from that vacant house—I didn't know it was vacant then—and went through the woods."

"Jesus!" Lee muttered, running his hand through his hair.

Behind her, Maggie heard her grandmother let out an unintelligible sound. Her grandfather went to her and helped her to the couch, where they both sat down. Her grandmother's face was white.

"What happened?" Seth's lips were set so tightly, Maggie was surprised he was able to get the words out. She didn't like upsetting her grandmother, but she had to admit she was enjoying the reaction from her uncle and Seth. They deserved to have their worlds rocked just a bit.

"I hid behind a tree and that line of shrubs we hid behind," she said. "Only further down. I didn't see anyone at first, but one of the upstairs windows was open and I could hear a radio. Turned out Lydia saw me from that window. That's why she came to me at the Garden Club meeting."

At the mention of the Garden Club meeting, Lee looked confused. He started to say something, but a glance from Seth stopped him.

"After a couple of minutes, I thought I saw something white move behind the patio doors. I was afraid to move. I hadn't planned on spying on anyone and had on a bright yellow shirt that day. And with my hair . . . anyway, I thought it best to stay still. After a few minutes, three men came out on the patio. One I assumed was Patrick Smith. The other two looked Middle Eastern. One was obviously the boss, while the other one looked like a bodyguard—all muscles and he didn't speak."

"Could you hear what the others were saying?" Lee's expression was all business. Seth sent him an irritated glance that seemed to say that should be the least of his concerns. Or, Maggie wondered, was she just choosing to interpret it that way? Maybe she wanted him to be more worried about her than about what Smith was up to and imagined it was so.

"They were too far away for me to catch more than a word here and there. At one point, Patrick and the boss man seemed to be arguing. The boss jumped up and accused Patrick of bungling something. It looked like that made Patrick mad and he started to stand up, but the muscle head looked like he wasn't going to let that happen so Patrick let it go. Then he asked the boss what he wanted him to do, but I couldn't hear what the answer was."

"Then what?"

"They eventually went back in the house and I got out of there."

She looked at Seth.

"You want to know what I thought?" she said. "I thought what Patrick had bungled was shooting you. I figured you and Lee worked for one of his competitors."

"Well, you're right in a way." Seth attempted a smile. "Christ, Maggie, if you had been caught . . ."

"I wasn't," she said. "So forget about it."

She turned to Lee. "You still haven't told me what is so important about Patrick Smith that it justifies breaking into his house and getting shot. And you still haven't told me what you meant when you said nuclear materials."

"Smith was in Germany last month with his wife. He was allegedly mixing a little import-export business with pleasure, but the import-export business he was conducting wasn't exactly the legal kind. We believe he was making arrangements to obtain weapons-grade plutonium for his client—probably the man you saw."

"You mean, like for a bomb?" Maggie was incredulous.

"Ever since the Soviet Union fell apart," Lee said, "there have been isolated incidents of nuclear materials finding their way into Europe. Security isn't the best in Russia and there's no way of knowing how much nuclear material has been stolen over the years. It's doubtful even the Russians know. What has been found in Europe hasn't been a lot in terms of total amount, but enough to scare the pants off anybody with any sense. Of course, anybody with any sense also realizes that a lot more has probably slipped through undetected. Can you imagine the price nuclear materials can bring on the illegal arms market?"

"Terrorists?"

"Among others. Also small countries looking to start their own nuclear weapons programs. For that matter, even countries trying to get their hands on plutonium to use for peaceful purposes in nuclear reactors for energy production—although I wouldn't want to bet the farm on an illegal buyer having peaceful intentions."

"But how does anyone get hold of this stuff to begin with? How do they get it out of one country and into another?"

"Like I said, security isn't as tight as it should be for nuclear materials, plus Russia's economy, which wasn't the best to start with, is going from bad to worse thanks to sanctions imposed after their invasion of Crimea. Bad combination. Plus, organized crime exists in Russia just like it does here."

"Viva la capitalism," Seth said.

Lee nodded.

"Organized crime is the unfortunate side effect of more freedom and of a market-based society. Rampant growth in organized crime occurred in the nineties. Since then, Putin has cracked down, but it still exists— just like we crack down on it here, but never seem to be able to wipe it out."

"How big is this stuff anyway? I mean, it just seems like something that could make an atomic bomb would be big enough to be noticed."

She remembered the Denver paper running an article once in the Sunday supplement about theft of nuclear materials and wished she had paid more attention to it. It was just after Tom had been arrested. She had been too caught up in her own drama to give a story about stolen plutonium and uranium a second glance. We always think everything bad only happens to the other fella, don't we, she thought. If what Lee and Seth were saying was true, the threat had come entirely too close to home.

"It only takes eighteen pounds of plutonium-239 to make a bomb the strength of the one that detonated at Hiroshima," Seth spoke up. "Or fifty-five pounds of uranium-235."

"To make a bomb from the eighteen pounds of plutonium," Lee said, "a lab has to first melt it down to something called a 'pit.' That's about the size of a tennis ball."

"My God! I had no idea."

"Of course, that's not all it takes to make a bomb," Seth said. "To set off a plutonium pit, for example, a person would need about eight-hundred pounds of conventional explosives and would have to have the know-how to pack them properly around the pit. But the nuclear materials themselves really aren't all that big or all that heavy. Pits could easily be smuggled into or out of a country. All you need is a lead-lined container."

Maggie sat for several moments, trying to assimilate the information. There was something very wrong, she thought, about something so destructive being so small. Apparently it wasn't just good things that came in small packages.

"What do you think Patrick Smith bought?" she said. "Plutonium or uranium? Or both?"

"We don't know," Lee said. "For that matter, we don't know if he actually bought anything, or if he was just making transport arrangements for something bought by his client. Interpol has had trouble getting details from their informants, and what they have gotten is conflicting. But one piece of very disturbing information didn't come from informants. It came from the Russian government."

"Russia?"

Lee nodded.

"Six months ago the U. S. received a report from the Russian government about missing plutonium pits. A facility in the central part of the country reported coming up short on their inventory. Three pits weren't accounted for."

"Could it just be a mistake with their paperwork?"

"It's possible," Lee said. "But they didn't seem to think so. And the fact that they do make mistakes with their paperwork from time to time points out that it would also be conceivable that other pits are missing and no one's noticed it yet."

Maggie sat for a few seconds trying to adjust to her view of the world being turned on its head by what she had just heard. Finally, she looked up at Lee, then Seth.

"So, what, you broke into Smith's house to get the pits?" she said. "And you were shot?"

Seth nodded. "I was shot. We hadn't gotten into the house, though—and we don't think the pits are in the house. After Elton told us what he'd overheard, a task force was formed. We have agents watching Smith's warehouses and shipping facilities all over the country. Interpol is keeping a watch on the overseas ones. Lee came here because of Dora and Everett, and I was assigned to come with him."

He smiled. "Except for getting shot, it's been one of my better assignments."

Maggie ignored the subtext in his statement.

"What happened the night you were shot?"

"Lee and I decided to get a look at the place. We came through the woods from the side opposite to where you and I entered—like Lee did tonight. We were surprised to find the driveway empty and no lights on. It looked like the house was empty. We decided to take advantage of the situation and see what we could find out. We pulled ski masks over our faces just in case we weren't able to find and scrub the security video, and started to use the lock gun on the patio door. Just like tonight. Only the house wasn't empty. A light came on and we took off—only I guess I didn't duck and weave as much as I should have. I was almost past the pool when I got hit. Lee held on to me and got me out of there. We came here."

"Why didn't you go to a hospital?" Maggie doubted she would ever forgive either of them for endangering her grandparents. Nothing was important enough to do that.

"We couldn't take the chance." Lee took over. "Like I told you, Smith has people everywhere. If he heard a federal agent was in the hospital for a gunshot wound, he'd know we were on to him. We preferred he thought he'd interrupted a burglary in progress."

"I don't think Smith is the one who shot you," Maggie said.

"What?"

"Lydia said that whenever her husband left with his guys to do whatever it is he does, he always leaves a guard with her. I'd say she was in the house that night, probably asleep, and the man who shot you was her guard."

She thought for a second before continuing. "I'm guessing there's another reason you didn't want to go to a hospital. What you were doing—breaking into a suspect's house—was your own idea, wasn't it? You'd have been in trouble with your bosses if they found out. Especially since you bungled it."

Lee and Seth looked at one another, and both started grinning.

"You were right," Seth said to Lee. "She is smart."

"You think it's funny?" Maggie's temper had been doing a slow burn, but now she felt it flame. "You and Lee put all of us in danger to keep from getting in trouble with your bosses? How dare you!"

"Maggie, stop." Lee held up his hand, his face serious now. "Trust me, our not wanting to get in trouble for screwing up something we weren't cleared to do in the first place was only a small part of the reason we didn't go to a hospital. The main reason was that we couldn't take the chance of Smith getting on to us. You say we put you all in trouble by coming here? You're right. But how much trouble do you think a lot of people will be in if Smith succeeds in delivering nuclear material to his client?"

Maggie started to speak, then stopped. He was right. She didn't like it, but she couldn't argue that maybe, just maybe, there had been some justification for what they did. Maybe some things were worth putting those you loved in danger. She wasn't entirely convinced, but she'd allow that it was possible.

"We knew from the start what we were getting into." Everett Jacobs spoke for the first time since Lee and Seth had begun their story. Maggie turned to him. "Your grandmother and I discussed it and decided it was safest for the boys to stay here. I could have patched Seth up enough to get to a hospital farther away, and maybe they would have been all right, but we didn't want to chance it. Besides, they still had important work to do here. And there was no reason Patrick Smith would suspect us. Why would he? As far as he knew, a couple of punks had tried to break into his home to get money for drugs."

Maggie had to admit he was right. As long as Smith didn't know who his burglars were, she and her grandparents had been safe. But she could have put them all in danger by spying on the Smith home. She had been lucky that only Lydia had seen her, and she had been lucky that Lydia wanted to get away from her husband instead of help him by telling him about the woman watching him from the woods. Suddenly she felt very foolish. As usual, she had acted without thinking.

"We're sorry, honey," Dora said. "We should have told you about Lee a long time ago. And we should have told you what was happening this time. It wasn't fair to you."

"No, Gran," Maggie said. "I'm the one who should apologize."

She looked around the room.

"To all of you. I've been angry with you, Lee, and you, Seth, for putting us in danger, but you're right. There was no reason for Patrick Smith to suspect us. But I almost gave him reason by spying on him that day. If he had seen me . . ."

Dora jumped up from the couch and threw her arms around Maggie.

"You didn't know," she said. "And that's on us. You weren't caught—thank goodness—so you don't need to apologize."

She gave Maggie a squeeze before releasing her.

"Now," she said. "Are we going to eat or did I make all those sandwiches for nothing?"

Chapter Twenty-Two

After they had all eaten, Everett went to the study to check on Lydia. Lee and Seth went out the back door. They said they just wanted to get some fresh air, but Maggie knew they were checking the house and area for anything that looked suspicious. She helped her grandmother clean up. There wasn't much conversation—both were too involved in their own thoughts, but the silence was companionable. For the first time in a long time, Maggie knew there were no more secrets in this house where she had grown up. She hadn't realized until now just how much those secrets had bothered her. She had felt like an outsider—had *been* an outsider, but no longer. Whatever was going to happen, she would be a part of it.

She was wiping down the counters when she heard the front door open, followed by the study door opening and closing. Lee and Seth were joining Everett, anxious for Lydia to wake up so they could question her as to what she knew of her husband's activities. A part of her wanted to intervene. Lydia had been through enough living with a husband who was insanely jealous and abusive to the point of drugging his wife to keep her from leaving him. But if what Lee and Seth had told her about Patrick Smith was even half true, Lydia's emotional wellbeing was the least of their concerns. Nuclear materials outweighed feminine fragility—and Maggie suspected Lydia wasn't all that fragile anyway.

After the kitchen was in order, Dora kissed Maggie on the cheek.

"I'm headed to bed," she said. "Too much excitement for an old lady."

Maggie was too keyed up for sleep. She poured a cup of milk, heated it for a minute and a half in the microwave, then started for the front porch. At the door, she hesitated. Was it safe, she wondered, before dismissing the thought as ridiculous. In spite of her having played the devil's advocate earlier, she thought Lee and Seth probably had managed to erase all the video footage at Smith's house. There was no reason for Patrick to suspect his wife was here. Besides, Lee and Seth had checked outside. If anything had looked suspicious, they would have raised the alarm.

She turned off the living room lights before opening the front door. The night was clear and the light from the full moon illuminated the porch and front lawn like a lamp on a dimmer switch. She had just closed the door when she realized she wasn't alone. A man was sitting on the glider. Her heart rate jumped alarmingly before she recognized the shape as belonging to Seth, not Patrick Smith or one of his thugs.

"I didn't know you were out here," she said.

"Lee and I thought it best if we keep a watch through the night," Seth said. "Just in case."

"You're not sure you scrubbed all the footage from the security cameras, are you." It wasn't a question.

"We were sure until you pointed out that we didn't have a lot of time. There could have been a backup system like you said."

"Do you really think Patrick Smith would come after his wife?" Maggie said. "It seems like he has a lot more to worry about than his wife leaving him."

"What he's involved in is even more reason for him to be worried if she leaves him. We don't know how much she knows, but based on what little she told you, I'd say she knows enough. Besides, when did jealous husbands think rationally? Until Lydia wakes up and your grandfather says it's safe to move her to the Indianapolis office, you and your grandparents could be in danger."

Maggie moved to the end of the glider. "Mind if I sit?" she said.

Seth hesitated, but finally nodded. "Sure. No problem."

Maggie sat down at the opposite end. They sat in silence for several minutes, the glider making low creaking noises whenever they shifted position. Maggie sipped her milk, not tasting it, and tried to think of how to frame the words she wanted to say.

"I want to apologize," she said finally.

"For what?" Seth sounded surprised, as if those words were the last words he expected to hear her say.

"For jumping to conclusions about you," she said. "I need to apologize to my uncle, too, but he's partly to blame for what I thought of him. If he hadn't kept secrets . . . well, we'll work that out. But I was wrong to think what I did about you. Especially after . . ."

She let the sentence drift off. He knew. She didn't need to say that after the wonderful night they had spent together, she should have known a man as gentle and loving as he had been could not be what she had thought he was.

"You don't need to apologize for thinking the worst of me," Seth said. He sounded amused. "I certainly looked suspicious."

"I need to apologize for more than just my thoughts," she said. "I need to apologize for my actions. I hope you won't be too angry with me when I tell you what I did."

"I'm not sure I could ever be angry with you, Maggie." His voice was low. She thought she detected a note of sadness in it.

"Don't commit yourself," she said, then steeled herself and came out with it. "When you found me in your room, I had been going through your things. Snooping. I found the guns hidden in your suitcase."

She was looking at Seth as she spoke. In the bright moonlight, she saw his eyes open wide in surprise. He stared at her for a moment, then threw his head back and burst into laughter.

"Well, I'm glad you find it so funny." She was a little miffed at his reaction. "Although I have to admit I expected you to take it more seriously."

"I'm sorry." He seemed to be struggling to get himself under control. "It's just that I never for a moment considered you doing that. Yet it's exactly what I would have done if the circumstances were reversed."

"You would?"

"Of course. I'm a cop. Remember? Suspicion is in our genes. If I had thought about you what you thought about me, I'd have been going through your things three days ago."

"Well, I'm certainly glad I was above suspicion," she said. She extended her hand and ran her fingers lightly over the side of his face. "So you're not mad at me?"

He shook his head, but didn't speak. She waited, expecting him to pull her to him, but he didn't move. He was staring at her, his eyes moving over her face as if he were trying to commit it to memory, but the sadness that she had thought she heard in his voice was in his gaze. The heck with it, she thought, and slid across the glider to him. It's the twenty-first century, she thought. We don't have to wait for the man to make the first move anymore.

"Can we kiss and make up then?" She brushed her lips lightly over his and heard the sharp intake of his breath.

"Maggie . . . ," he started.

"Shhh," she said and kissed him again, this time lingering.

It worked. He slid his arms around her and pulled her to him, his lips pressing hard and forcing hers open. Her entire body lit up with desire, the wave washing through her nearly bringing her to orgasm with just the touch of his lips. She pressed herself against him and matched his kisses with abandon of her own. It was going to be okay. The man she desired and loved—yes, loved, it was okay to admit that now—was not the wrong kind of man after all. He was one of the good guys.

Suddenly he pulled away and stood up, his breathing rapid. In the light, she could see his erection straining against his pants. He turned away from her and walked to the end of the porch where he stood gazing out at the lawn, obviously working hard to get himself under control.

"Seth?" She stood and went to him. She tentatively put her hand on his shoulder, but he shrugged it off with a violent gesture.

"No!" he said. "Don't!"

"Seth, what's wrong? I don't understand."

"We can't get involved," Seth said. "It won't work."

"Well, since you're not likely to end up in prison for burglary, I don't see why not." Her attempt at humor failed. She felt herself growing angry. "You certainly didn't kiss me just now like you didn't want me."

"Ah, damn it, Maggie!" He turned and glared at her. "Of course, I want you. What man wouldn't?"

"Oh, so that's it then? It's just a physical thing?" She was shocked at the hurt she felt. Stupid, she told herself. We've only known each other a few days. Why should it be anything more than physical? But it was for her and there was no sense denying it.

"It's not that." Seth ran his hand through his hair in a gesture of frustration. "It just wouldn't work."

"Are you involved with someone? Is that it?" She felt a pang of jealousy that made her angry with herself. She knew he was widowed, but had never bothered to ask if he had a girlfriend. Truth was, she hadn't wanted to know. And now she was paying for that head-in-the-sand attitude.

"Maggie, let's just drop it." He pushed past her, heading toward the porch steps. "You and I—well, there is no 'you and I.' There never will be."

He strode down the steps and disappeared around the corner of the house. Maggie stood dumbfounded for several minutes after he left. Did he not want her? Of course, he did. There was no questioning his desire when he'd kissed her. And did most men react so strongly when they didn't care for a woman? She didn't believe that for a minute. It was as if he did want her and cared for her, but was refusing to do anything about it. He was pushing her away and she didn't know why. There must be someone else in his life. It was the only thing that made sense. She had allowed herself to fall for a man who was already taken. Stupid! Stupid!

As she felt the hurt welling up and the tears threatening to break loose, she hurried in the house and up the stairs to her room.

**

As soon as he was around the corner and out of sight, Seth stopped and leaned over, his hands on his knees. His heart was racing and he ached with wanting Maggie. God, she had felt so good in his arms! He wanted to carry her into the house and up the stairs to the guest room bed and kiss her all over! It had taken every ounce of willpower he possessed to push her away and tell her to forget about him. He had hurt her, he knew. She has asked if there was someone else in his life, and without confirming or denying, he had let her think that there was. If that thought hurt her as much as it would have hurt him had the roles been reversed, then her pain was excruciating.

Better now than later, he thought with bitterness. She could—and would—recover from the pain of a broken heart. If she continued to be involved with him, she might suffer a pain she could never recover from. Being involved with him had cost one woman her life. He would not let it cost Maggie hers.

Besides, it was true, wasn't it? There was a "significant other" in his life that he wasn't sure he'd be able to give up, even for Maggie—his job. Diane had not been able to share him and it had killed her. He couldn't let it do the same thing to Maggie.

But did it have to? He could change his life, couldn't he? He loved what he did for a living, loved the excitement and the challenge and the knowledge that what he did made a difference. But what he loved doing took its toll on a marriage. His hadn't been the only one destroyed by it, but most only ended in divorce, not death. Extended periods away from home, the need to don other identities, the uncertainty whether a loved one would be hurt or killed while on assignment—it was more than most spouses could take.

He knew he could ask for a different assignment and he'd likely get it. The Burcau had plenty of tamer assignments. He could go back to investigating white-collar crimes. He'd done that for the first five years he'd been with the Bureau, and he'd been good at it. He'd been bored to tears, but he'd been good. He could investigate money laundering or maybe public corruption. Sure, there was always the potential for danger, but it was minimal. And agents usually worked normal hours. Could he tolerate the mundane life of a white-collar investigator for the twenty years or so until his retirement?

If it meant having a life with Maggie Fields and keeping her safe, maybe—just maybe—he could do it. Or was he kidding himself? Would he come to resent her for pulling him away from the work he loved? Which was worse, he wondered—losing her now or losing her later?

Chapter Twenty-Three

Something woke Maggie. She sat up in bed, confused, her heart racing. It was dark in the room, no moonlight coming through the window like it had been when she cried herself to sleep. The clock on her nightstand showed it was half past two. She sat still, listening for what had woke her. Then she heard it—the sound of voices floating up the stairs to her room, urgency in their tone, and the sound of a door being shut on the second level of the house.

She slipped out of bed, pulled her robe on over her nightshirt, and slid her feet into her slippers. She started toward the door, but a noise from outside directed her attention to the window. Looking out, she saw a car she didn't know in the drive. The headlights were off, but she could hear the faint sound of a running engine. As she watched, the front passenger door opened and a man got out. It was too dark to make out his features—the old maple tree in the front yard blocked the glow from the streetlight—but Maggie guessed there were only two possibilities for such a late night caller. Either one of Lee and Seth's cohorts had come to talk to Lydia or Patrick Smith had come to claim his wife.

She hurried to the door and down the steps. The door to the guest room was ajar, and she could hear men's voices behind it. She pushed it open. The only light in the room was from the overhead light, but the dimmer switch had dialed it down to a dim glow. Lee was fully dressed. Seth had on jeans, but was just slipping into a shirt with a button-front. In spite of what had happened between them on the porch and in spite of her concern about the car in the drive, she felt a warmth run through her body at the sight of his naked skin. She would give anything, she thought, if she could erase the memory of how that skin had felt against her own, anything to obliterate the sadness brought by that memory and the rejection that followed only days later.

"What's going on?" she said, pulling her eyes away from Seth.

"Smith." Lee reached behind him and pulled a gun from his waistband. As she watched, he popped the clip and checked its contents.

"Are you sure?" It was dark enough that Maggie doubted Lee had been able to make a positive identification.

"It looks like one of the cars registered to him," Lee said. "Besides, who else would it be at this hour?"

"Maybe someone lost? Or maybe one of the people you work with?" Maggie knew she was grasping at straws. If any other federal agents were coming, Lee and Seth would know about it.

"We'd know if it were one of our guys," Lee said, echoing her thoughts.

"Is Lydia awake yet?"

"When I checked on her ten minutes ago, she was asleep. But she stirred a little, so I think the drug is wearing off." Lee pushed the clip back into the gun and replaced it in his waistband. "I was making a check of the outside when the car pulled in."

"Were you seen?"

"I came in the back door. Nobody saw me."

"What do we do?" Maggie was finally starting to get scared.

Lee and Seth looked at one another.

"That's what we were just trying to decide," Seth said. "We don't want Smith to know we're here, which is why the light is turned down. We're hoping he'll think everyone is asleep and leave."

The sound of the doorbell punctuated Seth's statement. So much for pretending to be asleep, Maggie thought. The sound of heavy pounding on the door indicated Patrick Smith—if that's who it was and Maggie had little doubt about that—wasn't going to depend on a musical chime waking the house's occupants.

"Shit!" Lee muttered.

"We're gonna have to open the door," Seth said. "If we don't, he'll be suspicious."

"Let me," Maggie said. "I live here after all."

"No!" Lee and Seth said simultaneously.

"Why not?" Maggie said. "If it is Smith outside, he's here about Lydia. That's all. He just wants his wife back. I'll tell him I don't know anything about it."

"Maggie, you're not thinking." Lee sounded exasperated with her. "The fact that he's here tells me that he must have had a backup security system like you thought. He saw all of us."

"If he saw you," Maggie said, "wouldn't it be more likely that he would have fled the area? Wouldn't video of you two searching his home have clued him in that you were probably the law? He'd know you were armed and that there is the possibility that your buddies are here, too. Why would he walk up to the front door and knock? He'd either run or he'd storm the place."

"She's right, Lee," Seth said.

"Then how did he know to come here?"

"He must have seen me with Lydia," Maggie said. "Either at the Garden Club meeting or at the spa. Lydia said he always has people spying on her. Maybe his spies aren't just male. Maybe one of the women at the meeting or at the spa reported back to him."

The doorbell sounded again, followed by heavy pounding.

"Look," Maggie said. "You two can slip downstairs before I turn on a light. The drapes are pulled and the glass in the door is opaque. He won't be able to see you. One of you needs to make sure Lydia stays quiet. The other one can get behind the door to the kitchen. If Smith tries to force his way in or threatens me, you can show yourselves then. But if he believes my story and leaves—well, he'll never have to know you were here."

It was obvious from their expressions that neither of the men liked the idea, but that they also saw the wisdom of it. Finally Lee nodded.

"Okay. We'll do it your way." Lee started for the door, Seth behind him. He hadn't tucked in the shirt he'd been slipping on when she entered the room, and Maggie saw the bulge of a gun in the small of his back. "Give us a minute or two to get in place before you turn on the light."

"I'll let Gran and Gramps know what's going on." Maggie said.

She moved to the door across the hall as Seth and Lee started down the dark stairs. She knocked lightly and opened the door a crack. She heard whispering. Her grandparents were awake.

"Gran?" she said in a low voice.

"What's going on?" Dora Jacobs sounded frightened. "Who's at the door?"

"We think it's Patrick Smith," Maggie said. She heard her grandfather sit up on his side of the bed. A moment later the lamp on his side of the bed clicked on. Maggie squinted her eyes against the sudden glare.

She had been about to tell them to leave the lights off, but now she realized it was better if one did come on. Her grandparents' room was at the front of the house. Patrick Smith would see the light flash on and realize he had finally woken someone. Everything would appear normal.

"Where are Lee and Seth?" Everett slid his feet into his slippers and stood, while his wife stayed sitting in the bed, clutching the covers around her. She looked like all she wanted to do was pull them over her head and pretend none of this had happened. Maggie sympathized with the feeling.

"They've gone downstairs," Maggie said. "One is with Lydia and the other is getting into position in the kitchen. In a couple of minutes, I'm going to answer the door."

"You? No!" Dora dropped the blankets. "You can't! It's not safe!"

"It's for the best," Maggie said. "We don't want Smith to know that Lee and Seth are here. If he already did—like if he had seen us all on the security video, he wouldn't just walk up and knock on the door. So all he must know is that Lydia and I know one another. He probably had someone watching her at the spa the day we met and thinks I'm hiding her. I'm going to tell him I don't know anything about it."

"What if he doesn't believe you?" her grandfather said.

"I haven't thought that far ahead," Maggie said. "But if he tries anything, Seth and Lee are nearby and they're both armed."

"I'll get my shotgun," Everett said, starting for the closet. "And come down with you."

"No, don't do that," Maggie said. "Get the gun and have it ready, but stay up here. We want everything to look as normal as possible. If all this wasn't going on and someone knocked on our door in the middle of the night, you wouldn't open it with a shotgun, would you?"

As a small-town doctor, her grandfather had been used to emergency calls in the middle of the night, and occasionally a patient or a patient's family member had shown up at the door. Even though he was now retired, he still occasionally got calls from former patients. If Lydia Smith hadn't been downstairs in the study, she knew he would have opened the door without stopping to consider that the person doing the knocking might be a threat.

Everett looked at her for a few moments before nodding his agreement. "All right. But I'll be at the top of the stairs if anything happens."

"I know. And thank you." Maggie kissed him on the cheek and left the room.

At the top of the stairs, she stopped and listened. Except for the running car engine outside, she heard nothing. Lee and Seth were in place. Just as she flicked on the stairway light, the doorbell rang again.

"Coming!" she called out and took a deep breath. She started down the stairs.

Chapter Twenty-Four

Maggie flipped the switch that turned on the porch light, then opened the door a crack, the way she supposed anyone would do if someone knocked on the door at this hour. "Yes? Can I help you?"

"I'm looking for Maggie Fields." The man standing under the front porch light was the man Maggie had seen the day she'd spied on the Smith house from the woods. He was so tall she had to look up at him. Up close, she could see that his blond hair was streaked with gray. His blue eyes broadcast a range of emotions—frustration, anger, worry—but frustration dominated. They were the eyes of a man used to being in control, but finding that control slipping out of his grasp.

"That's me," Maggie said. She tried to look surprised, like the last thing she expected was to have someone come knocking on her grandparents' door at this hour looking for her. "And who are you?"

"You know who I am," Smith said, biting the words off.

"I don't. And I think you'd better leave." She started to close the door, but he stopped it with his hand. He looked as if he wanted to push it open and storm into the house, but he only held it in place.

"Wait. I'm sorry—that was rude of me." He didn't look apologetic. "My name is Patrick Smith. I'm looking for my wife, Lydia."

"I don't know anyone named Lydia," Maggie said. She decided it was time to look aggravated. It seemed the most likely reaction of someone woke in the middle of the night for nothing. "And I don't appreciate you beating on my grandparents' door at this hour."

"You do know my wife." Patrick ignored her aggravation and the comment about her grandparents. "She was seen talking to you at the Garden Club meeting and the two of you met at Eve's Fitness and Spa."

Maggie knew her surprise was showing on her face. This time it wasn't part of her act. She had theorized that Patrick's spies had seen her and Lydia at one or the other of the places he'd mentioned, but both? My God, she thought, what Lydia must have gone through all these years married to this nutjob! He had his wife followed everywhere. Lydia had thought the bodyguard she knew was the only person keeping tabs on her activities, but her husband must have one or more women in the town on his payroll. Did those women know what kind of man they were working for, or did they even care? Maggie knew some people were so desperate for money—or greedy—that they wouldn't bother to ask questions. She'd just never thought any of the women from her hometown were those kinds of people. Apparently she had been wrong.

"Oh," she said. There didn't seem to be much point in denying she knew Lydia now. She knew her face had given her away. "That Lydia."

"Yes, *that* Lydia!" Smith took a deep breath. "Now—can I see my wife?"

Maggie glanced at the car in the drive. She had seen Patrick get out of the front passenger side, so there was at least one other man in the car. Were there more in the back seat? What would Patrick and the rest of them do if she kept denying she knew anything? Patrick looked like it wouldn't take much for him to lose control and force his way into the house. His driver and any other men would doubtless follow, at which point Lee, Seth, and her grandfather would show themselves. She knew the men in her house were armed and had little doubt Patrick and his men were as well. She would end up in the middle of a gunfight. Time to get creative, she thought.

"Okay," she relented. "I do know your wife. But she's not here."

"What do you mean, she's not here?"

"She asked me to help her get out of town. I liked her and felt sorry for her." She glared at Patrick with disapproval. It wasn't entirely an act. "She said you were abusive and she wanted to get away from you."

Patrick made a growling sound in his throat and took a step forward. Maggie held up her hand and tried to look contrite.

"I'm just repeating what she told me," she said. "I'm not accusing you of anything."

"Go on." Patrick practically bit the words as he forced them out of his mouth.

"She asked me to pick her up at your house earlier tonight—well, I guess now it's last night—and I did. I drove her to Cincinnati."

"When I last saw my wife," Patrick said, the look on his face telling her he didn't believe her, "she had taken a sleeping pill and was fast asleep."

"Well, that explains that," Maggie said, forcing a nervous laugh. "I thought she seemed awfully groggy.

She wanted to stop on the way for coffee, but by the time we got to the MacDonald's, she was asleep. I kept going."

"To Cincinnati."

"Yes. That was—oh, I don't know—around eight or so. We got to Cincy around ten, I dropped her off, and drove home. That's the last I saw her."

"Dropped her where?"

"Downtown—at a cabstand in front of the Netherland Hotel. She said she'd get a cab to another hotel. I offered to take her, but she said she didn't want me to be in the position of having to lie about where she was if you came looking. I didn't think you'd come looking, but I guess she was right."

Patrick stood silently for several minutes. Maggie felt sweat trickle down her side. She was grasping the side of the door so hard her hand was starting to hurt. Finally he spoke.

"What kind of cab?"

"I don't know. I think there was more than one sitting there, but I didn't see which one she got in."

"Did she have any luggage?"

Maggie knew they hadn't packed Lydia a suitcase when they carried her from the house. Patrick had probably checked to see if any of his wife's things were gone.

"No. I thought that was strange and asked her about it when she got in my car. She said she didn't want anything out of that house, that she'd buy whatever she needed."

She took a deep breath and tried to look like a woman who was sorry she'd gotten mixed up in someone's marital problems.

"Look," she said. "I'm sorry. She asked me for help and I did what she asked. I don't know if anything she said was true, and I apologize for thinking it was. I'm sorry I got involved—really sorry. But, please, leave before my grandparents wake up. They're old and I don't like upsetting them. I've told you all I know. I don't want anything else to do with you or your wife. Okay?"

Patrick stared at her. She could tell he wasn't convinced she had told him the truth, but he also wasn't convinced she hadn't. Finally he nodded.

"Okay. I'm sorry to have bothered you, Miss Fields." He pulled a business card from his shirt pocket and handed it to her. "If you hear from Lydia again, please give me a call."

Maggie looked at the card. She had assumed the persona of someone not wanting to be involved. It might be wise to keep up the act.

"I don't know if I want to do that," she said. "Really. I should have stayed out of all this to start with . . ." She let her words trail off.

"I understand." Patrick's tone had turned conciliatory. "But my wife has mental issues. From time to time, she goes off her meds, unbeknownst to me or her doctor, and becomes paranoid. You'd be doing her a favor by calling me."

"Oh, I didn't know that!" Maggie made her eyes go wide. She put her hand to her mouth. "Oh, I'm so sorry! I didn't know she was sick. I just thought . . . of course, I'll call you if I hear from her. And, please, if you find her, please let me know if she's all right. I'd hate it if she got hurt and I was partly to blame."

"I'll do that." Patrick was all sweetness and light now. "I'm sorry to have bothered you. And thank you for the information. Have a good night."

He turned, went back down the steps to the car, and got in. As the car's lights came on and it started backing down the drive, Maggie closed the door. She fell back against it and began to shake.

Chapter Twenty-Five

"I'm nominating you for an Oscar!" Lee said, as he stepped from the door to the kitchen. He wiped his sleeve across his forehead, which was shiny with sweat. "I thought it was all over when he told you he knew you and Lydia had met."

Seth stepped from the door of the study, but stayed where he could still see into it. The expression on his face . . . well, the expression was fear. His features were set in hard lines, and as she looked at him, she saw a small tic at the corner of his eye. Like Lee, his forehead was bathed in sweat, a strand of hair plastered to it. These men were federal agents, used to dealing with the bad guys, but they had been scared half to death by Patrick Smith's nighttime visit. Looking at them, she suddenly felt more afraid than she had when Patrick Smith was still standing at the half-open door.

"That's my girl!" Everett Jacobs bounced down the steps, a big grin on his face. He was the only one who didn't look scared. Of course, Maggie thought, that could be attributed to his faith in the double-barreled shotgun he had in his hand. "You can spin a yarn better than I can!"

He crossed the room and hugged her, holding the shotgun in one hand, the barrels pointed at the floor, while he drew her to him with the other arm. She hugged him back and felt her own fear start to melt away.

"I had a good teacher," she said and kissed him on the cheek.

"Is it over?" A timid voice floated down from the hall above.

"Come on down, Dora," Everett called up. "It's safe now and I think it's going to take a while for any of us to get back to sleep. Didn't I see a pie sitting on the counter earlier?"

"It's supposed to be for dinner tomorrow—er, today," Dora grumbled as she came down the stairs. Maggie could tell that she was grumbling in an attempt to mask her anxiety. Her grandmother's face was pale and she held onto the bannister like a lifeline, support Maggie knew she didn't usually need. "But I guess we can cut it now. Coffee?"

"How about a pot of decaf?" Everett met his wife at the bottom of the stairs and hugged her. "We don't need any caffeine to jazz us up even more."

Dora looked at Maggie, a glint of tears in her eyes. "You okay?" It came out in little more than a whisper.

Maggie nodded and smiled at her. "I'm fine, Gran. A little shook-up, but fine."

Her grandmother nodded, then turned toward the kitchen. As she passed her son, she put her left hand on his shoulder and gave it a squeeze. He patted her hand in return. She went on into the kitchen, and a moment later, they heard a cabinet being opened and the rattle of plates being set on the counter.

"How's Lydia?" Maggie turned to Seth.

"Still asleep." He seemed to have trouble forcing the words through his clenched jaws. Now he forced them apart wide, and the pop could be heard from across the room. "She stayed asleep through the whole thing."

"I was sweating it," Lee said. "I was afraid she'd wake up while Smith was at the door and freak out when she saw she was in a place she didn't recognize with a man she didn't know. If she had let out a yell . . ."

His words trailed off. None of them wanted to think about what might have happened had Lee's fears come to pass.

"Do you think he'll be back?" Maggie said. "He looked like he believed my story, but maybe he's as good of an actor as you think I am. He knows Lydia was chained to the bed, not just drugged, so won't he wonder how she got loose?"

"I don't think he would have left if he hadn't believed you," Lee said. "He knows Lydia had planned this, so for all he knows, she secreted a handcuff key on her person just in case. It may not be the first time he's cuffed her. And he's got to wonder if she hid the Ambien under her tongue and just pretended to pass out. But that doesn't mean he won't come back when he doesn't find any sign of her in Cincinnati."

"It's a big city," Maggie said. "Surely a person could conceivably disappear."

"Smith's reach is wide," Lee said. "He'll have all his contacts scouring the greater Cincinnati hotels and motels, as well as the airport, train and bus stations. And once we take Lydia in to the Indianapolis office, the word will get back to him."

"You think he has people inside your agency?" Maggie was shocked. She could understand how members of local police forces might be convinced through money or threats to pass on information, but the FBI? Surely not!

"We can't be sure," Lee said.

"We can't take her into the office, Lee." Seth spoke up. "We can't take that chance."

"Where else can we take her?" Lee turned to him. "We can't leave her here."

"We need a safe house. We'll take her there and only tell the few people we trust that we have her. It shouldn't take too long to find out what she knows. If she knows enough . . . well, maybe it will be enough to move on Smith and get this over with."

Lee thought for a moment, and then nodded. "You're right. I'll call Mike first thing in the morning."

"Who is Mike?" Maggie said.

"Someone who can be trusted," Lee said. He obviously wasn't about to share any more details so Maggie let it drop.

The lights were still off in the living room and they had all been talking in low voices. Maggie glanced at the windows. The drapes were heavy and pulled close together, and she knew the blinds behind them were closed. Usually the blinds were all her grandmother closed at night, but because of Lydia's presence in the house, extra precautions had been taken the evening before. The blinds were closed in every downstairs room and curtains pulled. If Patrick Smith or any of his men slipped back and tried to peer in windows, she knew they wouldn't be able to see anything.

"Do you think it's safe to turn a light on?" she said now.

"Probably, but let's leave it on a dimmer," Lee said. "I can find Mom's pie in the dark."

"Maggie?" Dora called from the kitchen. "Help me carry these things to the dining room. The drapes are heavier than these curtains."

Her grandmother had obviously been listening to their conversation and didn't feel secure about eating at the kitchen table. Maggie went into the kitchen to help carry the pie, plates, forks, and coffee to the table. When she entered, her grandmother turned to her and threw her arms around her.

"I was so afraid something was going to happen to you," she whispered. Maggie could feel her trembling.

"You weren't the only one!" Maggie laughed, but it came out sounding like something else. "It's a wonder I don't have to change my underwear!"

Dora barked a laugh, surprised by Maggie's comment. "Oh, you!" she said, stepping back and smacking Maggie lightly on the shoulder. "You're as bad as your grandfather!"

"Thank you." Maggie smiled. "That's the nicest thing anyone has ever said to me."

Suddenly everything was back to normal—or at least as normal as could be expected after a middle-of-the-night visit by a thug. Maggie was glad her attempt at humor had relieved her grandmother's anxiety, at least for the moment.

Between the two of them, they quickly moved the apple pie, plates, forks, coffee cups, and napkins to the big oak table in the dining room. The leaf was still out. The men gravitated to the same chairs they had occupied at dinner a few days before. As Dora carried the coffee carafe to the table, Maggie debated whether she could get away with taking the chair her grandmother usually sat in, but knew her grandfather

LOLLI POWELL

would probably comment on it. Resigned, she pulled out the chair next to Seth and sat down. As she did, her arm brushed against his. She felt him flinch, but he didn't look at her. She couldn't help but compare the difference to the way he'd been the last time they had sat next to each other at this table, when he had brushed her hair back to examine the spot where his head had bumped hers. He'd promised then he'd never hurt her, but he'd already broken that promise.

The conversation died down as they ate their pie and sipped their coffee. Maggie felt herself growing tired, and based on the looks of the others at the table, they felt the same. The adrenaline rush brought about by Patrick Smith's visit was wearing off, and their beds were starting to sound very inviting. Maggie finished her pie. She had just begun clearing the table when a voice caused her to whirl around, nearly dropping the stack of plates she had in her hand.

"Where am I?" Lydia was standing in the doorway to the dining room. Her hair was disheveled and her eyes swollen. She looked at Maggie. "Who are all these people?"

Chapter Twenty-Six

Dora allowed Maggie to introduce Lydia to Lee, Seth, and Everett, but refused to allow her to be questioned until she'd had some coffee and a piece of pie. Lee had started to argue with his mother, but a look from her shut him up. Seth followed Lee's lead. They sat in silence watching while Lydia ate and Dora fussed. If the reason for Lydia being here weren't so serious, Maggie would have found the scene hilarious—the tough FBI agents cowed by the petite gray-haired woman. As it was, all she wanted was for it to be over so she could climb back in bed, pull the covers over her head, and forget about wife-beaters and terrorists and men in general.

After Lydia had pushed her plate away and Dora had refreshed her coffee, Everett stepped up to check her vitals one more time. As he removed the blood pressure cuff from her arm, he nodded at the others.

"BP's a little low, but that's to be expected with the drug," he said. "I think our guest is on the road to recovery."

"Are you up to answering a few questions?" Lee said after his father gave the all-clear.

"Do I have a choice?" Lydia said.

"Everyone always has a choice." Lee shrugged. "Of course, some choices aren't in a person's best interests."

"I get the message." Lydia sighed. "Fire away. I'll answer your questions as long as I can keep my eyes open—which may not be long."

"You already know Maggie here was watching your house the other day." Lee gestured to Maggie, and Lydia smiled at her. Even though she didn't feel like it, Maggie smiled back. "Who were the two men she saw meeting with your husband?"

"One of his clients and the client's bodyguard," Lydia said. "All I know is the client's first name is Kasim. I never heard the rest of his name or the name of the muscle."

"What were they meeting with your husband about?"

"I'd say you have a pretty good idea or you wouldn't be asking me these questions," Lydia said. "I'm not sure I can tell you anything you don't already know or at least suspect."

"Why don't you let us be the judge of that?" Seth spoke up. "When did your husband meet this Kasim?"

"Over a year ago." Lydia pushed her chair back from the table and stretched her legs. "I'm guessing you already know Patrick is a mover?"

The last was said as a question and Seth nodded.

"Kasim or someone working on his behalf approached Patrick. They offered him a lot of money to transport weapons." She snorted a laugh. "Patrick doesn't ask a lot of questions when there's a lot of money involved. I asked him once if it bothered him— what he did. His response was why should it? Said all he does is move items from point A to point B. What people do with those items once they arrive at point B is none of his concern. Said if he didn't do it, someone else would, so he might as well be the one to get rich doing it."

What a guy, Maggie thought. She was disgusted. Based on the expression on Seth's face, she wasn't the only one.

"It wasn't the first time Patrick had worked for clients from the Middle East," Lydia said. "And it wasn't the first time he'd moved arms for Middle Easterners. Sometimes he moved them to rebels that the U.S. sympathized with, but wouldn't support because of political reasons. Patrick said somebody had to help those people, somebody that wasn't worried about what the voters would think."

Lydia looked at each of them, an almost pleading look on her face. It was as if she wanted them to think better of Patrick than she knew they did. Was she still in love with the man who beat her? Or did she just want some small affirmation that her choice of a husband hadn't been an entirely brain-dead move on her part? An image of Tom being led away in handcuffs flashed unbidden into Maggie's mind, and for a moment, Maggie could identify with Lydia Smith. No woman wanted to admit that she had been stupid enough to fall in love with the wrong kind of man.

Then the moment passed. One thing Tom hadn't been guilty of was abusing his wife. Maggie knew that had he ever lifted a hand to her, she would have left him. For that matter, had she known how he was financing their posh lifestyle, she would have left him. Whether or not she would have turned him in to the police—that she couldn't answer, but she would not have stayed with him.

But had she known? Had there been a small part of her brain that wondered how they could afford all that they had? She had never questioned where the money came from, preferring instead to believe that Tom was simply a wildly successful investment counselor. Wouldn't most wives have questioned whether or not they were getting themselves deeply in debt with the cars and the clothes and the trips? Why had she never done that? Lydia had at least questioned Patrick about whether he was bothered by what he did for a living. She had never even asked Tom what exactly he did.

"We went to Germany last month," Lydia said, dragging Maggie's thoughts back to the present. "Pat was supposed to meet with the people providing the weapons for Kasim. He took me along. He said we'd do Europe after he concluded his business, but we never got any further than Frankfort. He met with whoever he met with and when he got back to the hotel, he was— well, how should I put it? He wasn't in the best of moods."

Lydia laughed, but there was no humor in the sound.

"He said to pack up, that we were going home. I made the mistake of complaining that I thought we were going to Paris. Said if I had known all I was going to get to do was eat sauerkraut and drink beer, I'd have stayed home." She looked down at her hands. "It was two more days before we left Frankfort, because I couldn't get out of bed. It worked, though. I didn't complain anymore about the trip."

She reached up and brushed her fingers across her cheek. She didn't look up or say anything for several seconds, and Maggie knew she was trying to get herself under control.

"Go on," Seth said finally, but his voice was soft.

"We came home as soon as I could move," Lydia said. "Usually Pat is all sweetness and charm after one of his temper tantrums. He feels sorry for whatever he says or does to me, and tries really hard to make it up to me. Not this time. He got worse after we got home. I got so I was afraid to say anything at all to him."

"He beat you again?" Seth asked.

"Not like in Frankfort," Lydia said. "But then I knew better than to antagonize him like I did over there. He smacked me around a little, but nothing bad."

She shrugged, as if a husband smacking a wife around, as she put it, was a mere blip on the screen of domestic life.

"Like I told you, he always leaves a guard with me when he goes out," Lydia said, looking at Maggie. "Usually it was Elton. Elton Jackson. He was a good guy, always respectful and polite. Sometimes we'd talk for hours while Pat was gone. One night Pat went out right after we'd gotten into it and Pat had slapped me. I was still upset and crying and told Elton I didn't know why Pat treated me the way he did. Elton said I should cut Pat some slack, that he was having a bad time of it. I asked what the hell did he think I was having? Elton kept telling me to take it easy on Pat, and I finally realized that he knew something. I kept after him and he finally told me that Pat had found out the weapons shipment he had agreed to move for Kasim was actually nuclear material. Pat wanted no part of a deal like that and had tried to back out, but was trapped."

She looked at each of them, one at a time.

"Pat's not a good person," she said. "I know that. But he never wanted to bring nuclear materials into the United States. He didn't know what he was getting into when he agreed to the deal with Kasim. He's not like that."

When no one answered her, she sighed and went on.

"A few nights later, Pat and I got into it again. I don't remember what set him off—probably something I said or didn't say. The way he was, it didn't take much. I finally had enough and I screamed at him to not take it out on me, that it was his own fault that he'd gotten involved with those Arabs. I'll never forget the look on his face when I said that. He was shocked and surprised, but then his eyes went kind of dead-like. I'd never seen him look like that before and it scared the hell out of me. He asked me what I meant. I told him nothing. Then he really went to work on me—and it wasn't long before I told him what Elton had told me."

She took a deep breath, her lower lip quivering.

"Elton was gone the next day. A few days later, I heard the guys talking and found out he was dead."

When the tears started this time, Lydia didn't bother to wipe them from her eyes. She looked at each of them, the tears trickling down her cheeks. "The only person in that house who was ever nice to me and I couldn't keep my mouth shut. It's my fault Elton is dead."

Chapter Twenty-Seven

It hadn't taken them long to calm Lydia down the night before, thanks in large part to the Ambien she had in her system. Elton's death was eating at her, but Seth and Lee tried to soothe her without giving away the fact that Elton had been their informant. They pointed out that it was doubtful Patrick would kill one of his men just because of what he'd told her—a beating, maybe, and certainly the man would not have been allowed to be her guard again. If her husband had killed Elton, they reasoned with her, there was likely another reason. When she pressed them for what that reason might be, they shrugged and said they couldn't guess. Maggie could tell Lydia wasn't convinced, but the drug she'd been forced to take reestablished its hold less than thirty minutes after they'd finished their questioning. Seth and Lee looked relieved when she told them she needed to lie down.

Maggie had also fallen asleep quickly, wanting nothing more than to block out all thoughts of Patrick Smith's nighttime visit, Lydia's predicament, and most of all, Seth's rejection. Maybe, she thought, as she drifted off, she could just stay asleep and avoid having to face worries about terrorists and nuclear bombs, abused wives, and the fact that the man she cared for belonged to someone else.

She woke to the sound of car doors shutting in the drive below. When she heard the engine start, she hurried to the window. Lee's car was backing out of the drive, her grandfather in the passenger seat. A glance at the clock told her it was nearly eight. She dressed, brushed her teeth, and ran a brush through her hair before hurrying downstairs. She found her grandmother in the kitchen starting breakfast.

"Morning, honey," Dora said. "Glad you made it up in time for breakfast. I wasn't going to bother you if you were still sleeping."

"I heard Gramps and Lee leaving." Maggie poured a cup of coffee. "Where are they going?"

"Lee's renting a van to take Mrs. Smith to Indianapolis," Dora said. "They want to keep her from being seen."

Maggie thought for a second. "Couldn't she just lie down on the back seat until they were out of town?"

"I don't think it's just here they're worried about," Dora said. "It sounded like they don't want her seen in Indianapolis either."

My God, Maggie thought. It was still hard for her to accept that Patrick Smith's reach extended as far as Lee and Seth seemed to think it did. They were the professionals, though, and if they thought it possible, then it probably was. She shivered, wondering how many other threats there were in her world that she didn't know about. Then again, maybe she didn't want to know. She might never get a good night's sleep again if she did.

She wandered out of the kitchen and into the living room, intending to check on Lydia in the study. Seth was sitting on the couch next to a folded pile of bedding. He had apparently spent the night on the couch, a vantage point from which he could both hear anyone outside the house and be close if Lydia had a problem. Or was he there to make sure Lydia didn't try to leave? For the first time, Maggie realized that Lydia might have exchanged one prison for another.

He looked up as she entered the room. For just a second, his eyes lit up with a warmth and tenderness that took her breath away. Just as quickly that warmth and tenderness vanished, almost as if a curtain had been pulled down over his thoughts. She stared at him, her coffee forgotten, knowing her surprise showed on her face. What was going on with him? He had been glad to see her. She couldn't have imagined that, could she? The only explanation was that in that unguarded moment, his feelings toward her had showed, but then he remembered he belonged to someone else. She would have grudgingly admired his commitment to resisting temptation if the memory of the night he hadn't resisted wasn't so fresh in her mind.

"Good morning," she said. "How was the couch?"

"Not too bad," he said, looking away. "I was awake most of the night anyway."

"Why?" Maggie's heart sped up. "Was someone outside? Or did Lydia have a problem?"

"No to both questions. It stayed quiet and Mrs. Smith stayed asleep." He smiled a little—not much, but a little. "Guard dogs don't find it easy to sleep. That's all."

"Oh." Maggie glanced at the study door. "Is Lydia awake?"

"She is. She finished in the bathroom a few minutes ago. She's getting ready so we can leave as soon as Lee gets back. He went to rent a van for the trip. We want to make sure no one can see our passenger."

219

"You're taking Lydia to Indianapolis already?" Maggie knew she shouldn't be surprised. She already knew Lee had gone to rent a vehicle for that purpose. She had hoped—she didn't know what she had hoped. Maybe that they would stick around until dark? Maybe that Seth would stay because he was worried they might still be in danger—or because he couldn't stand to leave her? Get a grip, she told herself. He's leaving and he won't be back. It was a one-night stand and nothing more.

Seth nodded. "Lee talked to Mike early this morning. He'll have a safe house set up by the time we're on the road."

"What about us?" Maggie thought she detected the hint of a whine in her voice. She took a deep breath before continuing in a stronger tone. "Do we have to worry about Smith or his friends coming after us?"

"Lee and I don't think so." Was she imagining things or did he look unconvinced by his own words. "Smith seemed to believe your story last night. By the time he realizes his wife never made it to Cincinnati, we'll have him locked up."

"Are you sure about that?"

He stared at her for several seconds. He looked exhausted. The whites of his eyes were streaked with red and the shadows under his eyes accented the paleness of his face and the stubble on his cheeks. As he looked at her, a small tic started near his right eyebrow.

"If we don't," he said. "I'll be back. I won't let anything happen to you."

He meant it. Relief flooded through her. Maybe he did belong to someone else, but he cared for her. The night they had spent together hadn't been a casual fling. Maybe there was still a chance . . . but, no, she couldn't think that way. Did she really want to be responsible for stealing a man away from another woman who loved him? Ruining someone else's happiness was a poor way to guarantee your own. But as they say, shit happens, doesn't it? People do sometimes fall out of love with the person they're with and in love with someone else. Maybe, just maybe, that's what was happening here.

He stood up and turned away from her, gathering his things that were piled on the chair next to the couch.

"I'd better get packed," he said, his tone all business. "Lee wants to head out as soon as he gets back."

And then again, Maggie thought, maybe shit doesn't always happen—at least not the way you hope it will. She turned back toward the study.

"I think I'll say goodbye to Lydia then," she said. "I probably won't see her again."

And I probably won't see you again either, she thought, and felt her heart break a little more.

***

The house was empty by nine o'clock. Well, not empty—her grandmother was in the kitchen and her grandfather had retired to his den to do some reading. But it felt empty. Maggie suspected that Lee and Lydia could have been there and it would still have felt empty. Seth was missing, and that was all that mattered.

What a pathetic case I am, she thought. What did I expect? I hopped into bed with a man I barely knew, a man I thought was a criminal, and I didn't even bother to ask if he was involved with anyone.

Was she the kind of woman other women hate—a woman so desperate for a man's attention that she buries her head in the sand and doesn't ask any questions? Well, she thought, maybe I deserve what I got, but it's time to get over it. Mental self-flagellation after the fact isn't going to change anything. She'd slept with Seth, she'd fallen for Seth, and now she was paying the price. All she could do was learn from her mistake.

Yeah, right, she thought. Like I learned from my mistake with Tom!

Pushing the thoughts out of her mind, she went to work on her room. She hadn't cleaned in a while, so she attacked the dust on the furniture, polished the bathroom fixtures until they shone, and ran the vacuum over the carpet so many times she began to worry the pile was going to come unraveled. Her laundry had piled up over the last few days, so she sorted the whites and colors into two piles and carried the whites downstairs to the laundry room. After she started the washer, she went looking for her grandmother and found her in the living room, sitting with a magazine in her lap, staring off into space.

"Oh, hello, honey." Her grandmother seemed startled at her entrance. "I thought you were still in the laundry room."

"Washer's running," Maggie said. "And I need something else to do. Want me to vacuum down here?"

"I did it while you were vacuuming upstairs." Dora smiled. "Guess we both have the same problem, don't we?"

"Yeah, I suppose we do." Maggie flopped down on the couch. She glanced at her watch. "Guess they'd be in Indy by now. Probably already at the safe house."

Dora nodded and laid the magazine aside.

"I pray they'll be safe," she said. "And that all this will be over soon."

"I'm not sure Lydia knows enough," Maggie said. "And that worries me. I was thinking maybe we should go away for a few days."

"Do you think?" Dora was wearing a light blue cardigan sweater and now she began twisting the hem of it between her fingers, a gesture Maggie had come to recognize over the years as a sign her grandmother was anxious.

"I think it might be the smart thing to do," Maggie said. "When Patrick Smith doesn't find Lydia in Cincinnati, he may very well come to the conclusion that I was lying to him."

"Oh, Lord!" Dora looked at the front door as if she expected Patrick to burst through at any moment.

"I don't think we have to worry right away," Maggie said. "I think we're safe for at least the weekend. But if he isn't in jail by Monday, I think we'd be wise to leave town."

"Where would we go?"

"Anywhere. Some place where no one would think to look for us. Not to relatives or friends—just drive somewhere and get a hotel room and wait this out."

Dora thought for a few moments, then nodded.

"You're right," she said. "I'll speak to your grandfather. He won't want to do it. You know how men can be—they don't like to look like they're afraid of anything."

Maggie grinned. Her grandmother certainly knew men—or at least her own husband.

"I'll tell him we're both frightened and we're too scared to go anywhere by ourselves." Dora chuckled. "That will work. Besides, it's not really a fib, is it?"

"No, it certainly isn't." Maggie stood. "Now that that's decided, I think the lawn could use mowing."

Chapter Twenty-Eight

Maggie was still full of nervous energy after mowing the lawn, so she decided to take a walk. She might not be able to do that in a few days, not after Patrick Smith started looking for her. She hoped Seth and Lee were right, that Lydia would be able to tell them all they needed to know to issue a warrant for Patrick Smith's arrest, but she wasn't betting the farm on it. While Lydia might know quite a bit about her husband's business, Maggie thought the FBI would need more than a wife's testimony. They'd need hard evidence, and unless Lydia could point them to the nuclear materials Patrick had been hired to move, they weren't likely to get any. Lydia had not given any indication of knowing where those materials were, and Maggie doubted a man as successful in his line of work as Patrick Smith had been, would have allowed his wife to know such an incriminating detail.

The day was overcast, but warm. Maggie's nose detected the promise of rain to come later in the day. She settled into a fast pace. She spoke or waved to people as she passed their houses or they drove by in their cars. In the way of small towns everywhere, Vichy was full of friendly people. The ones she didn't know waved or spoke as much as the ones she did. The town had an innocence about it, but also in the way of small towns everywhere, not all was sweetness and light. Maggie knew there was a drug problem in Vichy just like everywhere else in the country. Spouses were unfaithful, people occasionally abused or killed their loved ones, suicides happened, people stole money and cheated on their taxes. Terrorists and nuclear materials—well, that was a new stain on the fabric of the town.

As she came into the downtown area, she thought about stopping in at the paper. She could always find something to do there, but today she doubted she would be able to focus on articles about high school graduations or garden club meetings. She stopped and peered in through the glass door, but the office was dark. Jack apparently had better things to do with his Saturday.

It was nearing lunchtime so she stopped at Millie's for a bowl of vegetable soup and a grilled cheese sandwich. The place was nearly empty, and she didn't know any of the customers seated at the counter and the tables.

"Slow day, I see," she said.

Shirley Jenkins, the weekend waitress, nodded. "Sure is. Unusual, too. Most of the time Saturdays are busy until after lunch. Must be something going on in the area I haven't heard about."

Oh, if you only knew, Maggie thought, although I doubt terrorists and weapons smugglers are keeping the customers away. Once the news came out—well, that might boost business. The town was bound to be inundated with news crews and feds and the curious. An increase in business for the tradesmen of the town would be the only good thing to come out of this whole mess—and that might be temporary. The town would become infamous. How many companies would feel comfortable locating in a town known for its terrorist connections, and how many people would feel safe moving their families there? But, she told herself, there was no point in worrying about it now. It was what it was. Vichy would survive like it always had, and the people whose families had been here for generations wouldn't abandon it.

She paid her check and left. She decided to take the long way around to go home so she turned east out of downtown. She had only gone a couple of blocks when she realized she wasn't too far from Arcadia Avenue. Lester and Viola lived on Arcadia, and she had told Lester she'd stop in and see Viola soon. Today was as good a day as any. She'd promised Lester she would call first, so she stopped and took out her cell.

"Hey, Vi!" Maggie said, surprised to hear Viola's voice. She had expected Lester, although she didn't know why she thought ovarian cancer would stop a person from answering a phone. "It's Maggie Fields."

"Oh, hello, Maggie! It's great to hear from you. Lester was just telling me this morning that he'd seen you the other day."

"I told him I'd give you a call and see how you were feeling. I'd love to stop by and see you if today is good for you."

"Please, do!" Viola chuckled. "I am bored out of my skull here! Lester just ran out to pick up a few things, but he should be home soon. Where are you?"

"Actually not too far from your house," Maggie said. "I took a walk today and I just had lunch at Millie's. I was going to head toward home the roundabout way down Oak Street when I realized I was close to you. Do you need me to pick up anything?"

"Can't think of a thing. Lester is taking care of that. When you get here, just come on in. I can't make it to the door as quickly as I used to, so we leave it unlocked if Lester isn't here."

As Maggie disconnected, she felt sad. Viola Lewis was a truly nice woman. Maggie had known her since childhood. In fact, when she was five or six, Viola had occasionally been her babysitter when Dora was otherwise occupied. Vi had been in high school then, and Maggie had idolized the pretty teenager. Vi had been an attentive babysitter, shunning phone calls from friends in favor of playing games with the little girl she was tasked to watch over. She would have made a great mother, but she and Lester never had children. Now she was dying, betrayed by the same ovaries that had refused to give her a baby.

It wasn't fair, Maggie thought. Evil people like Patrick Smith are healthy and strong, and good people like Viola Lewis die young. The random wrongness in the world sometimes made it difficult to sit in church on Sundays and accept what the minister put forth. Of course, the answer the minister would give to such doubts would be that mere mortals could never know the mind of God. That might be so, but it did tend to make one wonder if God was a sadist with a sick sense of humor.

"It's me," she called out as she stepped through the front door.

"In here."

Vi's voice came from the door on the right at the rear of the foyer. From previous visits to the house, Maggie knew the door led to a small room that had always been used as a TV room. Viola was seated in a recliner to the left of a hospital bed that occupied most of the space. Now that the cancer had made Viola too weak to tackle the stairs to the two bedrooms on the second floor, the TV room had apparently been turned into a bedroom.

Maggie hoped her shock at seeing how thin and frail the woman had become didn't show on her face. Viola had a scarf tied around her head to hide the baldness caused by her chemo treatments. Her pale skin sagged on her face and her eyes were sunken, but they sparkled with life. Maggie found that amazing. She'd known Viola Lewis was a nice woman; she hadn't realized she was also a fighter.

Maggie leaned down and kissed Viola on the cheek. "It's good to see you, Vi," she said. "I apologize for not coming by sooner."

"Oh, you don't need to apologize." Vi waved the apology away. "Nobody likes to visit sick people. I never did. When my mother was still alive, she used to have to drag me to people's houses when they were sick or dying. Believe me, I get it."

"No, no, that's not it." Maggie felt herself blushing. "I just got busy . . ."

She stopped. Which was worse, she wondered. Being too busy to visit a sick friend or admitting that visiting made her uncomfortably aware of how tenuous life really was?

"It's okay, honey." Viola smiled. "Let's not waste your visit talking about that. Now, have a seat and tell me—what's been going on in your life?"

Maggie stalled for time while arranging herself in a comfortable position on the padded desk chair. Due to space limitations, it was the only other chair in the room. Maggie remembered that a large oak desk had been its companion, but it apparently had been moved out when the hospital bed was moved in.

She wished she could tell Vi about Seth. She knew her friend would love to hear all about him and how she felt, but she couldn't really say anything, could she? Vi might mention it to Lester, who might comment on it at the station, and if Seth and Lee's suspicions were grounded in fact, someone in Patrick Smith's employ might hear about it. That was too big a chance to take. She could come back later after Patrick was in jail and talk to Vi about it.

If she were still alive, that is, Maggie thought as she looked at the frail woman before her.

"Oh, not much," she said. "Just living the exciting life of a Sun reporter."

Vi laughed. "That bad, huh?"

"Hey, you know how exciting Garden Club meetings and high school graduations can be!"

"I guess there has been some excitement in the area, though," Vi said. "Lester told me about the break-in at the Smiths' house and about the body the deputies found."

Maggie nodded, not trusting herself to speak.

"Probably something to do with drugs." Viola shook her head. "I swear, drugs are going to be the death of this country. Why do people want to get high anyway? Don't they realize they miss out on life that way?"

"I guess some of them want to escape their lives," Maggie said.

"If they walked in my slippers for a day or so, they'd change their tune!" Vi's cheerful delivery offset the sadness of the remark. "I know I don't have much time, but I'd be damned if I'd miss a minute of it by 'turning on and tuning out,' as they say. I don't even take my pain pills unless it gets really bad—and then I only take them at night so I can sleep."

"Has it been bad?" Maggie surprised herself by asking the question, but Viola had a way of making a person comfortable talking about such things. Vi had always been an open person, unafraid to talk about things most people shunned away from in conversation. Maggie guessed her imminent death was no different.

"Sometimes." Vi nodded. "But most of the time, it's bearable."

Her expression grew sad.

"I think it's harder on Lester than it is on me," she said. "He keeps holding out hope that some miracle is going to happen. I know better and I tell him so, but he doesn't give up."

"He doesn't want to lose you," Maggie said. "And, who knows? Maybe there is something out there that will work. Lester said something about a clinical trial in California?"

Viola nodded. "He found the trial on a website and he's insisting we go. I don't want to—with my luck I'll drop dead in California and have to be shipped back. I'd rather die in my own home. But I'll probably do it for him. He's already bought space on one of those private jets people can lease for trips. He said he doesn't want me on a commercial liner with my immune system compromised the way it is."

"A private jet!" Maggie was surprised. She doubted Lester made the kind of money that could pay for a private jet, and when Viola was still able to work, she had been a secretary at the elementary school. "That must be expensive!"

"I'm sure it is, but he refuses to tell me how much. Just says it's too late to cancel." Viola sighed. "I worry about the debt I know we must be in. We have insurance, but we've still been hit with big co-pays. And some of the alternative stuff Lester has insisted I try isn't covered by insurance. Vitamins, massage, aromatherapy—you name it, we've done it. The cancer hasn't gone away, but it's sure been pampered a lot."

"I can understand his wanting to try everything to save you," Maggie said.

"Yeah, I guess I do, too, but I hate it that he's mortgaged his future—and this house—to do it."

"I'm sure he considers it money well-spent," Maggie said. "He would never be able to forgive himself if he didn't try everything."

"You're right, of course." Viola smiled and nodded. "Maybe what we've spent will buy him peace of mind after I'm gone. He'll know he did his best."

Before Maggie could reply, the front door opened and she heard Lester's voice.

"I'm back, Vi. Got everything you asked for and a little more."

"We've got company, sweetie," Viola called out to him. "Come on back and say hello."

Lester's face broke into a grin when he saw Maggie. "Maggie! Good to see you."

"I was taking a walk and realized I wasn't far from your place. I gave Vi a call and she said to come on over."

"Yeah, she's getting sick of looking at my ugly mug." He bent down and kissed his wife on the forehead. Maggie noticed he handled her as if she were a valuable and fragile thing that might easily be broken. "And I'm not much for girl talk either, so I'm glad you stopped by to give her a fix. You two want something to drink? I was planning on fixing a pot of decaf after I get the groceries put away."

"I'll have one," Vi said and looked at Maggie.

"Sounds good to me," Maggie said. "As long as it's better than the swill you serve down at the station."

"Hey! What's wrong with cop coffee?" Lester pretended to be offended, but Viola laughed.

"Don't worry, Maggie," she said. "I taught him how to make coffee—and we buy a better brand than that cheap stuff they use at the station."

Lester went into the kitchen and started the coffee, then began carrying the groceries in from the car. Maggie started to offer to help him, but stopped, knowing he would tell her to keep Vi company. It was obvious how grateful he was that someone had come to visit his wife and take her mind off her illness even if only for a few minutes. So Maggie settled back in while she and Viola exchanged small talk—gossip, her grandfather would call it—about the town and its people. It wasn't long before Lester came in carrying three mugs of coffee. He handed Maggie the single mug in his left hand, then carefully took one of the two mugs he carried in his right hand and gave it to his wife. He sat down on the edge of the hospital bed and took a careful sip.

"Pretty darn tasty, if I do say so myself."

Maggie took a sip and nodded. "Much better than the stuff at the station. You taught him well, Vi."

"Say, Maggie," Lester said. "Were my eyes deceiving me, or did I see Lee driving your granddad around town this morning?"

Uh-oh, Maggie thought. She took another sip of coffee while she thought how she should answer. Deny it? But then, wouldn't Lester find that suspicious? He knew Lee and her grandfather by sight, so he already knew the answer to his question. What he was really asking was what Lee was doing in town. The only answer she could safely give was, yes, he had come for a short visit. After all, nothing strange about that, was there? It was only natural he would occasionally visit his parents. Besides, Lester had no idea what Lee did for a living, and neither did anyone else in this town. Even if Lester mentioned seeing Lee to someone on his department, there was no reason to think it would set off alarms with any cop in Patrick Smith's pocket.

"Yes, that was my uncle," she said, hoping she'd made the right decision. "He was passing through the area and stopped in for a short visit."

"Lee Jacobs." There was a wistful tone to Viola's voice. "I had the biggest crush on him in high school."

"You did?" Maggie was surprised. Vi had never told her that.

"Oh, yeah! Of course, I was a lowly freshman and he was a senior, so he never paid any attention to me." She laughed. "I probably shouldn't tell you this, but being able to see Lee when he came home from college for visits was one of the main perks of babysitting you."

Maggie burst out laughing. "You're kidding? You had it that bad?"

"Oh, yeah." Viola smiled at her husband. "At least until Lester got my attention."

"Piece of cake," Lester said. "How could any man compete with the likes of me?"

The women groaned, and Lester grinned.

"So how long is Lee staying?" he asked. "I'd like to say hello to him—and thank him for not paying any attention to Vi when he had the chance."

"He left earlier today," Maggie said.

"Wow! That wasn't much of a visit! One night and he's gone?"

"I guess he's a busy man," Maggie said. She turned to Viola, anxious to change the subject. "I forgot to ask you—did you hear that Corey and Adelle Hudson's daughter is going to be on one of those talent shows on television?"

"No, I hadn't heard! How exciting!"

Maggie proceeded to tell Viola all about how Marla Hudson had auditioned for the show and won a spot. She glanced at Lester as she talked. He seemed interested in the news. The story she'd given him about why Lee was in town seemed to have satisfied him, because he never brought it up again during the rest of her visit.

It wasn't until she was a few blocks from the Lewis house forty-five minutes later that it occurred to her that she had confirmed that Lee had come in the night before. If Patrick Smith heard that there had been someone else in the house when he came looking for his wife, would that make him suspicious? Maybe not, she decided. Other than denying Lydia was there, she hadn't said who was or wasn't in the house. She was probably worrying about nothing. Still . . . well, she hoped that Lester kept his mouth shut down at the station.

Chapter Twenty-Nine

It took all the willpower she had to drag herself out of bed the following morning. It had been another restless night. No matter how hard she tried, she could not put Seth out of her mind. She alternated between chastising herself for falling for a man she didn't know to remembering how good and how right it had felt to make love with him. She supposed she'd get over it eventually, but she suspected she'd be thrown into his proximity for some time to come. Her years as a reporter had taught her how criminal cases were handled. If—no, *when* Patrick Smith was arrested, there would be a trial, but before the trial, there would be months, maybe years, of preparation. She knew she would be asked to go over her role in the affair many times. Lydia Smith had thrust that role upon her when she'd sat down next to her at the Garden Club meeting. Because they would both be witnesses in the case, she was likely to see Seth again.

She dragged herself into the shower, pushing him from her thoughts. That was a worry for later. For now, she needed to get fully awake and ready for church. Her grandmother didn't ask many things of her, but regular church attendance was one of them. As far as Dora Jacobs was concerned, fever, diarrhea, and puking were the only excuses for not going to church.

Breakfast was a quiet affair. The three of them ate their sausage and pancakes with barely a word exchanged. Dora and Everett looked as tired as Maggie felt, and she knew their sleep had been disturbed by concerns for their son's safety. And maybe for their own and hers, she suddenly realized. Maybe she wasn't the only one who was afraid that Patrick Smith might make a return visit to their home. When her grandfather suggested they have Sunday dinner out and her grandmother jumped at the chance, Maggie knew she had guessed right. Dora Jacobs enjoyed cooking a big meal on Sundays and usually sneered at the idea of going to a crowded restaurant to eat food that wasn't as good as her own. The fact that she accepted so eagerly told Maggie that she felt safer in a crowd.

A rush of un-Christian-like hatred for Patrick Smith surged through Maggie. It was bad enough that he helped terrorists and beat his wife, but scaring an old lady she loved so badly that she didn't feel safe in her own home—well, Maggie was going to have to pray for a lot of forgiveness for the thoughts she had about what she'd like to do to him for that!

After the service was over, it took them longer than usual to get away from the church. The nice weather had brought a good turnout, which resulted in a lot of socializing with people they hadn't seen in a while. Everett finally managed to pry his wife loose from her Sunday gossiping and steered his two "girls," as he liked to call them, to the car. As Maggie opened the rear door, she noticed movement in a car parked directly across the lot from them. The sun was glinting off the windshield of the silver sedan so she couldn't see the face of the person in the driver's seat. She couldn't tell if it was a man or a woman. Was he—or she—watching them, she wondered? Maybe Patrick Smith had tasked one of his people to follow them.

No, she thought as she watched their fellow churchgoers making their way to the parking lot. She was being silly. The person in the car was likely there to pick someone up from church. She was letting paranoia get the better of her. It was too soon for Smith to be sure Lydia wasn't where Maggie had said she was, and when he was sure, it wouldn't be hard for him to find her. There was no reason for him to have them tailed. She'd been watching too many bad TV shows.

***

They drove to Caney's Corner, a town ten miles from Vichy. Although small, the town had a plethora of interesting shops, charming bed and breakfast inns, and good restaurants. They'd wisely made antiques and crafts the town business, which attracted day-shoppers from Indianapolis and Cincinnati, as well as tourists passing through on their way to other better known destinations. On the way, the three of them discussed their dining options and decided on Hyde's, a homey restaurant known for a delicious Sunday brunch buffet.

The lot was already crowded when they arrived, but Everett managed to find a spot at the far end, three spaces down from the fence that separated the lot from the neighborhood behind it. He offered to drop Maggie and her grandmother at the door, but they declined. It was nice enough to walk. Besides, Maggie felt that it was better if they all stayed together. The paranoia again, she thought, vowing to start watching more sitcoms than crime shows.

They had a fifteen-minute wait for a table, but spent it in conversation with several people they knew. While they were waiting, Maggie glanced out the large plate glass window in the front of the restaurant and saw a silver sedan cruise by slowly. Although she couldn't make out his features, she could see it was a man behind the wheel. He was alone in the car and he was looking toward the restaurant. She fought a sudden urge to drop to the floor and out of sight. There were a lot of silver sedans in the world. It probably wasn't even the same one she'd seen at the church. Just because the vehicle was moving slowly and the driver was looking toward the restaurant didn't mean anything. He was probably trying to decide if the place was too crowded to get a meal. Still, Maggie kept a watch on the street until their name was called. The sedan never returned.

The three of them stuffed themselves at the buffet. Dora opined that Hyde's piecrust left something to be desired. Maggie thought the pie was every bit as good as her grandmother's, but there was no way she was going to tell her that. Maggie tried to pay for the meal, but her grandfather insisted it was his treat. They spoke to more people they knew on their way to the front door, but Maggie's attention kept returning to the window. As they exited, she looked around, but there was no silver sedan that she could see—well, that wasn't entirely true. There were several in the lot, but all were empty, their owners inside packing on the calories. She would have worried that the man she had seen had followed them inside, but she hadn't seen anyone eating alone. She was positive about that, because she had looked, unable to shake the feeling that they were being followed even though she knew it was silly.

She began to relax as they approached their car. It was a beautiful day and she'd just enjoyed a great meal with her family. She had no reason to be worried. Not yet, anyway. The coming week might be a different matter entirely, but this was now and they were safe. As they approached the car, Everett hit the remote twice to unlock the doors. Maggie opened the front passenger door for her grandmother, and as she waited for her to get settled in the seat, she looked over the car's roof at the neighborhood on the other side of the fence. A silver sedan was parked on the opposite side of the street from the fence. A sole occupant, a male, sat behind the wheel.

Chapter Thirty

Lack of sleep was starting to wear Maggie down. Between worrying about the man in the silver sedan and thinking about how good Seth had sounded on the phone, falling asleep Sunday night had become an exercise in futility. Exhaustion finally knocked her out around one and she slept soundly until her alarm went off at six-thirty, but five-and-a-half hours of sleep after two nights of not enough shuteye wasn't enough. She went mining in her bathroom junk drawer and found a cover-up stick among the discarded lipsticks and hairbands. While it didn't cover the dark shadows under her eyes completely, it helped. That was about the best she could do.

As she dressed, she thought about the day before. She had watched for the silver sedan all the way home, turning frequently to peer out the back window to see if it was following them. Trouble was, after-church traffic was heavy, and she couldn't see more than two cars behind them. A couple of times she caught her grandfather looking at her in the rearview mirror, but he didn't say anything. She hadn't thought her grandmother was aware of what she was doing, but just as they entered the outskirts of Vichy, Dora shifted around in her seat.

"What is the matter with you?" she said. "You've been squirming back there ever since we left the restaurant. Should we stop somewhere with a bathroom?"

Her grandmother apparently thought something she'd eaten had gone straight south. Better she think that, Maggie thought, than that I think someone is following us.

"I can wait till I get home," she said.

"Well, step on it, Everett," Dora said, chuckling. "We don't want a mess in the car."

Her grandfather caught her eye in the mirror. She saw a small smile on his lips and suspected he was grateful she hadn't voiced her concerns to her grandmother.

When they reached the house, Maggie went inside and headed for her room. Once there, she pulled her cell from her purse and punched in the number on the card Lee had given her. Maybe she was being paranoid, maybe not. She needed to let Lee know that there might be a problem. The phone rang four times, and just as she was expecting it to roll to voice mail, she heard Seth answer.

"Hello?" he said.

She tried to speak, but found herself tongue-tied. What was he doing answering Lee's phone? Or was this number to an office phone? God, he sounded good. A mixture of emotions ran through her—warmth at the sound of his voice, hurt at the memory of his rejection, sadness that she had found someone she knew she could love, but who belonged to someone else.

"Hello?" he said again and she disconnected.

She sat for several minutes staring at the phone. She should have told him about the car. She had done a stupid thing letting her emotions get in the way of her good sense—a common character flaw with her. She could just call him back and tell him she'd gotten a lousy connection the first time. Or maybe if she waited a few minutes, then tried again, Lee would pick up. Yes, that was the better choice, she decided. If Seth answered, she would go ahead and talk to him, but if she were lucky, she wouldn't have to.

She went back downstairs to let Dora know she was okay and that she was going to take a nap. Her grandfather was on the front porch with the Sunday paper. She wondered if she should tell him about the silver sedan, but decided not to worry him. He'd seen her looking out the window, but he didn't know she'd been looking for a specific vehicle. No sense upsetting him yet. Patrick Smith's man—if that's who had been behind the wheel of the sedan—wasn't likely to storm the house in the middle of the day.

Back upstairs, she exchanged the dress she'd worn to church for a loose pair of light sweatpants and a baggy tee. She stretched out on the bed, doubtful she would be able to fall asleep. When she woke, it was to the sound of her phone ringing and to surprise that the clock on her nightstand showed she'd slept the afternoon away.

"Supper time, sleepyhead," her grandmother said when she answered. "Come on down."

She ran a wet washcloth over her face to try to wake up and headed downstairs. Dora had fixed soup and ham sandwiches for a light dinner. As Maggie ate, she thought about the car and the call to her uncle. Now that she'd rested, she began to see her suspicions of the driver of the sedan as silly, a paranoia probably brought on by fatigue. There were probably hundreds of silver sedans in the area. Just because she'd spotted two or three—or even the same one three times—didn't mean they had been followed. She was glad she hadn't told Seth her suspicions. He would see them as ridiculous and probably suspect she was calling just to talk to him. She decided not to call back.

Now as she tried to make herself presentable for work, she wondered if she had made the right decision. Still, no one had invaded them during the night, so wasn't that proof she had imagined the threat? Then again, maybe Patrick Smith had someone keeping an eye on them until he could verify whether or not Lydia was where Maggie had told him she was. She decided she would take her grandfather aside before she left for work and tell him about the car. Maybe it was nothing, but it would still be a good idea to give him a heads up so he could keep a watch on traffic passing the house during the day.

At dinner the night before, they had agreed to leave after she got home from work. She wished they could simply pack the car and leave now. She hadn't decided yet what to tell Jack when she told him she was taking a few days off. She didn't think it would be a problem, but she felt she owed it to him to tell him in person. She just hoped they weren't sticking around longer than was safe.

After breakfast, she motioned to her grandfather to come out on the front porch. Once there, she quickly told him about the car.

"It's probably nothing," she said. "I don't even know if the car at the restaurant was the same one I saw at the church. That's why I didn't call Lee. But I decided this morning that I should at least tell you."

"Glad you did, honey. I'll keep an eye out today."

"Good." Maggie felt better and decided her decision to tell her grandfather had been the right one. "I'll try to get off early. I'll call once I know what time I'm getting home."

"We'll get things ready to go and come by and pick you up."

"Great! In that case, I'll leave the car and walk in. I need the exercise anyway."

She opened the door and called to her grandmother that she was heading in to the office. Setting off down the street, she put worries about silver cars, abusive husbands, and sexy FBI agents out of her mind, forcing herself to concentrate instead on what she needed to do at work to prepare for being off several days. Immersed in thought, she didn't notice the van pull up alongside her until it was too late.

Chapter Thirty-One

"Is Lee Jacobs there?"

The man on the other end of the call that had come in to Lee's desk didn't bother to say hello when Seth answered. Seth recognized the voice of Everett Jacobs and he didn't like his panicked tone. Something had happened and it wasn't good. Was it Maggie?

"It's Seth Brady, Dr. Jacobs. Lee's at the safe house with Mrs. Smith. What's wrong?"

"It's Maggie," Everett said and Seth's heart felt like it climbed into his throat. He swallowed hard.

"What's happened?" he asked, dreading the answer.

"She's disappeared," Everett said. "She left for work over an hour ago, but her boss just called to see why she hadn't come in."

"Could she just have stopped somewhere along the way?" Seth knew he was grasping at straws, but he couldn't help himself.

"No. She wouldn't do that. She always goes straight in."

"Have you called the local police yet? They can keep a lookout for her car."

"She didn't drive in today. She walked. We decided yesterday that we'd go out of town for a few days until all this foolishness was settled. Dora and I were going to get everything packed and pick her up at her office this afternoon."

Seth ran his free hand through his hair, causing it to stand up in spikes. What to do? Where to start? Smith's house? Would he be dumb enough to take her there? He doubted that. After his nocturnal visit to the Jacobs' home, Smith would know it was the first place anyone would look for her. So where? One of his warehouses? More likely, but which one? They knew of a lot, but the task force had suspected there were others they didn't know about.

"She should have called you about the silver sedan," Everett mumbled. "I should have told her to do it before she left this morning."

"Silver sedan?"

Everett told him about the car Maggie had spotted the day before.

"She thought she was just being paranoid," Everett said. "She wasn't even sure it was the same car every time."

The hang-up, Seth thought. He'd had a funny feeling that the hang-up of the day before had been Maggie, but he'd thought the call was of a personal nature. He should have called her back. If he had, he felt sure she would have talked to him. And if she'd told him about the car, he would have been on his way to Vichy before she'd had a chance to say goodbye. Now Smith had her. He would force her to tell him everything. She was in danger and it was all his fault for leading Smith to her in the first place.

"We're on our way," he said now.

"Should I call the police?" Everett asked.

Seth hesitated a moment, then said, "Yes. Go ahead and call them, but be careful what you say. Just tell them Maggie left the house for work, but hasn't shown up. Ask if there have been any traffic accidents or if they've seen her. If they haven't—and I don't expect they will have—just pass it off. Just say she's probably stopped off somewhere for a story that her boss had forgotten about."

"What's he saying?" It was Dora in the background. Seth could hear the fear in her voice.

"They're coming," Everett told his wife, then to Seth, "Hurry. Please."

Seth assured him they would. He hung up and ran out the door, ignoring the surprised looks of the other agents in the room. He'd call Lee from the road.

***

The two men who had pulled her off the street and into the van had thrown a scarf around her eyes as soon as the door slid shut. She'd only gotten a glimpse of one of them, a short stocky man with thinning hair and acne-pitted skin. She'd never seen him before. Then the scarf blocked her vision. Her wrists were pulled together. She felt cold metal encircle them and heard a ratcheting sound that she knew were handcuffs being tightened, then she was pushed down onto the floor. She struggled to sit up and was shoved roughly back down.

"Stay there," a voice growled. She felt a heavy foot settle on her midsection and she stopped struggling.

A few minutes into the drive, she heard the radio come on. The driver or someone in the front passenger seat scrolled through the stations until he found a country music station. A song was just ending.

"That's Brad Paisley and he's got *Moonshine in the Trunk*," the DJ said. "And we've got a winner. Cheryl

Jenkins, you're our fifth caller. Lucky lady, you've won yourself a dinner for four at Red Lobster!"

After the winner squealed her pleasure at being the fifth caller, the DJ gave the time and broke for the eight o'clock news. Maggie had known it was close to eight. She hoped her kidnappers would continue to play the radio until they arrived at their destination. It might give her some idea of how far away from town they were taking her. Not that it would do her much good, she thought. With a blindfold over her eyes, she didn't even know which direction they were going. They could drive her around for a couple of hours and end up a block from where they started. Still, she kept her attention focused on the radio and on the feel of the pavement. She might be fooling herself into thinking she could figure out where they ended up when they got there, but it gave her a feeling of being in control. Illusory, maybe, but it made her feel a little better.

The nine o'clock news came and went. Not long after, the van slowed and made a right turn. Maggie heard the sound of gravel crunching under the van's wheels, then it made a left turn and the crunching stopped as the vehicle came to a rest on pavement. The driver turned the engine off and she heard two front doors open. A second later, she heard the sound of the side door sliding open and a hand grasped her upper right arm roughly.

"Get up," a man ordered.

He pulled as she sat up and scooted toward the light she could see through the blindfold. She felt her heels slide off the edge of the carpeted van floor and onto the step, then off that into air. When she hesitated, the man yanked her forward and her feet touched pavement. She was stiff from having lain in the same position for over an hour, and she stumbled as he pulled her to her feet.

"Come on," he ordered. "Stop screwing around."

"I'm not!" She felt herself growing angry. They'd kidnapped her, but they were acting like she was inconveniencing them! "My legs are stiff."

The man didn't reply as he pulled her forward. When she tripped over her own feet, she heard him curse, but he steadied her and kept her from falling. She felt her muscles loosen as she took a few more steps. They walked only a short distance, then a door opened and she was escorted out of the light and into what felt like a cavernous space. It was cool and sounds echoed. A warehouse, maybe? That would fit with Patrick Smith's business.

"Stairs," the man holding her arm said, just as she felt the front of her ankle strike metal.

She lifted her foot and placed it cautiously on the bottom step. The step felt like it was a metal grid, not a solid surface. The man moved to one side and behind her, still holding onto her upper arm. He let her take her time rather than push her and for that she was grateful. Not so grateful that she didn't think about turning and kicking him down the stairs, but considering she was cuffed and blindfolded and he wasn't alone, she decided that wouldn't be the wisest course of action.

At the top of the stairs, he turned her to the right. She moved along what felt like an extension of the metal grid that formed the steps. Maggie had seen this type of stairs and walkways in warehouses before. She'd once covered a story in Denver that had taken her into such a warehouse and had learned the hard way never to wear heels when walking on a metal grid. Thankfully, she'd been wearing athletic shoes for her walk to work, planning on changing into the low-heeled shoes she kept in her bottom desk drawer, so she had no trouble keeping her footing even while blindfolded.

"Stop," her human guide dog said.

He leaned past her and she heard a door being opened before he pushed her on through. The space felt enclosed, not open like the one they had just traveled through. An office, she thought. She felt hands at the back of her head. The blindfold was suddenly gone and she saw she had been right about being in an office. It was a utilitarian and windowless room with a pressed wood and metal desk, a scratched wooden desk chair, two metal and vinyl chairs, and a four-drawer gray metal file cabinet. A pin-up calendar hung on the wall, but someone had forgotten to turn the page to the current month. Two doors broke up the cheaply paneled walls—one on the wall to the left of the door through which she had entered, the other on the right wall. The door on the right was closed, but the one on the left stood ajar a few inches. Through the gap, Maggie could see the edge of a toilet. Other than herself and the stocky man she had seen in the van, the room was empty.

"Where am I?" She didn't expect an answer, but asked the question anyway.

The stocky man huffed as if he recognized her question as the ridiculous utterance it was. He turned to leave.

"Wait," she said. "Please—can't you take these off?"

She turned and wiggled the handcuffs at him.

"Nope." He turned back to the door.

"I need to use the bathroom." She injected a pleading note into her voice. "I can't very well do that with my hands behind my back. Please—I mean, where am I going to go?"

The man hesitated a second, then said, "Turn around."

She obeyed and felt him removing the cuffs. She was a little surprised that her lie about needing to use the bathroom had worked to free her hands. The feeling of satisfaction at having conned the man quickly vanished as he cuffed her in front.

Without speaking, the man turned and left the room. She heard the door's lock engage, but went to it anyway and tried the knob. She was locked in.

She checked the closed door on the right, but it was only an empty closet. The small lavatory had only a toilet and basin. Suddenly her lie became real and she felt the need to pee. She pulled the door shut and pushed the button in the knob to lock it even though she knew the cheap lock provided no protection. Her abductors might grant her privacy while she used the toilet, but they wouldn't let her lock herself in to get away from them. Not that there was anywhere to go in the windowless room. She managed to take care of business with her hands together, flushed, washed her hands as best she could, and stepped out of the room, stopping in surprise when she saw Patrick Smith seated behind the desk.

"We meet again, Ms. Fields." He was smiling as if they were two friends who had just happened to run into one another. "And this time, you're going to tell me where you've hidden my wife."

He paused for a second and the smile disappeared from his face.

"That is, after you tell me how much your uncle and his FBI friends know about me."

Chapter Thirty-Two

The front door of the Jacobs house opened as Seth turned the car into the drive. Everett Jacobs stepped onto the porch, his wife behind him. Dora's eyes were red and she clutched a handful of tissues that were sodden with tears. Everett's face was pale. They both looked like they had aged ten years since Seth had last seen them, and he knew that transformation had taken place in the last couple of hours.

"I called the police like you said," Everett said to Seth as the two men hurried up the porch steps. "There's been no traffic accidents in town since yesterday. I called the ambulatory clinic, too, just in case, but Maggie hasn't come in."

Until he heard the words, Seth hadn't realized how much he'd hoped that Maggie had just had an accident—a minor one, of course. He wouldn't want her involved in anything serious. But he'd have much preferred finding out that she had been in a minor pedestrian accident than taken by Patrick Smith. For that's what he was now certain had happened.

Seth had called Lee from the car. Lee had been waiting a few doors down from the safe house and jumped in before the car rolled to a stop. Seth broke every speed limit between Indianapolis and Vichy, while Lee called Mike. Earl Samuels, the Special Agent in Charge, was in Washington for a high-level meeting, and thankfully, unreachable. As the senior agent in the office, Mike had the authority to make decisions when the SAC wasn't available. When Lee explained the situation, Mike assured him he would have agents checking every warehouse and residence known to Smith for any unusual activity and especially for any women matching Maggie's description.

Seth knew there weren't enough agents already read in on the Smith case to check all the possible locations simultaneously. Mike would have to bring in agents they weren't sure they could trust. While Mike had the authority to make decisions in the SAC's absence, it was generally understood that anything of major importance needed to be run by Samuels. Mike would probably be in hot water when the SAC learned that Mike had let everyone in the office know they were investigating Patrick Smith, but Mike had enough years in to retire. He'd be okay.

Was one of their agents in Smith's employ? Possibly, but there wasn't anything to be done about it. They had to check every place Smith might have taken Maggie, and they couldn't do that without help. An even bigger problem than Smith having one of their agents in his pocket was that they weren't sure they knew the extent of his holdings. He might have taken Maggie to one of his buildings they didn't know about.

"We'll find her, Ma." Lee was holding his mother close. He looked at Seth as he spoke, his desperate gaze making it clear that he wasn't convinced of his own words. "We've got agents checking all of Smith's places. If he's got her, we'll find her."

From your mouth to God's ears, Seth thought. He had never felt so helpless in his life. He should never have left her here alone. They had been wrong to assume Smith would spend a few days searching

Cincinnati for Lydia before realizing Maggie had lied. Maybe he hadn't been as convinced as he'd seemed by her story and had just been waiting for the right opportunity to grab her. Why hadn't he and Lee moved Maggie, Everett, and Dora to a safe house like they had Lydia?

He shook his head, trying to put the self-recriminations aside. There would be plenty of time for that later. He knew that from the years of self-recrimination he'd put himself through after Diane. He needed to concentrate on finding Maggie before it was too late, not waste his mental energy on berating himself for leaving the woman he loved in danger. Pitiful, he thought. Now you admit to yourself you love this woman, but you didn't have the courage to admit it to her when you had the chance.

"Lee," he said now. "I think we need to go public with this. We need to involve the local, county, and state cops."

Lee opened his mouth, Seth assumed to object.

"I know what you're going to say," Seth continued. "Smith is bound to have someone on those departments in his employ, but if he's taken Maggie, the cat's out of the bag anyway. He might not know about us, but he'll find out soon enough."

Because he'll torture it out of Maggie was the unspoken subtext in what he said. He saw Everett's eyes widen and knew he'd understood the meaning. Dora did not seem to have picked up on it, and for that, Seth was grateful.

"I wasn't going to object," Lee said. "You're right. The SAC might not like it, but if we go ahead and do it before he has a chance to nix the idea, he won't be able to do anything about it."

Samuels had been adamant about keeping the Smith operation quiet from most of his agents, but especially from local police. He wanted to find the location of the nuclear pits before moving on Smith himself, but they were no closer to pinpointing the location of the pits than they had been at the start of the operation. Speaking of nuclear, Seth knew that's what Samuels would go if he and Lee went to the police. Might be the answer to my dilemma, Seth thought. I might not have to decide between the woman I love and the job I love. That decision might be made for me.

Suddenly he realized that was okay. The job wasn't what mattered the most anymore. Maggie was. He prayed he'd have the chance to tell her that.

Chapter Thirty-Three

"FBI?" Maggie knew her surprise showed on her face. She could only hope that Smith would interpret it as the surprise of someone who didn't know what he was talking about.

He chuckled, but there was no humor in it.

"Don't waste my time, Ms. Fields. I'm not in the mood for it. My wife is gone, thanks to you and your family. Now I discover that your uncle is a fed and he's in town. I don't think that's a coincidence, do you?"

"I don't know what you're talking about." Maggie tried to add confusion to the expression of surprise on her face. Time to try to match the Oscar-winning performance of the other night. "My uncle did stop by to visit, but FBI? Where in heaven's name did you get that idea? And for that matter, why would you be concerned about the FBI? The last I heard, they don't arrest men who abuse their wives."

Patrick Smith's face darkened and he leaned forward as if about to get out of his chair. Guess he doesn't like being accused of abuse, Maggie thought.

"I don't abuse my wife," he said through gritted teeth, confirming her thought. "And I don't like being lied to."

"I'm only repeating what your wife told me," Maggie said, ignoring the comment about lying. "I don't know what's true and what isn't. But having your thugs abduct me tends to lend credence to what she says."

"We'll discuss where my wife is later." Smith settled back in his chair, but his expression didn't change. Lydia was a sore spot with him. Maggie didn't know whether that was a good thing or a bad thing. She might be able to use it to distract him from Lee and Seth, but if his emotions got the better of him, she might end up regretting it.

"I know Lee Jacobs is an agent with the FBI," Smith said. "And I can only assume he's in town because of me. What I want to know is, why?"

"You've got to be kidding!" Maggie forced out a laugh. "My uncle an FBI agent? My uncle is a no-good son-of-a-bitch who treats his family like crap! He calls Gran and Gramps every once in a blue moon and visits even less than that. Where did you ever get the idea that he's a fed?"

Maggie thought she saw a fleeting look of doubt cross Smith's face. Maybe she was being convincing—it was easy enough to remember the resentment she had felt for Lee all these years and use it to her advantage. It might not be enough to convince Patrick Smith that Lee wasn't a fed, but it might be enough to convince him that she didn't know anything about it. Would that help her? Or would he decide that she was no use to him? After having his men grab her off the street, he could hardly let her go.

As she stared at him staring back at her, she wondered how he had gotten his information. Neither she nor her grandparents had told anyone Lee was in town. Lester had seen Lee with her grandfather Saturday morning, so it was not out of the realm of possibility that others had seen him as well. If Patrick Smith had spies everywhere as Lydia, Seth, and Lee all believed, then one of them could easily have spotted Lee driving through town and reported it to Smith. But why? Why would anyone in Vichy think Lee was anything more than the prodigal son returning home for a rare visit? Who would know he was an FBI agent when she herself hadn't known until a few days ago?

"Perhaps your family has kept you in the dark about your uncle's affiliations." Patrick Smith leaned back in his desk chair and looked at her appraisingly. "Then again, you were very convincing the other night about my wife and I know you lied about that."

"I did not!" Maggie drew herself up and tried to look indignant. It wasn't easy to look indignant, she found, when your heart was about to beat out of your chest. "I took Lydia to Cincinnati, just like I said. Where she went from there, I have no idea."

"Well, you see, here's the problem. I've found no evidence of my wife ever having made it to Cincinnati."

"It's a big city."

"Not that big." He smiled. "I learned a long time ago, Ms. Fields, that it pays to have eyes everywhere. I'd know if my wife had checked into any hotels or motels other than fleabags. I know her well enough to know she wouldn't stay in those, not even to hide from me, and I know she hasn't taken a plane, train, bus, or rental car out of town."

"Maybe she met someone and they took her some place else."

Again, the look of doubt crossed Smith's face. He apparently hadn't thought of that. He shook his head.

"No," he said. "No one would be foolish enough to do something like that."

Maggie could tell what he was thinking—no one who knew him would be foolish enough to do something like that. But there was no way for him to be sure that Lydia hadn't met someone after she got to Cincinnati, someone who didn't know that she was fleeing an abusive husband with ties to criminals and terrorists.

"Well, I don't know anything about where she is now," Maggie said. "And I can assure you, my uncle is not an FBI agent. Why you think he is and why you think he's after you—well, I don't *want* to know anything about that! I just want to go to work. I'm already late, so I'd appreciate it if you could get your men to give me a ride back to town."

Patrick Smith's face burst into a huge grin. He started chuckling.

"You are really something, Ms. Fields! You've got spirit, I'll say that. Or you're dumb as a rock. I'm not sure which it is."

Me, either, Maggie thought.

"But one thing I am sure of," he said, his grin fading, "is that you're not going into work or anywhere else today."

Chapter Thirty-Four

"We need to see Lester."

The woman at the window of the police department's front desk looked up from the papers spread before her, no doubt preparing to ask what Everett's request was in reference to. One look at his appearance and the papers were forgotten.

"Dr. Jacobs? Is there something wrong?" The name tag on her shirt read "Cindy Barker."

Behind her, Seth saw a young male dispatcher working the radio. Through a windowed door in the back of the communications room, he could see a room with desks—probably where the detectives and maybe the clerical staff sat. The department was too small to have many detectives, so he doubted all the desks were for them.

"My niece is missing," Everett said. "I called earlier to see if she had been in an accident."

"Yes, you spoke to me," Cindy said. She motioned to a door to the left of the window. "Come on back."

As they moved toward the door, there was a loud buzz. Lee had moved ahead of his father and pulled the door open before the buzzer stopped. They passed through it into a small hall leading to the room where Seth had seen the desks. Cindy was just stepping out of the door to the communications room as they entered the larger room.

"The Chief's not here at the moment," she said.

She motioned to a desk. The chair behind it was empty and there was one chrome and vinyl chair sitting by its side. She pulled two more from the desk next to it.

"Have a seat," she said. "I'll call Bill to come in and talk to you."

She turned back to the communications room.

"Bill Reynolds is a detective," Everett explained. "He's a good fellow. He'll find Maggie?"

The last sounded like a question and he looked at his son as if begging for reassurance. Lee nodded and patted his father on the shoulder.

Seth glanced at his watch as he sat down, and again when a burly man with thinning blonde hair entered through a rear door. Only five minutes had passed, but Seth felt as if he'd been sitting there five years—years during which he could have been out searching for Maggie. He suddenly wished he weren't in law enforcement. He had seen too much and knew the endings to stories of disappearances didn't always end happily. If he were just a Joe Citizen, he could believe in miracles.

"Everett." Bill Reynolds shook Everett's hand, then turned to Lee. "Good to see you, Lee. Didn't know you were in town."

They shook and Lee introduced Seth.

"So tell me," Bill said, pulling off his suit jacket and slinging it onto the back of his chair before he sat down. He retrieved a small notebook and a pen from his shirt pocket.

The three of them filled the detective in on the sequence of events. Seth saw the detective's eyes widen when Lee showed him his FBI credentials, but he didn't interrupt. Lee and Seth had talked on the way to the station and decided it wasn't necessary to mention the nuclear pits. There was little chance something like that could be kept quiet once the local police knew. They would be duty-bound to do whatever they could to protect their citizens and would likely institute emergency measures up to and including evacuating the town. If that happened, the situation could rapidly spiral out of control. So all they told Reynolds was that they were investigating Patrick Smith for his ties to organized crime. They also told him about the domestic situation that Maggie had gotten herself into when she helped Lydia Smith.

"Oh, boy," Reynolds said when they finished. "Sounds like Smith is one crazy jealous fool. Domestics are the worst."

Lee nodded. He started to say something, but before he could, Cindy stepped forward. She had apparently been standing in the doorway to the communication room listening as they'd told the detective their story. She had an odd look on her face—a mix, Seth decided, of worry and confusion and something else? Maybe dread?

"Bill," she said. "Have you talked to Lester?"

"Not since this morning when I got here," Bill said. "Why?"

"I took a call this morning," Cindy said. "A little after eight. It was a man who lives over on Culver Street next to the playground. He said he'd seen a woman being forced into a blue panel van a few minutes before he called."

She swallowed hard.

"She said the woman had red hair."

"What?" Bill stood up, knocking his chair back a couple of feet in his haste. "How come that wasn't put out on the air?"

"Lester said not to," Cindy said. "He said he knew who it was and it was nothing. Said some local kids were making a video about self-defense or something for a college class they were taking. He said he'd go talk to them. I thought it seemed kind of funny, but he's the chief. You know? I figured he knew what he was talking about."

She looked at Everett.

"I'm so sorry. When you called an hour later, I didn't think to put it together. I mean, I'd pretty much forgotten the whole thing with the van and the college kids. You don't think . . . But then, why would the chief . . . ?"

Seth stood up. His voice was hard as he spoke. "Call Chief Lewis on the radio. Now."

Cindy shrank back from him and looked at Reynolds. The detective nodded.

"Okay. What do you want me to tell him when he answers?"

"Tell him I need to see him at the station," Reynolds said.

Cindy nodded and stepped back through the door into the communications room. A second later, they heard her voice going out over the air calling the chief. They waited, then heard her call again. From the look on the faces of the men standing next to him, Seth saw that none of them were surprised when the chief didn't answer.

Chapter Thirty-Five

"You can't just hold me here against my will!"

"Oh? And why is that?"

Patrick Smith was looking at her the way a father looks at a child protesting a grounding. It was the look of someone who knows he's in control of the situation and anyone who thinks otherwise is a fool. Maggie wanted to lash out at him and tell him it was only a matter of time before Lee, Seth, and the might of the United States government landed on him with full force and shipped him off to Guantanamo or wherever terrorists were being sent these days. Instead, she forced herself to sputter and stammer and act like a woman who didn't know how much trouble she was really in.

"Well . . . I mean . . . well, you just can't! It's kidnapping, that's what it is!"

"You know, Ms. Fields, I really am beginning to believe you're nothing more than a dumb broad." He chuckled, but there was no humor in it. "At least that explains why you were dumb enough to help my wife."

Maybe I should go into acting, Maggie thought—if I can live long enough to audition for my first part.

Smith stood up and came around the desk. As he came toward her, she shrank back in her chair. The fear she knew was on her face was not part of her act. He'd apparently decided she was telling the truth about not knowing Lydia's whereabouts and not knowing anything about her uncle's FBI connections. If she knew nothing, there was no reason to keep her prisoner, but he couldn't let her go. His only alternative was to kill her. She tried to think of something she could say that could keep her alive a little longer, but nothing came to mind. If she admitted she hadn't taken Lydia to Cincinnati or admitted she knew her uncle was an FBI agent, once he got that information from her, it would be the same scenario. No reason to keep her around.

No, she thought. I'm going to die either way, but I can at least do it on my terms. I'm not telling him a damn thing!

"Get up!" He took her by the arm and pulled her roughly from the chair.

"What are you doing?" She tried to pull away from him, but couldn't break his grasp.

"Shut up."

He pulled her toward the door and opened it. A man she hadn't seen before stood outside it. He wasn't much taller than she was, but he was built like a fireplug. He wore a short-sleeve tee, displaying bulging muscles that she doubted could be gotten from lifting weights alone. She wondered what his steroid bill was a month.

"Take our 'guest' downstairs and lock her up." Smith shoved her at the man.

The fireplug took hold of her upper arm, his fingers digging into her pitiful excuse for biceps.

"Ouch!" she said, pulling back. "You're hurting me!"

Instead of easing up, he grinned and pressed his fingers into her even harder. She looked away from him, her skin crawling from the sadistic glee she saw there. She knew if she continued to protest, he'd only hurt her more, so she tried to ignore the pain in her arm.

"You don't want me to take care of her?"

Maggie stole a look at the man. He was speaking to Smith and the look on his face was almost that of a child begging to be allowed to torture and kill the kitten he'd just found.

"Not yet," Smith said. "She might come in handy."

"Yeah. All right."

The man's disappointment showed. He turned back to her, glaring, and yanked her along as he headed toward the stairs. She had been right—Smith's office opened off a walkway overlooking the floor of the warehouse. The walkway and the stairs leading down were a metal grid. She could see three closed doors further down the walkway from Smith's office, which was to the left of the stairs at the end.

Because the stairs were too narrow for them to walk side-by-side, Smith's thug started down ahead of her, his grip still tight on her left arm. She tried to steady herself and counteract his tugging by holding onto the railing with her cuffed right hand. On the third step from the top, she stumbled and fell into him.

"Watch it, bitch!" His fingers dug even deeper into her arm. Maggie knew she would have bruises where his fingers were, but bruises were the least of her worries.

Smith had just started back into his office when one of the closed doors further down the metal walkway opened.

"Hey, boss," a man called out. "We got a problem."

The man pulling Maggie down the steps stopped and they both turned to look at the man who had called out. It was the man who had taken Maggie from the van to the office. He had a cell phone in one hand and a worried look on his face. The grip on her arm loosened, and Maggie stole a glance at the man holding her. He had turned to look at the man who had called out, his back toward the bottom of the stairs, his attention momentarily on something other than her. It was now or never, she thought.

She gripped the right-hand railing hard with her hand, lifted her left foot, and kicked the man in the stomach as hard as she could. He had only been holding her, not the railing, and he instinctively grabbed for it as he began to fall. She felt herself being pulled down after him and hung onto the railing with all her strength. Finally she felt his grip leave her arm. He screamed like a girl as he started down the metal steps backward, still on his feet, but unable to stop his descent. Halfway down, he began to fall, his arms and legs flailing as he tried to regain his balance, but as he neared the bottom, he went backward. There was a sickening thud as his head hit the cement floor of the warehouse.

Maggie hadn't waited for his fall to be over before she started down after him. The men on the grid above must have been momentarily stunned at what had happened, because she was two-thirds of the way to the bottom before she heard their shouts and the sound of their feet pounding down the stairs after her. She reached the bottom. There was a pool of blood spreading from the downed man's head. His pants leg had pulled up and she saw a gun in an ankle holster. She unsnapped the strap holding the gun in place, pulled it out, and whirled to point it at the two men who had just reached the bottom of the stairs.

"Get back!" she shouted as she backed toward the door.

Patrick Smith glowered at her. If looks could kill, she thought. She saw the stocky man behind him start to ease his right hand behind his back.

"Keep your hands where I can see them," she said, knowing he probably had a gun in his waistband. "Better yet, put them on top of your head."

He hesitated, then raised his hands and clasped them on top of his head. Patrick Smith kept his on the railings of the stairs.

"Give me the gun, Ms. Fields," he said. "Before you get hurt."

"You take another step toward me, it's not going to be me who gets hurt," she said.

She risked a quick glance behind her. The door was less than ten feet away. As she looked back, she saw Smith stepping quickly off the bottom step, while the stocky man's hands dropped from his head, the right one going behind his back. She pulled the trigger—and nothing happened. She pulled it again. A safety, she thought, it must have a safety and it must be on. The only thing she knew about guns was that you pointed them and pulled the trigger. This wasn't a good time to try to learn more. She threw the gun and saw the stocky man duck as it sailed by his head.

Time to run, she thought, turned and bolted for the door. As she pushed through it, she heard a shot ring out behind her.

Chapter Thirty-Six

The woman who opened the door was a contradiction. Her body was rail thin, her skin sagging on her face and dangling from the stick-figure arms that poked out of her short-sleeved blouse, and she had to support herself by leaning on a walker. Her eyes, however, were full of life. I'm not ready to shuffle off this mortal coil just yet, they seemed to say. I'm going to go out kicking and screaming.

"Viola," Bill Reynolds said. "Sorry to bother you. We're trying to find Lester, but he must have his radio and cell turned off or he's out of range. Is he here?"

"He was."

She hesitated and Seth realized her eyes were full of something besides life, and that something was concern. She stepped back and to the side. "Come in."

The four men, the woman and the walker crowded the small entrance foyer. To the right was the living room and Viola motioned them into it. They entered and stood awkwardly, trying to decide how best to approach the subject of the dying woman's husband being a dirty cop. She solved the problem for them.

"I know something's wrong," she said. "Lester has done something wrong and he's trying to make it right."

She looked at each of them, one at a time, and again Seth was surprised by the intensity of her gaze.

"He's a good man," she said. "He was only trying to help me."

She was leaning hard on the walker and Seth saw her arms begin to tremble. He stepped forward and took her arm gently.

"Here," he said. "You need to sit down."

"Before I fall down," she said and laughed. "Lester tells me that all the time."

Seth helped her to an upholstered chair that had arms and looked firm enough that she wouldn't sink into it and be unable to get up. Each of the men then took a seat—Everett and Lee on the couch, Bill on the matching loveseat. Seth took the remaining chair.

"Tell us," Bill said gently. "We want to help, Vi."

Viola took a deep breath and let it out slowly before she spoke.

"Lester came home a few hours ago," she said. "He was upset. He said we needed to pack some things, that we were going to California now."

She looked at Everett.

"I think he told you about the clinical trial out there."

Everett nodded.

"We weren't supposed to leave until the end of next week, but he said it had been moved up. At first, I believed him. I mean, it's not exactly a sure thing that I'll still be here at the end of next week, is it?"

She said it matter-of-factly. Seth marveled at the woman's poise in the face of her own death.

"But he just didn't look right," she said. "I know my husband. Something was wrong. I kept after him until he finally broke down and told me."

Her eyes started to fill with tears. She stopped talking for a moment and wiped at them with her fingers. Another deep breath and she continued.

"He's been taking money from someone—I don't know who. He did it for me. The medical bills have been piling up. We have insurance, but the co-pays and the deductibles are outragcous. And this trial—well, he doesn't want me flying commercial, because my immune system has been zapped by the chemo and he's afraid I'll catch something on a plane. So he arranged space on one of those private jets people can lease. I don't know how much it cost, but I know it's a lot. I thought he'd borrowed it from our home equity line-of-credit, but I'm not sure even that would be enough. So he was vulnerable when this—this—vulture approached him."

Viola looked angry now. Someone had taken advantage of the man she loved.

"Anyway, he said the man didn't want much from him. He just wanted to know any time someone showed interest in him or any time federal investigators showed up in town. Lester didn't have anything to tell him for the longest time, but he still got paid. Then this weekend, he saw you."

She looked at Lee.

"He saw you and Everett driving somewhere. He said he knew you were FBI. Are you?"

Lee nodded.

"I was surprised. I always wondered what you did. Tell the truth, I thought you were the black sheep of the family. I don't know how Lester knew that you were FBI, but he did. He did what he'd agreed to do and reported to the man."

Lee leaned against the back of the couch and ran his right hand through his hair.

"It's my fault," he said. "I told him a long time ago, right after I got accepted. I was bragging, I guess. I swore him to secrecy and forgot about it."

"Well, he never told me and I don't think he told anyone else. Until now. He said the man he'd been taking money from was more dangerous than he thought and that he'd done something that Lester hadn't expected."

She looked at each of them.

"He wouldn't tell me who, but he said someone was in danger. I told him we couldn't just leave town, that he needed to make it right. I thought he was going to the station to get the rest of the department to help him. But he didn't, did he? He's trying to make it right on his own."

Her voice broke and Seth saw a tear trickle down her cheek. She ignored it.

"Help him," she said. "Please. He shouldn't die before me."

She put her face in her hands and began to sob.

Chapter Thirty-Seven

Maggie stopped for a second to get her bearings. The warehouse seemed to be in the country. A wide empty paved area separated the building from the gate; beyond that she could see a gravel drive and open fields dotted here and there with trees. There was no way she could make it across the lot and out the gate before Smith and his man exited the warehouse. They would shoot her in the back and that would be the end of that.

The warehouse wasn't wide on this side—she guessed fifty yards at most. She had a chance to make it to either corner. She turned left and ran as hard as she could. It was awkward with both her hands in front of her, but she made it to the corner without losing her balance. The warehouse stretched out in front of her, its length five or more times its width. A smaller building sat about thirty yards from it; between them, two semi-trucks were parked, their engines silent. Behind her, she heard a door open.

"Damn it!" Smith sounded angry. "That way."

They must be splitting up, she thought. They knew she had to have gone around the building. One would go to the right, one to the left. She didn't have much time. She ran across the lot to the smaller building and tried the door. It was unlocked. She pulled it open and left it that way, then backtracked to one of the semis. Dropping to the pavement, she rolled under the trailer and scooted behind the front double axle. The tires would block her from the view of whoever ran around the building.

Within seconds, she heard running footsteps. A man's feet hurried past the truck and into the open door of the smaller building. She hoped and prayed it was filled with merchandise and cubbyholes that she could have hidden in. She needed the man inside searching for as long as possible. She waited a few seconds, but the feet didn't reappear. She slid out from under the truck. Hoisting herself up on the running board, she looked inside the cab for keys, but nothing dangled from the ignition. She quickly checked the other cab, but no keys there either.

What now? Try to make it to the gate and as far away as she could before they came after her? There was no cover for as far as she could see. Even if she had her hands free and could move faster, she'd never make it. But they wouldn't expect her to go back inside the building she had escaped from. While she hadn't seen a phone in Smith's office, there was bound to be one somewhere in the building. She could call Seth and he could trace the number. The FBI could do that, couldn't they? She felt the sting of tears as she thought of Seth. She didn't want to die before she could tell him how she felt about him. Even if he didn't want her, she wanted him to know. God, she wanted so badly to feel his arms around her again!

Enough, she thought, and shook her head. This isn't the time to go all girly-girl—not if you want to stay alive! She ran across the pavement, expecting to hear a shout behind her at any moment. When she got to the corner of the building, she stopped and peered around it. It was clear and the door she had exited was standing open. She covered the distance to it in seconds and ducked inside, leaving the door the way she'd found it.

The man she had kicked down the stairs lay where she'd left him. That told her two things—one, she had killed a man, and two, there must have only been two men with Smith. Otherwise, someone would have moved his body or at least joined in the chase. She wasn't sure yet how she felt about the first thing, but she was relieved about the second. That meant she only had to elude Smith and one of his employees long enough to either get away or be rescued. She'd been a fool to throw the gun she'd taken from the dead man. With only Smith and one other man to contend with, she might have had a chance to shoot her way out.

Yeah, right, she thought. This isn't a TV show. The last time I fired a gun was when I was twelve and shooting tin cans with Gramps's rifle. And I didn't hit many of those.

She knelt and quickly went through the man's pants pockets, trying to ignore the fact that she was searching a corpse. In the right one she found what she was looking for—a handcuff key. She cupped it in her hands and stood up.

She looked up the metal stairs. Should she go up and try to find a phone in one of the offices? From where she stood, it didn't look as if there were any way off that platform except down the stairs. When Smith and his man came back, she'd be trapped. She stepped to the side and peered under the platform into the dimly lit first floor of the warehouse. The area between the stairs and the door was clear, but beyond the stairs, crates were stacked halfway to the ceiling, with wide aisles on either side. She stepped over to where she could see down one of the aisles. It looked like a door at the far end, maybe more offices, and if she were lucky, a phone.

She crossed the concrete floor, and keeping close to the stacked crates, started down the aisle.

Chapter Thirty-Eight

"I'll get the info on Lester's car out to the patrol units," Bill said, reaching for his cell phone.

"Wait." Lee held up his hand. "Let's not do that just yet. We don't know if there are other officers on Smith's payroll."

Seth saw Viola wince when Lee said "other officers." Lee picked up on it, too. He looked like he wanted to say something to her, but instead turned back to Bill.

"Let's check Smith's house first," he said. "Unless Lester knows where Smith is, that's the most likely place he'd go."

Bill nodded.

"That makes sense," he said. "Okay. Dispatch knows we were trying to find Lester anyway—just not why. If he surfaces at the station or on the radio, Cindy will let me know."

"I'll call Dora to come sit with you," Everett said to Viola. "You shouldn't be here alone."

"I'm fine." Viola waved his concerns away with a flap of her hand. "Just find Lester."

"Nonsense," Everett said. "Dora needs to be with someone now anyway. It will help her as much as it helps you."

They hadn't told Viola that Maggie was missing and that someone had reported seeing a red-haired woman being abducted earlier in the day. The men looked at one another, the question in their gaze.

Everett gave his head a slight shake. They didn't have the time to break the news to her. Seth guessed he would explain it all to his wife when he called her from the car. It would be up to her whether or not she filled Viola in on the seriousness of what her husband was involved in. From what Seth had seen of Dora in the short time he'd known her, he had no doubt she could handle the assignment. She was tough—a lot like her granddaughter.

Maggie. Seth felt his heart lurch every time he thought of her. She was tough, but was she tough enough to survive until they could find her? He had no doubt they *would* find her. The question was, would it be in time? Would he ever get to hold her again and tell her he loved her? Or would they be too late?

No, he thought, refusing to let his mind dwell on the unthinkable. He wouldn't—couldn't—lose her. Negative thoughts didn't accomplish anything other than interfere with clear thinking and what had to be done. He would proceed on the assumption that she was still alive. It was up to them to make sure she stayed that way.

When they turned into the drive leading to Smith's house, Seth saw that they'd made the right call. Lester's marked unit sat in the drive. The front door of the house stood open, the jamb splintered where Lester had kicked it open. They told Everett to wait in the car and approached the house.

"Chief?" Bill called as they entered the front door. "It's Bill Reynolds."

He had his weapon drawn, as did Seth and Lee, but the look on Bill's face was one of dread. Lester was not only his boss, he was his friend. Seth knew he was afraid he'd have to use his weapon and was praying that he wouldn't. The look on Lee's face, on the other hand, was one of determination. His first concern was finding his niece; his second was preventing the nuclear pits from getting into the hands of the enemies of his country. Lester Lewis's well-being was way down in the list of Lee's priorities, at about the same level as it was on Seth's list.

They found Lester in Smith's office. He had been going through the file cabinet and the drawers. Papers were strewn across the floor and Smith's laptop was standing open. Seth saw the screen blinking with the message that the machine didn't recognize the user name or password. Lester had been unsuccessful in accessing whatever was on the machine. Their IT people could probably break it, but that took time— time they didn't have.

Lester looked up as they entered the office. He glanced at the guns in their hands.

"You don't need those," he said. "I'm on your side."

"Is that so?" Lee said.

"I screwed up, Lee. I screwed up big-time and I know it. I did it for a good reason, but that doesn't excuse it. I know Pat has Maggie. I don't know *why* he has her, but I know he does." He turned in a circle, looking at the mess in the room, his expression one of frustration. "I can't find anything that might tell me where he's taken her. I'm trying, I really am."

Bill holstered his weapon. Seth and Lee lowered theirs to their sides, but didn't put them away.

"Sit down, Les," Bill said, his voice gentle. "We're gonna figure this out."

He pulled Smith's executive desk chair from behind the desk and guided Lester to it. The police chief's face was pale and his hands were shaking.

"I knew I should never have gotten involved with Pat," he said. "He always claimed it was no big deal, that all he did was go round some regulations when it came to imports. Nothing serious, he said. I knew better, though. I figured it was drugs. I confronted him about it. He never admitted it, but he never denied it either. He just promised to keep his business out of Vichy."

His shoulders slumped.

"I told myself it didn't much matter if he brought drugs into the country or not. If he didn't, someone else would. If I didn't take his money, Vi wouldn't get the treatment she needed." He looked at them. "That's all I cared about. I never thought anyone would get hurt."

"You must have a way to contact Smith," Lee said.

His face was hard. Seth could see Lee had no sympathy for the man in front of him. Seth, on the other hand, did feel for Lester. Had he been in Lester's shoes and Maggie needed medical treatment to save her life, he knew he'd sell his soul to the devil to save her.

"I've got a number to call," Lester said. "A cell phone."

"Call it," Lee ordered.

"He's not going to tell me anything," Lester said.

"You're not going to ask him anything. You're going to tell him that I know he has Maggie and that I came to you. You'll say that I've got agents scouring his house and moving on his warehouses."

"Lee, wait a minute," Seth said. "That could put Maggie in more danger."

"I don't think so," Lee said. "I think he'll hang onto her for leverage. Meanwhile, we can get a trace on his cell that will lead us to him—and hopefully her."

Seth didn't like it, but the awful truth was, it was the only chance they had. As it stood now, they didn't know where to look for Maggie. They had agents checking Smith's known warehouses, but they'd always suspected he had facilities they didn't know about. If he had Maggie at one of those, they'd never find her—at least not until it was too late and her body turned up in the woods like Elton's had.

"Let's do it," he said.

Chapter Thirty-Nine

The crates were stacked three-high in rows, the sides of the rows facing the narrower ends of the warehouse. Between them were aisles wide enough for forklifts. The stacks didn't go all the way to the high ceiling, but they towered above Maggie's head. She estimated each crate to be about five feet high, making the entire stack approximately fifteen feet high. She moved carefully down the side aisle, pausing at each cross aisle and peering down it to make sure it was empty before she moved past. She was pretty sure there were no other men in the warehouse, but it would foolish to take chances based on that assumption.

Halfway down the rows, she ducked into a cross aisle. Holding the handcuff key between the index finger and thumb of her right hand, she twisted her hand around, straining to fit the key in the lock. While her hand cramped, she prayed she wouldn't drop the key. The light between the stacks of crates was dim and she couldn't be sure of finding it before Smith and his man came back. Just as she was about to give up and reconcile herself to trying to escape with cuffed hands, the key slid into the lock on the left cuff. She turned it and let out a sigh of relief when she heard the click. Another second and she had the right cuff off. She tucked the handcuffs and the key into the pocket of her slacks.

She had moved past two more rows of crates when she heard voices behind her. Smith and his man had returned. She picked up her speed. She moved rapidly between each cross aisle, and when she verified each was empty, she ducked into it. She could hear the men talking, but she could only pick up the occasional word, usually when Smith, who sounded angry, raised his voice. She kept moving toward the far end of the building, praying there was another way out back there or a phone or, better yet, both.

She was nearing the end of the crates when she heard the sound of a ringing phone. Her heart felt like it lurched into her throat. There was a phone, but someone was calling it and that meant Smith would be heading her direction to answer it! Then reasoning kicked in and she realized the sound had come from the front of the warehouse where the men were. It was probably Smith's cell phone that she heard ringing. That was good, because it meant Smith would be occupied—at least temporarily—by the phone call. She peered around the corner of the crate she was hiding behind. No one was in the aisle, so she moved quickly into it. Only two more rows to go.

She heard the sound of talking as she moved to the end of the stacks of crates. She was pretty sure it was Smith's voice. He was still at the front of the building, and she could only hope his man was as well. As she ducked in behind the last row of crates, she found herself looking at a wall broken by three closed overhead doors and the single door she had seen when she first looked down the side aisle. If she used that door, she would be visible from the front of the building if anyone looked down the aisle, but what choice did she have? She couldn't go back. There might be a phone or another way out on the other side of that door. She took a deep breath, peeked around the corner of the crates, didn't see anyone looking back at her from the front, and hurried across the ten feet of concrete floor separating the door from the crates. It will probably be locked, she told herself, but the door opened when she twisted the knob. She slipped through and pushed it shut behind her.

She looked around. She appeared to be in a loading area. An office occupied the far left corner, the top half of its walls made of glass to enable whoever worked there to see the rest of the space. It was empty. Three forklifts were parked in the far right corner. Two closed overhead doors occupied each of the side walls and the wall directly across from her. She knew there were likely loading docks on the other side of the doors. The crates she had seen in the other room were unloaded here and moved by forklift through the overhead doors leading into the warehouse. And when it was time for the crates to be moved elsewhere, the process was reversed.

She didn't see a phone on any of the walls, but the office was bound to have one. She moved quickly across the empty space and into the office. If anyone came into the loading area, they wouldn't be able to miss seeing her through the glass of the office walls, but she could duck down behind one of the desks to make her call. She looked around, but there was no sign of a phone. It didn't make sense—an office should have a phone. Unless, she thought, they didn't trust them.

Of course. It made sense that Patrick Smith wouldn't trust a landline. He probably conducted all of his business via burner phones—the cheap, untraceable phones that could be bought at any big-box store. She felt tears of frustration burn her eyes. She hadn't realized until this moment how badly she wanted to hear Seth's voice. Maybe he wouldn't be able to get to her in time, but if she had to die in this crappy place, she at least wanted to hear his voice before she did.

No! She shook her head. She wasn't going to give up that easily. So there wasn't a phone to call a man for help. So what? She'd get out on her own. Those overhead doors led to the outside. Smith and his man would doubtless hear the door as she raised it, but if they were still at the front of the building, she'd have a head start on them. She could still get away.

She turned to leave the office when suddenly she registered the three drums standing against the back wall of the office. They were the size of most 55-gallon drums, but appeared to be made of stainless steel. The international symbol for radiation—three black fan shapes spreading out from a black circle on a yellow background enclosed in a black triangle—were affixed to each of the drums. There were words painted on the drum below the symbols. They weren't in English. Maggie couldn't read the words, but unless she was very much mistaken, the language was Russian. She had found the plutonium pits.

Chapter Forty

"It's me," Lester said. "What the hell have you gotten me into?"

Lee had called the office in Indianapolis to set up a trace on the call. They hadn't been sure the number Lester had would still be active, but apparently Smith hadn't switched burners yet. Sloppy and stupid, Seth thought, but he supposed Smith had wanted a way to keep in touch with Vichy's police chief. Lee had stayed on the line with Indianapolis, monitoring the progress of the track.

Lester listened for a moment, then interrupted.

"Did you kidnap Maggie Fields?" he asked. "No, no, don't give me any of that! I want an answer! Vichy's gonna be crawling with feds and state cops before the day is out! What am I supposed to do? I didn't agree to any of this!"

He listened again, then made a thumbs up gesture. Patrick Smith was buying his story.

"Did you grab her?" he asked again, then after a few moments, "Have you hurt her?"

He listened while Seth held his breath, waiting for the answer. A look of relief crossed Lester's face, and Seth let out the breath.

"Thank God!" Lester said. "Pat, you gotta let her go! I don't know what's going on and I don't want to know, but you gotta let her go. It's bad enough that you took her, but if you hurt her—well, there won't be any place in the world where you'll be safe."

He listened again and a puzzled look crossed his face.

"No, I haven't seen Lydia. Isn't she with you?"

Again, a few moments of listening, then, "Oh, Christ on a cracker! Is that what this is about? You and your wife get in a squabble and you go and kidnap the woman you think helped her—a woman who just happens to be the niece of an FBI agent? I gotta say, Patrick, that's one of the dumber moves you've made!"

The men standing around Lester could all hear Patrick Smith shouting into the phone as Lester yanked it a few inches away from his ear. Apparently he'd hit a sore spot.

"Hey, hey, calm down!" Lester moved the phone back to his ear. "I'm sorry, okay? I shouldn't have said that. Hell, if it was Viola, I'd probably have done the same thing."

"Anything yet?" Lee spoke in a low tone into his phone, his back to Lester. He listened a moment, then turned and motioned to Lester to keep the conversation going.

"Okay," Lester said, speaking into the phone and nodding at Lee to indicate he understood. "What should I do? Lee Jacobs has called in his buddies. I'm going to have to put on a good show and help them look for you. If you tell me where you are, I can do a better job of sending them in another direction."

Oh, crap, Seth thought. Don't push it, chief! He's going to get suspicious. Let the techs do their job and track the call.

"So don't tell me," Lester said. "But don't blame me either if they show up on the doorstep of whatever hole you're hiding in."

He sent a desperate look at Lee. Smith must be trying to end the call. Lee muttered something into his phone.

"Wait!" Lester said. "Please, Pat, please don't hurt Maggie. She's a good person. If she helped Lydia, she only did it because Lydia convinced her to do it. Yeah, yeah, of course. Okay, call me with the new number."

Lee said something into his phone and gave a thumbs-up to Lester. Seth let out the breath he hadn't realized he was holding. They had a location!

"We got it!" Lee said as soon as Lester disconnected the call with Smith.

"Where?" Seth said.

"About an hour south," Lee said. "A location in the country a couple of miles from the Ohio River. A warehouse—one we didn't know about."

"Now what?" Everett said. "What do we do now?"

"Now," Seth said, "we go get Maggie."

"It will take us an hour to get there," Everett said, his voice rising. He looked like he was starting to lose it. "That's too long."

"It will take less in a police car with lights and siren," Lester said.

Lee and Seth stared at him, then they both nodded at the same time. The four of them headed for the door.

**

She had to get out of there now and somehow, some way, get in touch with Seth or her uncle to tell them the location of the pits before the terrorists got their hands on them. She would have to open one of the overhead doors, noise be damned, and make a run for it. If she didn't get away in time to prevent the pits from disappearing, who knew how many Americans might die? She ran through the office door and started for the nearest overhead door. A box beside it held two buttons, one conveniently marked with an upward-pointing green arrow, the other marked with a red downward-pointing one. Just as she reached for the button with the green arrow, she heard men's voices just outside the door to the loading area. Without stopping to think, she cleared the distance to the parked forklifts in three strides and ducked down behind the one farthest from the door.

She had hidden herself just in time. The door opened and a very angry Patrick Smith strode in, followed by the man Maggie had seen on the platform, the one who had interrupted them with an important phone call, giving her the opportunity to kick the other man down the stairs. Patrick sounded angry, but the other man sounded scared. He also sounded out of breath.

"We gotta get out of here! She got away and she's gonna have the cops down on us!"

"She didn't get away!" Patrick sounded like he was speaking through gritted teeth. He also sounded out of breath as if the exertion of looking for her had worn him out. "She's hiding somewhere in one of the buildings or on the grounds."

"It don't matter! We don't have the time to find her! Now the feds are bringing in reinforcements to look for her—if she gets away and makes a call, we're toast."

Reinforcements to look for her, Maggie thought, feeling her spirits lift. That meant Seth knew she'd been kidnapped. One of the phone calls that had come in must have been a warning from someone in Smith's employ. As quickly as her spirits lifted, they fell. Seth knew she'd been taken, but he had no idea where to start looking for her. She closed her eyes, picturing the way he'd looked the night they made love, and wished with all her heart she could send him a telepathic message with directions to her location—or at the very least, the words "I love you."

"And we're worse than toast if we leave before passing off the package," Smith said. "They'll be here soon. After that . . . ," he hesitated, then continued, "after that, we'll leave. I can call from the car and have the plane readied."

"What about . . . ?" The man didn't finish his question. Maggie guessed the word he didn't say was "Lydia."

"I'll take care of that later." Smith's tone indicated he didn't want to discuss the matter further.

The sudden and loud whir of an overhead door being raised startled Maggie into letting out a small yelp of surprise. Fortunately, the noise from the door covered the sound. One of the doors to the left of the office was being raised, and she silently said a prayer of thanks that it hadn't been one of the doors nearer the forklifts. As the door came to a stop, she heard more voices and huddled lower. Patrick's reinforcements had arrived.

"Get rid of him," Patrick said. "Take the body out the back way. They'll be coming from the front and I don't want them knowing there's a problem. Tony, go up front. Let me know when you see them coming."

So that's why they had sounded out of breath, Maggie thought. They'd dragged the body of the man she'd killed to the back rather than take him out the front and risk running into—who? Certainly not the police or the FBI, she thought. They would know that the authorities wouldn't know where to start looking. Smith had mentioned "passing off the package" and said "they'll be here soon." That could only mean the men Maggie had seen at Smith's house or other men from their organization. Lydia had said Patrick was in over his head and was afraid of those men. He didn't want them to know there had been a problem, but he was still willing to deliver the pits to them. He would save himself and the hell with the people who might be killed in the future.

He'd also told them to take the body "out the back way." There must be another road or drive leading out of the back of the compound. If she could manage to get out, maybe there would be more cover in that direction. But how was she going to get out? Not only were Patrick's men at the rear of the warehouse, so were the pits. When Kasim and his men got here, they would be coming to the rear of the warehouse to collect their goods.

Another thought occurred to her. How heavy were plutonium pits? The drums themselves looked too heavy to move by hand. And why would they bother exerting themselves that way when they had access to three forklifts?

Chapter Forty-One

Everett Jacobs was white-knuckled by the time they reached their destination forty minutes later, but Seth felt like they'd been moving in slow motion. Lee had ridden with Lester in the cruiser, lights and siren going; Seth, with Everett and Bill as passengers, had followed in his and Lee's car. Lee had told Seth he would make calls to Indianapolis on the way. They had decided against calling for local backup. Since Smith had a warehouse in the area, he was bound to have one or more locals on his payroll. The man was like a spider, Seth thought, spreading his web far and wide. He was also like a spider in his patience, willing to pay people even when he didn't see any immediate benefit. Viola had said Smith had paid Lester for a long time, but Lester hadn't had any information for him until Lee showed up in town. Smith had patience and that patience had paid off.

No, they couldn't trust the locals and they couldn't wait for the agents they did trust to get there. Maggie might not have that much time. If she wasn't already dead, an ugly little voice in the back of Seth's mind chattered at him, and he quashed it into silence. She wasn't dead. She couldn't be.

Lester shut off his lights and siren five miles out. He pulled his cruiser into an empty parking lot in front of a closed gas station a mile or so outside of the town nearest the warehouse. Seth pulled in behind the cruiser and got out. He stumbled with his first step, his legs stiff, and only then realized how tense he'd been while driving.

"I pulled up satellite photos of the location," Lee said. He enlarged the picture on his iPhone. "It looks like the compound consists of three buildings, one of them larger than the others. They're surrounded by a chain-link fence and sit on what looks like four or five acres. There are two roads in on opposite sides of the compound. We'll have to split up. Dad, you ride with Lester and me. We'll take the front. Seth, you and Bill take the back road here."

He pointed to the road visible on the map. It didn't have a name and Seth guessed it was probably gravel or dirt. It led off a county road that was named, but the only thing on it was the warehouse compound. The road that Lee referred to as going to the front was the same—unnamed and leading only to the compound.

"Call when you get to the start of the road," Lee said. "We'll go in at the same time. Dad, you'll stay in the car and I want you laying low."

"Like hell I'll stay in the car!" Everett Jacobs patted the shotgun he'd brought with him. "I'm ready."

"Dad . . . ," Lee started, then let out an exasperated sigh. "We'll talk on the way."

He turned to tell Seth to get going, but Seth was already opening the door of his car. He nodded to Lee, got in, and pulled out of the lot with a squeal of his tires.

"Lee's gonna have a hard time convincing Everett to lay low," Bill said, chuckling. "Lee forgets who he got his hard head from."

"Everett could get hurt," Seth said.

"Sure," Bill said. "We all could. But I've hunted with Everett Jacobs and he can shoot."

"Hunting animals isn't the same as shooting a person," Seth said.

"Guess Lee never told you his dad did two tours in-country during the Vietnam War," Bill said. "And not as a doctor."

"Didn't know that," Seth said and focused on his driving.

Less than ten minutes later, they were at the junction of the county road and the drive leading to the compound. He'd been right—the drive was hard-packed gravel. It cut through a small stand of trees near the paved road, but he could see the roof of a building approximately three-quarters of a mile away. Probably the largest one, he thought. The trees appeared to thin out not far down the drive. They would have no cover from that point on and the car would be visible to anyone who looked that direction.

"I think we should go in on foot," he said.

Bill nodded. "I was just thinking the same thing."

Seth stopped the car and hit Lee's speed-dial number.

"Hey," he said. "We're here, but it's too open to drive in. We're going to leave the car and go on foot."

"Same here," Lee said. "Even on foot, we'll be out in the open, but at least we'll be less noticeable than in a car. We passed a pull-off a half-mile back. We'll leave the car there and hike in. I'll call when we get back to the drive."

They disconnected, and Seth pulled into the drive. When he reached the trees, he pulled off the gravel and parked behind the trunk of the largest one. It wasn't ideal, but it did provide some concealment from anyone who might look toward the road from the compound.

His cell phone rang and he saw it was Lee. That was quick, he thought. Too quick. Something's wrong.

"Yeah?"

"We just passed a black Navigator with tinted windows. It turned into the drive. A box truck was following and turned in behind it."

"The Navigator sounds like the one Maggie saw at Smith's house," Seth said. His mind was whirling. The Middle Eastern men Maggie had seen were doubtless in the SUV and they'd brought a truck with them.

"You know what that means," he said.

"Yeah," Lee said. "I do. I think we've found the pits."

Seth's heart did a flip. They had planned on a small army of heavily armed men to recover the pits if and when they found their location. They were two FBI agents, two small-town cops, and a doctor with a shotgun. Were they enough to face down an arms dealer, an unknown number of his men, and an unknown number of terrorists? The life of the woman he loved hung in the balance, but they couldn't let the terrorists leave with the pits or the lives of many more would be threatened.

They didn't have a choice. They had to go in and they had to go in now.

Chapter Forty-Two

A cell phone rang, the sound shrill in the nearly empty space of the loading area.

"Yeah?" It was Patrick. A second later, he said, "They're here."

The men removing the body had driven away not more than a minute before. Maggie had hoped they would still be here when Kasim and his people arrived. Patrick hadn't wanted Kasim to know about the dead man. She wondered, had the body still been there, what explanation he would have given Kasim. Probably not the real story. She doubted a man like Kasim would look favorably at a man who kidnapped a woman, then let her get away and kill one of his men in the process. No, he wouldn't have told Kasim the truth, but no matter what story Patrick fed him, Kasim would have been suspicious. She might have been able to escape during any fight that resulted.

Or, she thought, I might have been killed in the crossfire that would doubtless have resulted. She hunkered down lower behind the forklift, wishing she could just melt into the concrete floor.

"You two, come with me."

Maggie heard the door to the warehouse open. Patrick must have gone to welcome Kasim. Based on the order she'd heard him give, he'd taken two of his men with him. That meant there were still others in the loading area and there was still no chance for her to get away.

She was crouched between the wall and back of the forklift closest to the rear overhead doors. Kasim would have brought a truck or van to transport the barrels, and it was likely it would back up to the side door that was already open. On the other hand, the rear doors were closer to the office door. There was always the chance they would decide to take them out the rear. If that happened, she would be exposed if anyone glanced her way. Her best bet to stay unnoticed was to move into the middle of the forklifts. She would be better shielded from the rear, and if the men used a forklift to move the barrels, they would probably take one from the end.

She listened. The men Patrick had left in the loading area sounded like they were near the open overhead. She caught a whiff of cigarette smoke. They were smoking and talking, although she only caught a word here and there. This might be her only chance. She began to scoot over behind the middle forklift, moving slowly and carefully so as not to make any sound. She had just made it when the door to the warehouse opened again and the conversation by the open overhead ceased.

"They're in the office," Patrick said.

She heard their footsteps crossing the concrete floor to the office. She risked a peek from her hiding place behind the forklift and saw the silver-haired man she had seen on Patrick's patio, the one Lydia had identified as Kasim. He was followed by four men; she recognized one as the bodyguard she had seen at Patrick's house. The other three were just as muscular and mean-looking. Kasim had come with some serious protection and there was probably more out front. It looked like he didn't care for Patrick any more than Patrick cared for him.

Kasim and the bodyguard she had seen before followed Patrick into the small office. The others stayed outside, their backs to the office, their eyes on Patrick's men. Maggie ducked back behind the forklift, afraid they might catch a glimpse of her as their eyes scanned for potential danger to their boss.

She couldn't hear more than the occasional word or two from the conversation taking place inside the office. Once she heard Patrick say something about a transfer being confirmed. For a second she was confused, thinking they were talking about the barrels, then realized he was probably talking about a money transfer. In this day and age, people like Kasim and Patrick wouldn't deal with cash in a briefcase. This was the electronic age and payoffs for illegal goods were done through wire transfers. It sounded like the sale was complete. Patrick Smith had just sold nuclear materials to a terrorist group.

The men came out of the office.

"What are you going to use them for?" Patrick said.

"Why do you want to know?" The voice she assumed came from Kasim was cold.

Patrick laughed, but there was no humor in it.

"I'd just like to know where I should stay away from," he said.

Kasim didn't bother to answer and Patrick didn't push it. Maggie felt sick. She needed to do something to stop this, but what could she do? If she showed herself, she'd end up dead. Her only hope was to stay hidden and try to get as much information as she could. She already knew the pits were contained in three barrels and that they had been sold to Kasim. She also knew Patrick had a plane fueled and ready to get him out of the area and probably out of the country. She could also describe the other four men who were with Kasim. It wasn't much, but it might help.

The sound of an engine reached her ears. It was probably Kasim's truck or van, she thought. It stopped outside the open overhead door and she heard the beep, beep sound of a backing truck. She breathed a sigh of relief. Apparently they were going to use the door that was already open. She heard Kasim say something to his men in a language she didn't recognize, then footsteps heading in the general direction of the office.

"When they get them out of there," Patrick said. "We can use a forklift to get them in the truck."

Chapter Forty-Three

"Hold up."

Seth and Bill had started down the drive toward the warehouse. They had just reached the edge of the grove of trees. Once they stepped out, they would have no cover from the view of anyone from the compound who looked in that direction. A smaller building sat between the rear gate and the main building. Assuming Smith and his men were in the main building, the smaller one provided some protection from being seen, but not much. They had decided to go in quickly. If someone happened to be looking, they were toast anyway, but if they moved quickly, they would be exposed for a shorter period of time. If luck were with them, no one would be looking.

"What is it?" Bill said.

"I hear something—a car engine," Seth said.

Bill listened for a second, then nodded. "I hear it, too. And it's getting louder."

Just as Bill spoke, they both saw a blue panel van appear around the side of the smaller building. They ducked back into the cover of the trees and hurried back toward their car.

"Now what?" Bill said.

"We don't have time to move the car," Seth said, thinking that he wouldn't move it even if he had the time. Maggie was somewhere inside that fence and he was going to get her out. "They'll stop to check it out. When they do, we'll take them."

They moved to the opposite side of the drive from where they had left the car and positioned themselves behind two trees a few feet from the drive. The trees weren't large, only providing them partial concealment. If either of the men looked carefully at the trees, they would be seen, but Seth was counting on their attention being focused on the car.

The van slowed and came to a stop as it came to the edge of the stand of trees. He'd been right—both men's heads were turned away from them and toward their car. The driver put the van into Park. Both men opened their doors and stepped out. The one on the passenger side slipped his hand into the pocket of the canvas hunting vest he was wearing. Seth had no doubt they were both armed and suspected that slight bulge at the driver's rear waistband was a gun hidden under his loose-fitting shirt. But they would hesitate to pull their weapons until they were sure there was a reason to do so. For all they knew, someone's car had broken down. Patrick Smith liked to keep a low profile; he wouldn't want his men drawing guns on the local citizenry.

The driver moved around the van to join his partner and they started toward Seth's car. There could be someone else in the van, but Seth doubted it. If there had been others, they likely would have hopped out the back by now. He motioned to Bill and they moved from behind the trees. The van concealed them from view of Smith's men and they hurried over to it, moving to opposite ends of the vehicle. Seth peered around the front of the van. The two men had approached the car cautiously and were a few feet away from it.

"I think it's empty," he heard the driver say. "Probably somebody just broke down and left it here."

"Looks that way," the passenger said. "We'd better check it, though. Go ahead, I'll cover you."

The driver moved to the car and walked around it. He opened the driver's door, reached in and activated the trunk release. The passenger moved slightly to the side so he could see into the trunk, while the driver came to the rear of the car, looked in, shrugged his shoulders, and closed the lid. He moved back to the open driver's door and pushed it shut.

"Indiana tags," the driver said, returning to the rear of the car. Both men's backs were to Seth and Bill, who moved as one around the van. "We oughta call Pat."

"He's a little busy right now," the passenger said. "I doubt he's gonna wanna be bothered for this."

"I think you're right," Seth said.

Both men whirled, the passenger's hand coming out of his vest pocket with an automatic. The driver's right hand went to the back of his waistband.

"Uh-uh," Bill said. "Bad idea, boys. Drop it."

The passenger hesitated for only a second before dropping his weapon on the ground. The driver brought his hand back around to his side.

"You know the drill." Bill motioned up with his weapon. The men hesitated, then raised their hands and clasped them on top of their heads.

"Turn around," Seth said.

When the men had complied, he moved forward while Bill covered him. He kicked the passenger's weapon away from the men and toward Bill, then removed the weapon from the driver's waistband and kicked it away. He did a one-handed pat-down of each of the men, keeping his own weapon trained on the one he was searching. He knew Bill would have the other one covered. He removed another weapon from the passenger's ankle holster and a switchblade from the driver's jeans. He also took cell phones off each of them. Satisfied they carried no other weapons or means of communication, he motioned Bill forward. Within seconds, they had both men cuffed behind their backs.

"Now what do we do with them?" Bill said. "We can't take the chance of calling the locals for a transport."

"I've got just the place for them," Seth said, moving to the side of the car and opening the driver's door. He reached in and popped the trunk release.

After they had stowed the men in the trunk and slammed the lid on their curses, Seth turned to the van. It fit the description given by the citizen who had called the police to report seeing a woman pulled into a blue panel van. Could Maggie be in the back? Maybe the men had been moving her to another location. Seth moved toward the van, alternating between anticipation at finding her bound and gagged in the rear of the van and dread that instead he would find her body concealed there. Bill said something, but Seth couldn't hear over the pounding in his ears. He forced himself to take another step toward the van, then another, until finally he broke into a jog. He had to know. One way or the other, he had to know.

The rear doors were unlocked. He pulled them open and let out a cry. A form was wrapped in a tarp, unmoving. Maggie was dead. They had killed the woman he loved and had been on their way to dump her body the way they had dumped Elton Jackson's body. With trembling hands he reached out and pulled the tarp back, wanting to look at her face one last time before he went to the warehouse and put a bullet between Smith's eyes.

When he saw the bloodied face of a man he'd never seen before, his legs gave out and he caught himself on the edge of the van.

"Jesus!" he said. "Thank God!"

"You know him?"

Bill had come up beside him. He didn't seem to notice Seth's near collapse—or if he did, he was being nice and ignoring it.

"Never saw him before."

Seth took a deep breath and straightened. It wasn't Maggie. That was all that mattered. She might still be alive. He would do whatever it took to make sure she stayed that way.

"Well, he's not going anywhere," Bill said. "We'll leave him for the forensics people. Now what?"

Seth thought for a moment.

"We'll take the van," he said. "If someone looks out, they'll just think it's those two guys coming back for some reason."

He took out his cell and pressed Lee's number. When Lee answered, he quickly filled him in on what had happened and what they'd found in the back of the van. He listened for a minute, agreed to whatever Lee had said, hung up and turned to Bill.

"Lee wants us to create a distraction," he said.

"What do you have in mind?"

"Noise," he said. "As much as we can make."

He slammed the rear doors of the van and headed for the driver's door.

Chapter Forty-Four

Maggie tried to melt into the floor as one of Smith's men moved to the forklift closest to the interior of the loading area. She was thankful she'd chosen neutral colors for her clothing that morning, but with her red hair . . . well, there wasn't much she could do about that except get as low as possible and hope for the best. She closed her eyes, knowing she was acting like a child who thought if he couldn't see the boogeyman, the boogeyman couldn't see him. She heard the man climb aboard the forklift, make some adjustments to something, then heard the motor turn over once before it died. The man tried again with the same result. After the third try, Patrick Smith spoke.

"Try another one." His tone was sharp, an undercurrent of anxiety running through it. Smith wanted Kasim and his men out of his warehouse as quickly as possible. "We don't have all day."

Maggie felt her heart drop. She was going to be found. She crawled to the back of the row of forklifts, knowing it would do no good, but hoping luck might be on her side. It wasn't.

"Hey!" The man tasked with finding a forklift that would start grabbed her arm and she was yanked to her feet.

"Let me go!" she said and tried to pull away.

"Who is this?" Kasim demanded, not taking his eyes from her. Maggie saw his men change their posture, their legs further apart for balance, their eyes alert, hands resting on waistbands near the guns she had no doubt were there. "Why is this woman hiding and spying on our business?"

Patrick Smith's face went pale as he stared at her. She could imagine the thoughts going through his mind. If he admitted she was a captive who had escaped his custody, he would have a lot of explaining to do to Kasim. Why he had kidnapped her, how he had let her escape, why he ran such a sloppy operation. And he had to know she might broadcast to Kasim and his men that her brother was an FBI agent who was looking for her. He didn't want Kasim to know who she was any more than she did. That might work in her favor.

"I'm his wife, that's who I am!" she said, gambling that Kasim had never met Lydia. She lifted her chin in the way of a woman used to getting her way. "Tell your errand boy to release me immediately, Patrick!"

Smith's eyes widened in surprise and a couple of his men glanced at him. She could see they weren't sure how they should respond and were looking to him for guidance.

"Your wife?" Kasim looked at Smith.

Patrick hesitated for a second, still staring at Maggie.

"Yes," he said. "And she is a hard one to handle."

Kasim looked from him to Maggie and back, then chuckled.

"Women with hair the color of fire often are," he said. "It takes a strong man to tame them."

The implication was that Patrick Smith was not a strong man. Patrick shifted his stance and a scowl crossed his face. He looked like a man who didn't like the insinuation that he couldn't control his wife.

Maggie wasn't sure if he was acting for Kasim's benefit, or if he was thinking about Lydia.

"Tame? Tame?" Her voice grew shrill. "I am *not* some animal that needs to be tamed! If you'd treat me with as much respect as you do your men, I wouldn't have to run and hide from you!"

She directed her rant at Patrick, hoping she was giving a convincing portrayal of an angry wife.

"That's enough. I'll deal with you later." He gestured to two of his men. "Take my wife to my office and make sure she stays there."

The men stepped forward, one on either side of her and took her arms. She made a show of trying to break free, but she wanted to be escorted out of there as badly as Patrick wanted her escorted out. While she didn't hold out much hope of getting away from Patrick's two goons, she had no hope of getting away from both his and Kasim's.

"Let me go!" she shouted as the men pulled her toward the door leading to the storage area of the warehouse. "Patrick! Tell them to let me go!"

"I must apologize for my wife," she heard Smith say as the man on her right opened the door. "I assure you I will take care of her later. But first . . . business."

The men forced her through the door. As it closed behind them, she heard a forklift motor start up.

"Come on." The man on her left yanked her arm hard.

"Figures we get stuck babysitting this broad," the other one said. "I don't like not knowing what's going on back there."

"Maybe you should just let me go to the office by myself and you go back and help your boss," Maggie said.

"Shut up." The man yanked her arm harder than before, and she decided it might be wise to do what he said. He wasn't in the mood for cracks like the one she'd just made.

They were halfway to the front of the warehouse when the sound of a honking horn reached them. It sounded as if it was coming from the direction they'd just left. The men stopped and turned toward the rear of the warehouse, their heads cocked to one side as if that would help them identify the source of the sound.

"What now?" one said.

The horn honked again, this time closer than it was before, then someone leaned on it, the blare growing louder as its source came closer to the warehouse. The men were focused on the sound, doubtless trying to decide if they should continue to the office or go back to the loading area. She felt their grips loosen and she twisted backward suddenly, taking them both by surprise. Before the one on the right could turn, she kicked him hard behind the knee. His leg buckled and he stumbled into the other man, knocking him off balance. Before they could recover, she was sprinting down the long aisle leading to the front. Their curses were followed by the sound of their pounding footsteps as they ran after her. She ran even faster, but could hear them getting closer. She wasn't going to make it to the door.

She had no sooner thought that when the door flew open and two men stepped through. She could only make out silhouettes framed against the light from outside. They had guns in their hands and they were pointed in her direction. She stopped, gasping for breath. It was over. She wasn't going to get away.

"Get down, Maggie!"

She recognized her uncle's voice at the same time she heard her two pursuers just behind her. She dropped to the floor and the sound of gunshots blasted through the cavernous warehouse space. She put her arms over her head and closed her eyes, trying for the second time in less than an hour to melt into the concrete floor.

In seconds it was quiet, but she was too busy trying to determine if she'd been shot to raise her head.

"Maggie?" Lee sounded worried. "Are you hurt?"

She raised her head and he smiled, the relief evident on his face.

"I don't think so," she said.

She raised herself to a sitting position and looked behind her for Smith's men. They were both lying motionless on the warehouse floor. The man who had come in with Lee kicked the fallen men's weapons out of their reach, although from the look of them, it wasn't necessary. They would never pick up another gun. The man turned toward her and she saw it was Lester. His left sleeve was soaked with blood.

"Lester? Lester's been shot," she said to Lee.

Lee turned, surprised. He'd been so focused on her, he hadn't noticed the bleeding.

"It's nothing." Lester flexed his arm. "Less than I deserve."

"What?" Maggie was confused.

"It's a long story and we don't have time for it," Lee said to Maggie. He turned back to Lester. "Can you hold a gun?"

"The bullet just grazed me. I can still use my arm. Besides, I'm right-handed."

Maggie stared at them, knowing she had missed something, but then she remembered the barrels.

"Lee," she said, tugging at his arm to pull herself to her feet. "I found the pits. They're in barrels in an office in the loading area back there."

She motioned toward the rear of the warehouse.

"Kasim is there with a bunch of guys. One of Smith's guys was just getting ready to load them onto a truck when these two dragged me out of there. Then we heard a horn honking. I think something's happening."

"Somebody is happening," Lee said. "Seth and Bill Reynolds."

Maggie's heart skipped a beat. Seth was back there with Kasim, Smith, and a lot of armed men. She whirled, crossed the floor quickly and bent to pick up one of the fallen men's guns. She knew the safety was off this one. Maybe she would have more success pointing and shooting at terrorists than she'd had with tin cans.

"Let's go," she said, starting toward the loading area.

"You're not going anywhere." Lee grabbed her arm. "Dad's outside. Go out there and wait with him."

"No!" She yanked her arm away. "You don't understand. There are a lot of men back there and they all have guns. Seth and Bill are not going to be able to handle them alone. I'm going and you're wasting time trying to stop me—time they don't have."

Lee started to object, then gave it up.

"Stay behind me," he ordered. They started toward the rear of the warehouse.

Chapter Forty-Five

Lee and Lester, with Maggie behind them, were two rows of crates away from the door leading to the loading area when the stocky man Maggie had first seen in the van during her abduction burst through the door, followed by two other men she recognized as being in Smith's employ. The stocky man had an assault rifle, its strap over his right shoulder; the other two men had automatics in their hands.

"FBI!" Lee shouted.

The stocky man began to raise the assault rifle, but Lee and Lester already had their weapons aimed at him. They both fired and the man went down, his finger spasming on the assault rifle's trigger. The sound of the weapon firing was deafening and chips of concrete blasted off the floor where the bullets struck flew toward them. Maggie felt something strike her shin. For a second, she thought she'd been shot, but when she looked down, she saw only a trickle of blood and realized it was concrete shrapnel. The two men behind the stocky man raised their weapons, but the hail of bullets from Lee's and Lester's guns stopped them before they could get off a shot.

Lee pulled her behind the row of crates second from the back of the warehouse, while Lester quickly moved forward and took position behind the row nearest the back.

"You okay?" Lee was looking at the blood on her leg, a concerned expression on his face.

"Just a piece of concrete," Maggie said. "I'm fine."

"Did you get a good look at how many are in there?" Lee said.

Maggie thought for a second. She'd been hiding most of the time, and when she'd been dragged from behind the forklifts, she'd been too focused on how to get out of the situation. She hadn't bothered to count the men.

"Not sure," she said. "But at a guess—I'd say Smith had ten guys with him, minus the five that are out here. Kasim didn't have as many—maybe six. I didn't see any more than that, but there may have been some outside."

"There were two out front," Lee said. "But they're no longer a concern."

His face was grim. She hadn't heard any gunshots as she ran toward the front of the warehouse. However Kasim's lookouts had met their deaths or been otherwise incapacitated, it had been up close and personal.

The sound of running footsteps crossed the loading area toward the door, then the door was slammed shut. Smith had realized any of his men who tried to enter the warehouse would be cut down as they came through the door. He was trying to switch positions with them, forcing them to storm the door where they would be sitting ducks. Maggie had a thought.

"What if he sends some of his men out to come around to the front of the building?" she said. "They'll have us trapped."

"I doubt Seth and Bill will let any of them out," he said. "We can simply keep them contained in the loading area until reinforcements get here."

"Reinforcements?"

"We've got agents on the way," he said. "The last time I spoke to them, they were less than twenty miles out. We can hold them in that long."

Suddenly shots rang out from the loading area.

"Seth!" She jumped to her feet and ran into the aisle and toward the door.

"Maggie! No!"

She heard Lee, but she ignored him and kept running to the door, the gun that had belonged to the fallen man down at her side. She felt invincible at that moment, although a part of her knew that was a stupid way to feel. The odds were against her making it more than a couple of feet inside the door before she was shot, but that might be enough to draw attention away from Seth and give him a chance. She didn't want to die, but even more, she wanted him to live.

Just as her hand closed on the knob and started to turn it, Lester grabbed her and yanked her to the hinge side, forcing her flat against the wall. She tried to pull away from him, but he held her still. In seconds Lee was there, glowering at her.

"What the hell do you think you're doing?!"

"Trying to help Seth," she said, as more gunshots rang out from the loading area. "What are we going to do—wait here until Smith and Kasim kill him, then send their goons around the building to surround us?"

Lee started to argue with her, but stopped. She was right and he knew it. They had to do something.

"Stay here." The words came out as almost a growl. She nodded as if agreeing, but she had no intention of obeying him.

He motioned to Lester to move to the other side of the door. When Lester was in place, Lee reached out, grasped the knob, and pushed the door open, careful to do it in such a way that it wouldn't slam against the inside wall. Maggie knew he was hoping that the attention of the men inside would be focused on Seth and Bill, but when a shot rang out and a bullet embedded itself in a crate a few feet away, Maggie knew Smith's and Kasim's men were apparently capable of multitasking.

"Shit!" Lee said.

Before he could say anything else, Lester leaned forward and pulled the trigger of his gun, then ducked back again. A cry from inside, then a thump, told Maggie he'd hit his target. More bullets smacked into crates across from them while they huddled against the walls to the sides of the doors. Maggie wondered if the concrete wall separating the loading area from the warehouse was enough to stop all bullets. If someone used an assault rifle, would the bullets penetrate the wall and their bodies?

There was a lull in the hail of bullets coming through the door and smacking into the concrete on either side of it. Lee swung around and fired several rounds, then ducked back.

"I saw one go down," he said, as the men inside fired through the door again.

Maggie could hear gunfire from the direction of the open overhead door and prayed that Seth was okay. She felt so helpless pressed up against the wall with no way to help him.

Over the next few minutes, Lee and Lester managed to get off a few rounds whenever the men inside stopped to reload or whatever they were doing. Suddenly, there was complete silence from inside. No firing through the door to the warehouse and no firing from the direction of the overhead door.

"What's going on?" she asked Lee. "Are they all dead?"

"I doubt that," he said and risked a look through the door. He pulled back quickly.

"Was there another way out?" he asked Maggie.

"Just the overhead doors," she said. "One was open when they pulled me out of there. The others were closed, but we would have heard them if they were raised. Wouldn't we?"

Lee didn't answer her question, but instead motioned to Lester. "Stay here," he said to her and moved quickly through the door, his gun at the ready. Lester followed.

Maggie closed her eyes and cringed, waiting for the bullets to start flying, but all she heard was the beating of her heart in her ears. She opened her eyes and moved to the edge of the doorframe and peered around. It looked like the proverbial war zone inside. Men were down everywhere, most groaning and bleeding, but some not moving at all. She hadn't expected that, but when she thought about it, Smith's and Kasim's men had been in a vulnerable position— shooters on either side of them and very few places to hide. What was the saying—like shooting fish in a barrel? She brought her gun up and followed her uncle and Lester inside. She saw Lee's mouth tighten, but he kept his attention on the men spread out before him.

"Go," he said to Lester.

While Lester moved forward to kick weapons out of reach of the still moving men, Lee covered him. Maggie held her gun at the ready and looked around the room at the bodies on the floor. Where were Smith and Kasim? None of the men on the floor looked like either of them.

"They're not here," she said to Lee. "I don't see Smith or Kasim."

"Lee?" It was Seth's voice and Maggie felt her spirits soar. He was alive!

"Yeah. You see Smith or Kasim come out that way?"

"Nobody came this way."

Seth sounded like he was closer. He was heading into the warehouse. A second later he appeared at the top of the concrete steps that led off the loading dock, and Maggie felt her eyes mist with tears of happiness. Their eyes locked and the look of relief that crossed his face told her all she wanted to know. Then he looked away, holding his weapon out at arm's length as he inspected the loading area.

"The forklifts," Maggie said. "I hid there. And they could be in the office, below the windows."

Bill appeared behind Seth and moved into the loading area. The four men fanned out.

"Stay with me," Lee ordered. Maggie nodded, relieved that he'd given up on expecting her to hide out in the warehouse.

They moved slowly, their attention divided between the men on the floor, the forklifts, and the office. Lee and Maggie were nearest the forklifts. As they approached them, Maggie moved a few feet away from Lee to gain a different line of sight. He started to object, but kept silent, apparently deciding it was a wise move to gain an extra vantage point. He moved in front of the two parked lifts, while she moved to a position where she could see behind them. There was no one there.

The third forklift sat a few feet from the office, its engine quiet. Maggie saw the barrels containing the pits had been manhandled out of the office and were sitting just outside the office door. The only place left for Smith and Kasim was in the small office. One or two of their men might also be in there, but it was a small room. There couldn't be many people hidden there. All it takes is one, she reminded herself, one with a good aim.

The five of them began converging on the office, Seth and Bill from the left and Lester, Lee, and Maggie from the right. Suddenly two figures shot up from below the windows. Lee pushed Maggie, knocking her onto the floor and jumping on top of her as Kasim and Smith began firing. Still leaning on her, Lee began firing back. Maggie felt him flinch and then felt something wet on her hand. It was blood! Lee had been shot! She squirmed out from under him and saw that his leg was bleeding. The blood was running out, but it wasn't spurting; the bullet had not hit an artery. She raised the gun she was holding, pointed it at the office, and pulled the trigger again and again until it clicked on an empty cylinder.

Suddenly there was a loud boom, then another, and Maggie saw blood spray inside the office. She turned to find the source of the sound and saw her grandfather standing a few feet from the door leading to the warehouse, his shotgun in his hands.

"That'll teach 'em to shoot my boy," he said and hurried to Lee.

While Everett and Maggie tended to Lee, the other men checked the office. Maggie could tell by the way their posture suddenly relaxed that Smith and Kasim weren't going to do any more shooting. The three men spread out and cuffed the men who were still breathing and moved all the weapons into a corner. Maggie tried to focus only on her bleeding uncle, but her eyes kept being drawn to Seth. He was alive and he wasn't bleeding. Maggie thought it was the most beautiful sight she'd ever seen.

Chapter Forty-Six

"Looks like you didn't need any backup, Jacobs."

Maggie didn't have to be introduced to know the man looking down at her bleeding uncle was in charge of the agents who had arrived within five minutes of the last wounded man being cuffed. She guessed him to be in his fifties. He was tall and fit with a military bearing. His black hair was liberally streaked with gray and his blue eyes didn't miss a thing as he surveyed the carnage on the loading area floor.

"Yeah, we figured you guys were never going to show, so we started the party without you."

"This must be your niece," the man said directing an appraising gaze at her. "I've heard a lot about you. Were you harmed in any way?"

"No," she said. "I'm fine."

"Or at least as fine as a recently rescued kidnap victim can be?" He looked concerned. She guessed he was expecting her to fall apart—if not now, then later.

"I'm not sure she needed rescuing," Lee said, wincing as he shifted his position. "She was doing a pretty good job of escaping when we showed up."

"Let me guess," Maggie said. "You're Mike, right?"

"That's me. I'm in charge of these two cowboys." He turned serious. "Good job, Lee. I mean it. If those pits had gotten to wherever they were headed . . ."

He didn't finish and he didn't need to. A lot of people had died today, but none of them were the innocents who would have died had Kasim gotten away with the plutonium pits.

Maggie became aware of a siren drawing closer to the warehouse. It stopped, and a few seconds later, two paramedics entered the loading area, escorted by what she assumed was another agent. She stepped back while her grandfather conferred with the paramedics. One took Lee's vital signs, while the other cut away his pants leg and examined the wound.

"I think the bullet's still inside," he said.

He ripped open a package of sterile gauze, pressed it against the wound in Lee's leg, then secured it with tape, while his partner inserted a cannula into the back of her uncle's hand to provide access for an IV unit. The one who had bandaged Lee's leg stood and turned to the door. He'd apparently intended to get the wheeled stretcher, but stopped when he saw an agent wheeling it in. The two men loaded Lee onto the stretcher and wheeled him through the door and into the warehouse. Everett followed with Lester in tow. His arm seemed to have stopped bleeding, but it was obvious from the way he cradled it that it hurt.

Maggie turned to look for Seth and found him in conversation with the tall man. His eyes were on her, however, and when she looked his way, he broke away from the man long enough to nod and say, "Go." She nodded back and followed her grandfather through the door.

Another agent approached them as Lee was being loaded onto the ambulance.

"Come with me," he said. "Seth told me where they left their car. I'll take you to it."

As they pulled up to the car Seth and Bill had left parked in the trees, Maggie saw two cuffed men being pulled from the trunk and walked to a waiting sedan. The agent wouldn't let them get out of his car until the men were safely ensconced in the back of the sedan. As the sedan pulled away, he held up the keys Seth had given him, looking from Maggie to Everett. Maggie took them and her grandfather didn't object.

As they pulled out onto the road, he took his cell phone from his pocket and called his wife.

"It's over. Maggie's with me and she's fine," he said when she answered. He listened for a moment. "No, they didn't hurt her. But Lee was shot in the leg . . . now hold on, Dora, there's no need for all that. He's going to be fine. He was shot in the leg, but it didn't hit an artery. He's on his way to the hospital now, and he'll be fine. We're on our way to pick you up, then we'll head on over there."

They talked for another minute, then he said, "We'll be there shortly. I love you . . . and our boy is going to be fine."

"Is she okay?" Maggie said when he disconnected.

"Other than bawling her eyes out, she's good," Everett said. "I don't know if they're tears of worry for Lee or tears of relief for you. Probably a bit of both."

Dora was standing in the open door when they pulled into the drive, her purse in her hand. When she saw them, she closed the door behind her and hurried toward the driver's side of the car. Maggie put the car in Park, stepped out, and was immediately enveloped by her grandmother's arms.

"Oh, thank God," Dora said as she hugged her granddaughter. "I was so worried! They could have killed you!"

She stroked Maggie's hair and Maggie felt tears sting her own eyes. She felt like a loved little girl, and it felt good.

"I'm okay, Gran. Really. They didn't hurt me."

"But they hurt Lee." Dora released her, stepped back, and looked at her in a way Maggie recognized from childhood. It was the look her grandmother had used when she suspected Maggie had been up to something and she wanted the truth—Maggie called it the "lie detector" look. "Is Everett being honest with me? Is Lee going to be okay?"

"I think so," Maggie said. "He was shot in the leg, but it wasn't bleeding too badly, and he was able to joke with one of the other agents."

"I want to see him," Dora said. She opened the rear door and climbed in. "Let's go."

When they arrived at the hospital, they were informed that Lee was being prepped for surgery. The staff allowed the three of them to see him for just a few minutes, but Maggie knew those few minutes did wonders for her grandmother's piece of mind. Dora visibly relaxed within seconds of entering the emergency room cubicle where Lee was being treated.

After their short visit, they were shooed out and Everett led them to the surgical waiting room. He excused himself to get cups of coffee for all of them, but Maggie suspected his main reason for the coffee run was to have a chance to talk to the doctor in private. She searched his face when he came back with the coffee and was reassured when she saw he was relaxed and smiling. Barring some unexpected surgical complication, Lee was going to be okay.

Less than an hour later, the door to the waiting room opened and Seth stepped in. He smiled at her, his eyes warm, and she felt a surge of happiness that took her breath away.

"Dora, Everett." He nodded at them. "How's Lee?"

"Still in surgery, but the doctors say he should be okay," Everett said. "Until they get in there, they weren't sure how much damage might have been done to bone or muscle. He might have a permanent limp, but he'll live."

Seth let out the breath he'd been holding.

"I'll wait with you. But first I need to call Mike and let him know."

He stepped into the hall to make his call. In a few minutes he was back. He sat down next to Maggie, leaned back in the chair, and closed his eyes.

"Are you okay?" she said.

A moment passed before he opened his eyes and looked at her.

"I am now," he said and took her hand.

They sat like that, hand-in-hand, not talking for the next hour until the door to the surgical unit opened. They all jumped up, eager to hear the news, but judging from the smile on the doctor's face, Maggie knew the news was good.

"Mr. Jacobs is fine," the doctor said. "We were able to repair the soft tissue damage. He did have a break in a bone in his thigh, but it was a clean break— no splintering—and we were able to repair it. With time and therapy, he should be as good as new."

"Can we see him?" Dora's expression told them all that she wouldn't believe her son was all right until she saw it for herself.

"As soon as he's out of recovery and in a room," the doctor said. "I'd say that will probably take another hour. Why don't you get something to eat while you're waiting?"

He left after more assurances that Lee would be fine. Dora protested that she wasn't hungry, but her husband talked her into accompanying him to the cafeteria.

"How about you two?" he said.

"Not me," Seth said. "They want me in Indianapolis. They need me to go over what went down, and of course, deal with a mountain of paperwork. By the way, they'll also need statements from you and Maggie. If there wasn't so much to be done at the warehouse and the jail, there'd be an army of them here by now, not just to talk to you, but also to check on Lee. With all they've got to do, though, you might be home before someone can get to you."

"Any time they're ready is fine with us," Everett said. "Come on, Dora. Let's get some food."

The second the door swung shut, Seth turned to Maggie and pulled her to him. She started to speak, but he pressed his lips to hers and all thoughts of speech vanished. By the time they came up for air, her lips felt almost bruised. She loved the feeling.

"I never told you how I felt . . . ," she began at the same time he said, "I was sure I'd lost . . ."

They both laughed. By unspoken agreement they separated a few inches, Seth's hands resting on her shoulders, his eyes tender as he gazed at her face. She reached up and placed her fingers against his lips.

"Not now," she said. "You have too much to do. We can talk later."

He pulled her to him again and wrapped his arms around her, hugging her close. Her face was pressed against his shoulder and she could feel the bandage that covered the wound that had brought him to her. She had believed he was a burglar, shot while trying to commit a crime. Instead, he was a hero, a man who risked his life to make sure others were safe. He wasn't the wrong kind of man after all—he was very much the right kind. He was holding her now, thankful that she was alive and unharmed, but he had held her before all during one long and wonderful night, yet still pulled away at the light of day. Once the relief at finding her safe subsided, would he pull away again?

Chapter Forty-Seven

The week following the shootout in the warehouse was a bustle of activity, while the night of the shootout was one of sleep interrupted by nightmares. When Maggie returned home with her grandparents, she'd gone to her room and laid on her bed, thinking over all that had occurred, both at the warehouse and with Seth at the hospital. She had been surprised that she didn't feel traumatized by the violence she had witnessed. She had no idea how many men had been injured or died, but even one would have been more than she'd ever seen. She was even responsible for the death of one. She finally decided that she wasn't bothered because they had "asked" for it. They were criminals who didn't care who they hurt, so why should she care if they were hurt.

Her subconscious apparently felt otherwise. The first time she woke up was just after midnight. She came awake, a scream just starting to work its way out of her throat. She could only remember snatches of the dream—a monster of some kind in a large empty building and it was coming for her. She got up, helped herself to a glass of water, told herself the dream was to be expected, and went back to sleep. Twice more she came awake with a start, but couldn't remember if she'd been dreaming or if some sound in the house had woken her.

Based on the bags under her grandparents' red eyes, they hadn't slept any better than she had. The three of them sat around the table picking at their breakfast and drinking coffee. Finally, Maggie broke the silence.

"I had a nightmare," she said. "About the warehouse."

Everett snorted. "You're not alone."

"I didn't have one about the warehouse," Dora said. "Mine was about your uncle."

"I didn't think it bothered me," Maggie said. "Those men deserve what they got. So why am I having nightmares?"

"Ever heard of PTSD?" Everett said. "Soldiers aren't the only ones who get that, you know. Most people who've gone through a situation in which they feared for their lives experience at least a little of it. You were kidnapped by thugs, bullets were flying all around you in that warehouse, and you were afraid for your life and the lives of people you care for. If you didn't have a nightmare or two, I'd be more worried about you."

He patted her hand.

"Don't worry too much about it," he said. "It will pass. If it doesn't, then we'll see about getting you someone to talk to professionally."

Her grandfather had been right. The first night was the worst, but after that the sleep disturbances lessened until she was sleeping soundly four nights out. It was a good thing, too, because her days were busier than they'd ever been. Jack was over-the-moon at having his reporter able to write firsthand accounts of the biggest news to ever hit Vichy. Her stories were picked up by the Associated Press and published nationally. A local news show out of Indianapolis sent a reporter to interview her on camera; shortly after, the national TV newsmen arrived. The town was crawling with news trucks, reporters, and cameramen, and Maggie remembered predicting just that the day she visited Viola.

The town was also crawling with federal investigators—another prediction come true. The first investigators showed up at their house late on the evening of the day of the shootout. She and her grandfather both gave statements, but two different pairs of investigators showed up over the next few days. They all covered the same ground. Maggie knew that was standard procedure, used to make sure a witness was telling the truth or wasn't confused about the sequence of events. She knew it was also a way to evaluate how good a witness would be at trial. Although Smith and Kasim hadn't survived to stand trial, several of their men had.

Viola called toward the end of the week.

"Hi, Maggie," she said when Maggie answered her cell. "It's Vi. I just wanted to call and see how you're doing. I also wanted to say how sorry I am for what you went through."

"I'm okay," Maggie said. "And thank you. I need to thank Lester, too, for helping to rescue me."

Maggie heard a voice in the background that sounded like Lester, but she couldn't make out the words.

"He was just doing what he needed to do," Viola said. "Another reason I called is to say goodbye."

"Goodbye?"

"Yes. Remember the clinical trial I told you about? We're leaving early tomorrow morning for California." Vi laughed. "Wish me luck."

"I definitely wish you luck," Maggie said. "And I'll be saying a prayer for you. So Lester's going with you?"

"Yes. We were afraid he wouldn't be able to and I'd have to go alone, but Lee talked to his bosses. Lester will be going with me and staying until I get settled. We are so grateful to Lee. I think once I get there and adjust to whatever they do, I'll be fine, but initially I need the support."

They talked for a few minutes more before hanging up. Maggie made a mental note to give her uncle a hug and a kiss for clearing it for Lester to leave town. Based on the number of times she and her grandfather had had to answer questions, she was surprised the feds hadn't insisted Lester stay in town in case they wanted to talk to him again.

Four days after her first article appeared nationally, she began getting calls from big city papers and the national news services offering her a job. She didn't turn any of them down, but she didn't accept any either. She needed more time to decide what she was going to do with her life. Lee called nearly every day to check in on how they were doing, but there were no calls from Seth. She knew he was the main reason for her hesitancy to make decisions about her professional life, and she knew it was stupid of her to put her life on hold for a man she barely knew. But stupid or not, she had to know if there was a chance for them or if it was over before it had even begun.

Monday afternoon, a week to the day after she'd been kidnapped and her world turned upside down, she stepped out of the Sun and came face-to-face with Seth. He was leaning against a car that screamed "government issue" a few cars up from the Sun's front door. He was wearing a gray suit and a conservative tie, and he'd gotten a haircut. He screamed government issue, too—a far cry from the way he'd looked that first morning in the guest room bed. He smiled when he saw her and she felt her own face break into an answering smile.

"Need a ride home?" he said.

She stared at him for a few seconds, her smile fading as she thought about how he had pulled away from her before. Did he think that he could just show up and act like nothing was wrong? Or was he here to have a "Dear Jane" talk with her?

"Not really," she said, and felt satisfaction when she saw his smile disappear. Served him right. "But I'll accept one."

She walked past him and opened the passenger door before he could do it for her.

"Might as well get this settled," she thought to herself. "Then maybe I can move on."

Chapter Forty-Eight

"How are you doing?" he said, as he fastened his seat belt and started the car. "Lee said you'd had a few nightmares."

"Only one," she said. Her grandfather or grandmother must have told Lee about her dream. "I'm fine now."

"You went through a lot, Maggie," he said. "What happened to you never happens to most people. It does things to a person."

"Is that why you're here? To check on my mental condition?"

He glanced at her and smiled. "Among other things."

And what, she wondered, does that mean? He looked back at the road and didn't say anything else. She looked out the side window so she wouldn't have to look at him sitting next to her. Her hands ached with wanting to touch him, but she'd cut them off first. He was here to give her the "Dear Jane" speech—she just knew it. There was no future for them and there never had been. He had come to Vichy to do a job. Now that the job was finished, he would be moving on. She probably wouldn't have heard from him at all, but he wanted to stay in Lee's good graces. Not the best move to do a wham-bam-thank-you-ma'm job on a friend's niece.

They left the city limits and drove into the countryside. At first Maggie didn't pay a lot of attention to where they were going, but then she realized they were heading in the direction of Patrick Smith's house. Suddenly a question occurred to her. It had been bugging her all week, but her grandparents had monopolized their visits with Lee and she'd never had the chance to ask him.

"How did you find me?" she said. "Was there some clue at Smith's house?"

He hesitated. She had the feeling he was trying to decide how to answer.

"It was Lester Lewis," he said.

"Lester? How would Lester know where to find me?"

"He didn't. Not until he called Smith."

"I don't understand."

After a few moments hesitation, he told her about Lester's involvement with Smith. She was stunned. She found it hard to believe that the dedicated police officer that was Lester had ever taken money from a man like Smith. She knew she should be angry and maybe she would be later. Lester's telling Smith that Lee was an FBI agent had resulted in her being kidnapped. But now she couldn't bring herself to feel anything but sorrow that her friend had been so desperate that he'd gotten involved with a man like Patrick Smith.

"What's going to happen to Lester?"

"He'll have to answer for what he did," he said. "But he did the right thing at the end. If it hadn't been for him, we might not have found you—at least not until it was too late."

"I spoke to Vi. She said she and Lester are leaving tomorrow for California."

"An agent is going with them," Seth said. "Because of his help taking Smith down, Mike agreed to let him go and get his wife settled. Mike wouldn't let him go without an escort, but I doubt one is necessary. Lester's not a bad person. He was just desperate to save his wife. I think he wants to face up to what he did. He's already resigned from the police department. Most people will figure his wife's declining health is the reason. The rest of it will come out eventually, but for now, his involvement with Smith isn't known around town."

After hearing Seth's story, she had a pretty good idea why Viola had said she was sorry for what Maggie had gone through. It was her way of apologizing for what Lester had done, but without coming right out and saying it. Vi wasn't sure she knew yet, and she couldn't be sure how Maggie would react once she learned Lester's part in her kidnapping. If she reacted badly, the FBI might withdraw their permission for Lester to accompany her.

"Did Bill know about Lester?"

"He found out when we did."

"And he's okay with keeping quiet for now?"

Seth nodded. "The two of them have been friends for some time."

A criminal like Smith, terrorists, and FBI agents were the talk of the town now. Maggie hated to think what the talk would be when the townspeople discovered their own police chief had been involved. Lester had always been well liked, but Maggie wasn't so naïve as to believe all the town's residents would feel forgiving toward him. Not that it mattered, she guessed. They had no children to suffer from their father's shame and their parents were dead. Viola was dying from cancer and Lester would probably serve some prison time. The reaction of the citizens of Vichy was the least of their worries.

The car slowed. Maggie recognized where they were—the abandoned house and barn on the other side of the woods from Smith's house. Seth turned in, drove to the spot behind the barn where they had parked the car before and stopped. He put the car in Park and shut off the engine.

"What are we doing here?" she said.

He unbuckled his seat belt and turned to her.

"I wanted to talk to you," he said. "And I wanted to do it where we wouldn't be interrupted."

Here it comes, she thought. Why couldn't he have broken her heart in town? She could have run away from him there; now she would have to sit in the car with him while he drove her home. She didn't know how strong she could be. She was afraid she would break down and make a fool of herself in front of him.

"I love you," he said.

She stared at him, unable to respond. Those wonderful words weren't what she had expected to hear come out of his mouth.

"You . . . you do?"

He looked at her tenderly and took her hand.

"You sound surprised. Surely you had a pretty good idea of how I felt about you."

She shook her head.

"No. I didn't. How could I? I thought I did after that night, but then you pushed me away. I thought you regretted . . ."

She couldn't finish.

"I did," he said and she gasped. "I did regret it. But it was too late to change how I was feeling."

He shook his head and looked out the windshield.

"I should never have let it get this far."

"Let me get this straight—first you say you love me, then you say you regret it? I don't get it." The man was infuriating. Was he going to tell her he loved her and still give her the "Dear Jane" speech?

He took a deep breath. "You remember I told you I'd been married and my wife had died."

She nodded. "Of course I remember."

He was still looking out the window, but Maggie had the feeling that he no longer saw the trees and the sunshine outside, but was instead looking back into his memory. He was silent and she waited, knowing he would begin when he was ready.

"I met Diane while I was in the service," he finally said. "The Air Force. Her father was a one-star general, and she was an only child. I think her parents had hoped she would marry a little better than she did, but they never really objected, not once they knew I was what she wanted. They had always seen to it that she got what she wanted, and I suppose they figured it was too late to change their method of child rearing."

He smiled bitterly.

"She was a fragile woman. I think that appealed to me at that point in my life. She had never been a strong person, physically or emotionally, and I guess I needed to feel like the big macho man protecting the helpless little woman. Maybe that's what she needed, too. I don't know. Anyway, we were married my last year in the service."

He paused for a moment, thinking. Maggie tried to picture his fragile dead wife, the woman he had wanted so much to protect. Somehow she couldn't see him with a weak person. He emanated an almost overpowering strength that she was sure would swallow up anyone who didn't match his power. Was that what had happened to Diane, she wondered?

"After I was discharged, we returned to Philadelphia. I have always been a bit of a rebel. I come from a long-line of conservative upper-class Philadelphians—my father is an attorney with his own firm—and I've never been comfortable with it. So I work hard, maybe too hard, at removing myself from that kind of life. I was in the Security Forces—that's the Air Force's military police—and I knew I wanted to stay in law enforcement. When I got out, I applied to every federal law enforcement agency that was taking applications. The FBI was my first choice and I was lucky enough to get accepted."

He chuckled. "Although I have to admit I wasn't sure I'd been so lucky last Monday while the bullets were flying. Anyway, Diane stuck by me through Quantico, then the long hours and the undercover assignments most new agents get. I loved it all. When I wasn't working, I was hanging out with other agents talking shop. Oh, she threatened to leave me a couple of times, but she never did. I guess she always thought deep down inside that sooner or later she could bring me back to the fold. Especially when she got pregnant."

He stopped talking, his eyes growing sad. Maggie felt a sudden pang of sadness for the children she and Tom had always wanted to have, but now never would. Oh, she might go on and one day have children, it was true, but those people that only she and Tom could have created would never exist. She found that terribly sad.

"It almost worked, too," Seth went on. "I gave serious thought to settling down and acting like the respectable family man I was about to become. My father offered to put me through law school, all expenses paid. After I passed the bar, I would have become a junior partner in the firm. No hassles, no problems, just a quick easy path to riches and respectability." He smiled. "I thought about it, I really did. But I thought too long."

The smile faded.

"Diane miscarried in her third month. Just one of those things, the doctor said. Happens all the time. Only it didn't happen all the time to Diane. Like I said, she had always been delicate and she didn't handle the loss well. I helped her all I could, but I was still wrapped up in what I was doing and I couldn't always be there. Even when I was, I don't think I gave her what she needed." He shook his head. "I'm not even sure I knew what she needed. But time passes and wounds heal even if the scars are still there. We finally got the nerve to try again."

Maggie suddenly knew with sickening certainty what the outcome of the story was going to be and wished with all her heart that she could avoid hearing the words.

"This time we were careful. We took all the precautions. Her doctor ordered bed rest, especially during the first three months of the pregnancy, and we listened to him. We hired a girl to stay with her when I couldn't be there, which was all too often, and Diane didn't have to lift a finger for anything. But it didn't make any difference. No difference at all, except that this time she miscarried in her fourth month instead of her third. And this time the doctor told her she could never carry children, that she would be endangering her own life too much to take the chance."

He closed his eyes and sat silent for a few minutes, his Adam's apple working in his throat.

"She was never the same after that," he said, opening his eyes. "Or maybe that's not quite right. She was the same, only worse. Her health grew worse, small irritating maladies, the kind that I know now can be brought on by stress and deep depression. I tried to be understanding, but I grew impatient with her. I began to think she was a hypochondriac, that she was inventing illnesses just to punish me and to avoid having to grow up and be my wife. I started staying away from home more and more, leaving her alone with her medicines and her illnesses. I was gone the night she finally did it, playing poker and drinking beer, would you believe it, with a bunch of guys I worked with. I was playing poker and drinking beer while my wife was killing herself."

He was silent for a minute, still staring out the window into his past.

"She did it the painless way," he continued. "With pills. God knows she had plenty of them at hand to choose from, pills to calm her, pills to make her sleep, pills to wake her up. Her doctor was very generous with his prescription pad. She took the ones to make her sleep and that's what she did. When I finally came home, tired and drunk, and tried to wake her up, it was too late."

He stopped talking. Maggie waited, looking at her hands twisting in her lap. They sat in silence for what seemed an eternity. Finally he spoke, his voice soft.

"I wanted to tell you this," he said. "To explain why I pulled away from you and why a part of me regrets what happened between us. I love my job and I love you. I learned from bitter experience the damage the job's demands can do to an agent's personal life. I wasn't sure I could give up the excitement of it for you—that is, if you wanted me. But when you were taken and I didn't know if I'd ever see you alive again—well, I got my answer."

He took her hand and brought it to his lips.

"I love you more than I love my job, Maggie Fields," he said. "If you'll have me, I will be glad to give it up."

"Leave the FBI?" She was shocked.

"Maybe not leave the Bureau," he said. "But I can request a transfer to something with better hours and less danger—like white collar crime."

"But why would you think I'd want you to give up something you love?" she said.

The look on his face was that of a small boy who had just opened a wrapped present only to find clothes instead of a toy.

"You don't . . . ," he started, but she shushed him.

"I don't love you? Is that what you started to say?" She leaned forward and kissed him lightly on the lips. "Of course I love you, you idiot! I love you so much I can hardly breathe! But what kind of love would it be if I asked you to give up something else you love?"

"You didn't ask me to do it. I'm volunteering."

"Well, un-volunteer," she said. She raised her chin and stared defiantly at him. "I'm not fragile, Seth. I will not be destroyed by you working long hours or by worrying that you're going to be killed. What you do is important. You're a hero."

He started to protest, but she shushed him again.

"You are. As is Lee and I have a lot of apologizing to do to him. I'm proud of what you do and I want you to keep doing it as long as you still want to."

"You don't know how hard it can be . . . ," he started.

"I've gotten several job offers myself from news organizations that often send reporters into conflict zones. If I accept one of them—and I might, then it could be harder on you." She grinned at him. "And you don't know how hard I can be to live with either."

He pulled her to him and hugged her.

"I'm looking forward to finding out." He pulled back and held her at arm's length, "But you have to promise me one thing."

"And what is that?" she said.

"That if the demands of my job do become too much, you'll tell me. I'll give it up in a heartbeat."

"I can promise that," she said. "Ask anyone—if something bothers me, people know about it. I do have one request, though."

"And what is that?"

"Kiss me," she said.

He did.

###

About the Author

I live with my husband, four dogs, and two cats inside Daniel Boone National Forest in Kentucky. I divide my time between writing romances and writing mysteries (as Laurel Heidtman). I love to hear from readers and can be found at: www.lollipowell.com.

If you enjoyed this book, please leave a review at your favorite online retailer. Readers depend on reviews to guide them to books they might enjoy and authors depend on them to spread the word to readers.

Lolli Powell

~~~ **Also By This Author**~~~

THE BOY NEXT DOOR

When Laney Mitchell was fifteen, she babysat the cute four-year old who lived next door. His family moved away when he was five. Twenty-six years later, he's all grown up, but he still wants to cuddle with his babysitter!

Laney's daughter has other plans for him, while a hunky friend of a friend and Laney's ex-husband both have other plans for her. By avoiding romance in the three years since her divorce, Laney has kept things simple. Now life has suddenly gotten very complicated!

Available at Amazon and other online bookstores.

www.ingramcontent.com/pod-product-compliance
Lightning Source LLC
Chambersburg PA
CBHW061321170626
46817CB00001B/252